NEVER ENOUGH

Books by Joan Elizabeth Lloyd

THE PRICE OF PLEASURE

NEVER ENOUGH

Published by Kensington Publishing Corporation

NEVER ENOUGH

JOAN ELIZABETH LLOYD

KENSINGTON BOOKS

KENSINGTON BOOKS are published by

Kensington Publishing Corp.
850 Third Avenue
New York, NY 10022

ISBN: 0-7394-3531-0

Printed in the United States of America

This book is dedicated to three wonderful people who push, pull, and otherwise encourage me to write bigger and better books.

To John, Meg, and Annelise, my sincerest thanks.

And as always, to Ed.

NEVER ENOUGH

Chapter

1

"Give me that again," Tracy McBride said, dropping into a leather chair in her sister's living room, her hand over her pounding heart. She had driven the three quarters of an hour to Kim's house to hear some "terrific news" her sister had promised her. Tracy was six years younger than her forty-one-year-old sister, yet once they'd reached adulthood, they could have been mistaken for twins. Both women had sandy brown hair, soft pale brown eyes, and similar builds, each five foot three with a trim figure. As they had when they were younger, they had coincidentally selected similar outfits— light blue T-shirts and well-washed khaki jeans. Although they looked very much alike, Tracy saw now that Kim seemed softer somehow and her smile almost split her face.

"You heard it right the first time. I'm going to have twins," she said, breathless with excitement. "The doctor did a sonogram this morning and he's sure. I'm more than twelve weeks, due the end of February." Her grin was infectious and Tracy shared her joy, tinged just slightly by envy. She'd always wanted children but it just wasn't to be. Until about five years earlier, when Tracy had moved to Washington State with her then-husband Andrew, the sisters had been close. Since her return, alone, two years before, Tracy had spent a lot of time by herself and saw her sister only occasionally. There seemed to be some kind of a barrier, a soft wall that Tracy couldn't seem to penetrate. Now years of separation slipped away and Tracy delighted in the sisters' suddenly reestablished closeness.

"Holy shit, sis," Tracy said, her head spinning. She jumped up and grabbed her sister's shoulders. "Oh, my God." As she started to jump up and down as they had done when they were teens, she suddenly dropped her hands to her sides. "Sorry. I don't want to hurt the baby. I mean babies. Oh my God. I'm going to be an aunt. Twice."

Kim hugged her sister hard. "Don't worry about the pregnancy. Hug as hard as you like. Me and the kids," she giggled, "are pretty indestructible." Kim's face became serious, a slight frown replacing the complete joy of a moment before. "But it's only the end of the first trimester so I'm not buying baby clothes or anything. As a matter of fact, you're the only one other than Elliot and his parents who know about this." She placed her hands across her still-flat belly. "And it's going to stay that way until I start to show." Again her expression changed as she grinned at her sister. "I just couldn't hold out on you."

"I can't believe it," Tracy said, as she dropped back into the chair and Kim settled onto the couch. "You said you wanted at least two kids but I didn't expect you to do it all at once."

Kim McBride Ryan swung her shapely legs around and propped her feet on the glass-topped coffee table. "Neither did I, Trace, believe me."

Tracy looked at her sister carefully. The last time they had met for lunch, almost two months earlier, Kim had been pregnant yet she hadn't said a word. She forced down her slightly hurt feelings and accepted the fact that Kim hadn't wanted to tell anyone until she was more sure that things would work out all right. She and her husband Elliot had been trying for a baby for most of the five years they had been married.

"So how did it happen?"

Kim giggled. "The usual way."

"Don't be a wise guy, sis. I meant did you go for fertility drugs or anything like that?"

"Sorry. Teasing you is an old habit." Kim's face settled into a soft smile. "No, no drugs. Just plain old-fashioned hard work."

"Hard work? Making love?"

"When you take your temperature all the time and go through every trick the doctors and a zillion magazines suggest, sex becomes work rather than a pleasure. I douched with baking soda every day for one month and with vinegar another." Kim giggled. "That month Elliot said my pussy had a permanent pucker and I smelled like a salad. Some months I would call him up at work when the time was right"—Kim sneered at the term—"and he'd hurry home. No preliminaries, just enough foreplay to get him erect then bang. Literally. Afterward, I'd lie on my back for half an hour with my feet up on the headboard. It was a disaster."

Tracy had never heard her sister say a bad word about sex. She'd always been so free and now . . . "I guess I can understand how all the fun went out of it."

Kim shook her head slowly. "Me. The sexpert, with the sex life from hell. Finally, we just gave up and for two months remembered what good sex was all about. That's when I got pregnant. I remember the evening well."

Slightly embarrassed by Kim's obvious recollections, Tracy said, "Okay, okay, no details, please. How are you feeling?"

"Surprisingly well, actually. I read the *What to Expect* book and I was somehow disappointed that I haven't been suffering much morning sickness. Just a few bouts of queasiness."

"Why in the world were you disappointed?"

"I guess throwing up each morning would have made it more real. I would have been more sure that this was really going to happen."

Tracy watched her sister's right hand gently rub her belly. The years of almost reading each other's minds when they were teenagers told her that something wasn't quite right. "There's a catch here, isn't there?"

"Yeah," Kim said, her voice sounding dismal. "It's not going to be quite as easy for me as it would have been five years ago. I'm not a kid anymore and I've got to be extra careful. After all, I'm over forty and this is my first pregnancy so I'm what they refer to as high risk. Now, with the two babies . . ." Her voice trailed off, then after a moment's silence, she continued, "The doctor had had an inkling and had warned me even before the sonogram that twins were a possibility and that, because I'm older, they would mean additional complications."

Tracy considered her sister. Although they had both wanted it, until today they had not reestablished their previous openness. Every time they got together, they swore to stay in closer touch, but Tracy's teaching schedule at the local campus of the State University of New York and Kim's work on her weekly sexual advice column took up a lot of their time, so it was often several weeks between phone calls and sometimes six or eight weeks between visits. There was something else, too, something Tracy couldn't put her finger on, that kept a distance between them. Now, she couldn't help but wonder whether the babies would further separate her from her sister. And with the added risk, she wondered whether Kim's getting pregnant so late had been a good idea. Not my decision, she told herself. Just be supportive.

"God, I can't get over it." Tracy looked around her sister's small, one-bedroom condo and shook her head. "Where are you going to put twins?"

Kim and Elliot's rented condo was comfortable for two but

was going to be impossible for four. The small living room had been tastefully decorated in shades of off-white, cornflower blue, and rose, with a wide white wall unit and pastel floral paintings on the walls. The dining area contained a small rose laquer table and chairs with a mirrored wall behind in an attempt to create the appearance of size. The bedroom was almost filled by a queen-sized bed and twin dressers.

Kim's shaking head mimicked her sister's. "Lord only knows. I think we'll have to consider renting or buying a house, or at least something larger than this." Again Kim's mercurial mood shifted and she frowned. "That's one of the other reasons that we didn't tell anyone. We'll have to make so many changes it boggles the mind. Elliot and I have done nothing but make lists and try to figure out where the money's going to come from."

Money had always been a delicate issue between the sisters so Tracy rose and headed for the tiny kitchen. "I'm going to get a soda," she said. "What are you drinking?"

"For now, just ice water. I'm off caffeine, alcohol, and most of the rest of the things I enjoy. Except sex, of course."

As Kim started to rise, Tracy said quickly, "Just sit. I'll fetch. But don't expect this being-waited-on stuff to continue. I'm just being nice to you because you've fulfilled all my aunt-type dreams at one time." As she poured herself a Diet Pepsi in the tiny kitchen, she spoke loudly enough for Kim to hear. "You know what makes me sad?"

"It's probably the same thing that gets to me. Mom."

"You always did read my mind. Have you told her?" Their mother, Ruth, had been older than many when her children were born and had lost her husband just before Tracy's fifth birthday from a sudden heart attack. She had been afflicted with the first signs of Alzheimer's disease four years earlier, and now at almost seventy-five, she had no real connection to the outside world. At least once a week each of the sisters dropped in at the upscale nursing home in which she had been placed. In the past several months those visits had become increasingly difficult and Tracy often had to grit her teeth and force herself to make the long drive. While at first Ruth had been glad to see her, now she didn't recognize her daughter and Tracy would leave never having made any connection with the older woman. Tracy returned to the living room, handed her sister a glass of ice water, and settled back into the chair with her soda.

"She's really gone now," Kim said. "I told her about the baby when I first found out but she didn't really understand and she hasn't make any reference to it since. She hardly speaks at all."

Tracy settled back into the chair, picturing the lovely sun porch on which she often found Ruth, seated in a wheelchair staring into space. "She usually doesn't recognize me either. Sometimes, when I introduce myself, she looks totally blank. Several weeks ago, when I said I was her daughter, she shook her head as if to say that she had no daughter. Since then she hasn't responded to me at all." Tracy blinked several times to suppress her tears.

"I know," Kim said. "Mom presents me, us, with a large problem."

Tracy cocked her head to one side and, when Kim seemed hesitant to continue, said, "Which is?"

"Coming up with the money to keep Mom at Willow Grove isn't going to be as easy as it used to be."

Tracy's stomach tightened and she felt the familiar guilt that she couldn't spare more than the check she wrote each month. "You know I'm contributing all I can," she said. "Assistant professors . . ."

Kim put up her hand, palm out. "Stop apologizing, Trace. I know you're doing all you can. So am I, and up to now Willow Grove has been possible. I'm afraid that, because of the babies, there may have to be changes. We may have to find a less-expensive place."

Tracy nodded. "Having twins will be quite a strain on your pocketbook."

Kim idly rubbed her belly. "It's not just the cost of the babies. For the moment I'm on what the doctor calls restricted activity. I have to rest and even take naps. I have to be in bed by nine. Short-distance walking is okay but I should be sitting and resting with my feet up or lying down most of the time. Writing my column is going to be an increasing problem."

"Why? It's just writing, right? And most of that is done in your head. A few taps on the keyboard and you're done."

Kim sighed. "It's not as simple as that, I'm afraid. Even Elliot underestimates the amount of work it takes to put *Ask Miranda* together. He's at work so much that he isn't really aware of the hours I spend opening and reading my mail, writing answers for some, and putting the column together each week."

Ask Miranda had begun around the time of Kim's marriage. In addition to taking ads and doing general office work for a local newspaper, Kim had been a part-time reporter. When the advice columnist had eloped, her editor had asked her to fill in and complete Miranda's unfinished column. After much reluctance, she had decided to take a crack at it and the column had seemed to work. It had soon become her regular job and she had rapidly developed a devoted readership. The column had become more and more successful until *Ask Miranda* was now syndicated in more than twenty newspapers. "It takes me several hours at the computer each day just to keep up."

"You answer your mail? I thought the only letters you answered were the ones that appear in your column."

"I don't answer every one, of course, but I do write to dozens of troubled people each week. Lots of it is boiler plate, but when people take the time to pour out their troubles, I try to find the time to reply."

"I guess I never really thought about the responsibility you have."

"Sometimes it's a bit overwhelming. So many really sad people write, thinking I have all the answers, and I don't. All I can do is give them some common sense and maybe a slightly different way to look at a problem. Often I suggest that they seek professional help. And sometimes I know they aren't really looking for advice, just a shoulder to cry on."

Kim sighed, then continued, "I'm not whining about it. For the most part I enjoy it and most of that work can be done sitting down and resting. Unfortunately, although I'm going to have to make minor changes in the way I handle the column, that's not the biggest problem."

Following her sister's train of thought, Tracy said, "Shit. The weekends."

"The weekends." Three years earlier, Kim had joined forces with the manager of a small resort and convention center in the Catskills about an hour and a half away to run Creative Loving Weekends. From what Tracy gathered from her conversations with her sister, the weekends ran from Friday evening to Sunday morning and involved workshops on all aspects of good sex. Being a bit reticent to discuss it, Tracy knew little more than that.

Kim sipped her water, then said, "The weekends are tremendous undertakings and the proceeds are what I use to keep Mom at Willow Grove."

Tracy reflexively tucked an errant strand of stick-straight hair behind one ear. "I didn't realize. What are you going to do about them?" Tracy was suddenly worried that her mother's days in Willow Grove might be numbered. Eighteen months before, when Ruth had become unable to care for herself and with neither sister able to take over, they had searched for several weeks until they found a nursing home that would be able to keep their mother the way they wanted. A caring staff, resident medical personnel, activities that she had enjoyed until she'd become too far gone to do anything but sit, all cost dearly. How would they find someplace as good, but less expensive?

"Where we go from here is going to be up to you," Kim said, breaking the silence.

"Me? I told you that I can't contribute anything more." She was already writing the nursing home a check for almost a quarter of her take-home pay each month. She lived in a less-than-stellar neighborhood in a one-bedroom apartment on the second floor of someone else's house. She drove an eight-year-old car and spent next to nothing on nonessentials. "I just can't."

As Tracy fought rising tears, Kim said quickly, "I know that and I understand. You're doing more than anyone should have to. I'm not thinking in terms of more money, it's more 'you.' "

When Kim seemed to debate what to say, Tracy said, "Meaning?"

"Look. I can handle the next meeting, the weekend of the twentieth of September, but that's the last one I'll be able to do. I was hoping that you could take over and at least run the one next January."

"Not a chance," Tracy said quickly. Kim had to be kidding. Tracy? Sex expert? Talking to couples about good, creative sex? She was the last one to undertake that kind of thing. How could she advise people on something she could only dream about?

It hadn't always been that way. Tracy remembered all the discussions she and her sister had had about sex as kids growing up sharing a bedroom in their small house in Westchester County, New York. Although Tracy had known she could go to her mother with any question, a softly spoken "Where do babies come from?" in the dark after lights out usually elicited a long explanation from her older and much more knowledgeable sister, one she could listen to without having to react, without anyone seeing her beet red face.

When Tracy first got her period, Kim had been the one to teach her how to use sanitary pads and answer all her embarrassed questions. Kim told her about breasts and the risk of letting a boy touch them. Because of Kim, Tracy knew early on about arousal and intercourse. By the time she dated, Kim had told her sister all about condoms and had put a few in her purse, "Just in case." She had even demonstrated, almost strangling on gales of laughter, the proper way to put one on, using a banana. Since then, bananas had been a running joke between the two girls.

Tracy remembered calling Kim, then in her senior year at college, to tell her of her first sexual experience, on the sofa of her current boyfriend's parents' house during her junior year in high school.

"So? How was it? I hope you were careful and the banana skin didn't split."

Tracy laughed. "I was. You taught me well, sis. Austin had a fit when I insisted he use one but I wouldn't let him even touch me until he agreed."

"Was it wonderful?"

After a slight pause Tracy admitted, "Not really. He begged and I let him do it."

Kim's concern was clearly audible through the phone. "Any pain, blood, that sort of thing?"

"No. It was just . . . Nothing."

Tracy could hear her sister's long exhalation. "That's not unusual," Kim said from a thousand miles away. "It will get better, I promise." But it hadn't. Not really. There had been moments, of course, but in general, sex for Tracy had always been a nonevent.

"Come on, sis, be real," Tracy said, snapping back to reality. "I'm hardly queen of the creative lovers or creative talkers for that matter." No way in hell. "I'm sure there must be lots of folks who would be willing to run the weekend for you."

"There probably are, but I don't know of anyone else who I would trust with it."

"You'd trust me? Don't be an idiot. I don't know much about the weekends, but I know you give advice and teach people about kinky sex. That's not me. Not a chance."

"I've known you all your life and I probably understand you better than you know yourself. I know what's under that professorial straight-arrow image."

"Yeah. A professor who's a straight arrow."

"One who wears outrageously sexy underwear."

Tracy reflexively slipped her finger under the strap of her wispy cobalt blue and off-white lace bra, her face heating. When Kim raised a slender brown eyebrow, Tracy said, "Okay, you're right. But . . ."

"No buts. We must have spent hundreds of hours talking about sex years ago." She let out a long breath and lowered her voice. "What happened to you, Trace?" she said sadly. "Was it Andrew?" Tracy watched a strange expression flash across Kim's face, then disappear.

They hadn't talked about Tracy's personal life for many years and she wasn't about to begin now. Her disastrous marriage was her own business and she wasn't going to admit her problems, especially to someone who might analyze the relationship and realize what a failure she had been. "Nothing. Things just didn't work out the way I thought they would."

"You don't have to tell me about it and I certainly won't ask, but that was then and this is two years later. Why haven't you just thrown off whatever went wrong that made you so reclusive? From what I've seen, you just placed yourself under house arrest. Every woman needs friends, especially men friends, and good sex occasionally."

"Is that Miranda talking or my sister?" Again that skeptical eyebrow, and Tracy's blush deepened. "Sorry. I had some bad experiences and that's the end."

"Everyone has a bad experience at one time or another. I could tell you stories of my dating years. The women who write to me also have tales both tragic and hysterical. There are highs and lows, mind-bending sex and mind-numbing boredom. It's never the same from one man to another," Kim said, "or even from one encounter to another. Listen, Trace, I haven't said anything because, after all, it was none of my business, but now it is. I don't know what happened to sour you on men, dating, and sex, but I don't think you've really changed, not underneath it all. Now I need you to remember what you once were. You need it, too."

"Sis, I'm not that person anymore." She felt her voice rising. "Period. It won't work and none of Miranda's preaching will change that." Kim looked so crestfallen that Tracy said, "I'm sorry. That was a low blow."

"I know you didn't mean that the way it sounded."

Didn't she? This time it was her brown eyebrow that lifted.

Kim smiled as she admitted, "Okay. I do get a bit preachy from time to time, but usually it's with someone I care deeply about, like you. If doing the weekend won't work, fine. But I'm not ready to give up on you or on between twenty and thirty thousand per."

Tracy felt all of the air whoosh out of her lungs. When she got her breath back, she said, "Per weekend? Thirty thousand? Dollars?"

"Dollars. Where do you think the money comes from to keep Mom at Willow Grove? Santa Claus?" There was an edge to Kim's voice.

Tracy's mind was boggled. "I guess I never thought much about it. I wrote a check each month and I thought you did about the same."

Kim's eyes bored into her sister's. "Well, think about it now.

Neither Elliot nor I make anywhere near the kind of money Mom needs so we need the proceeds from the weekends. It's just that simple. I could probably find someone else to run them and pay him or her a hefty part of the fees. I'd also have to trust that whoever did it would handle it so as not to lose the weekend's reputation or steal the idea and all the planning that's gone into it to run something of their own."

"Thirty thousand dollars?"

Kim's face softened and she grinned. "Maybe closer to twenty after taxes. Didn't think I had it in me, did you? Somewhere around fifty couples pay a thousand dollars each for the weekend. Of that thousand, two hundred fifty goes to expenses, mostly to the hotel, and almost all of the rest is taxes and profit. I also get a commission on space that the vendors take."

"Vendors?" Tracy had never given the weekends much thought but it seemed now that there was more going on than she had realized.

Kim sipped her ice water. "There's so much you don't know and I'll explain it all in due time. For now, I need you to reconsider. Just think about it."

"How can I? You're the expert. I'm Little Miss Prim and Proper in comparison."

"I wasn't born knowing, and as you well know, I have no official credentials. I read, listen to people, and use the common sense we were both born with. You counsel students. You understand people. Sex is just people and I can give you a lot of help."

"I counsel students on job placement, grades, getting along with professors."

"Getting along. That's what sex is all about."

Tracy twisted her fingers in the hem of her T-shirt. "Not really."

"I know your hands, sis," Kim said, taking pity on her sister.

"You tangle your fingers like that when you're embarrassed or confused. Relax. No one's going to force you to do anything. Honest."

Tracy concentrated on unwinding her fingers. "We see each other at most once a month and now you're reading my body language." Tracy swallowed hard around the lump in her throat. "You're right. I'm confused and, if you must know, embarrassed, too. You know so much. I could never be Miranda."

Kim sighed. "You wouldn't become Miranda and everyone going to the weekend in January would be told that it's not me, but rather my sister, who'd be running it."

"I know you wouldn't cheat anyone, sis, but I don't think I can do it, even for all that money." She heard herself shift from *I can't* to *I don't think I can* and from the look on Kim's face, she had heard it, too.

"Okay, here's a compromise. You don't have to agree to anything. Come with me on the twentieth and spend the weekend at the lake. You don't have to say anything or do anything, just observe. Then, if you decide that you can run the January weekend, we can spend time talking and working with my mail. You can read all my old columns and lots of books on sex and relationships. If we work together, you'll know everything I know by January. From then on it's just a matter of honesty and caring."

There was a thread of panic in the back of Tracy's mind, but she forced herself to concentrate on the money and the fact that Kim needed her. "I don't know, sis." It felt good to be needed.

"Go home and think about it. Call me over the weekend and let me know. Remember it's just a weekend. If you agree, I'll have Dave set aside a room for you."

"Dave?"

"Dave Markov, the owner and manager of the hotel. I need to alert him to the possibility of not doing the January weekend. It will be tough for him financially, losing fifty rooms at two hundred and fifty dollars apiece, too."

Feeling a bit overwhelmed, Tracy said, "Lay off the pressure, Kim."

Kim's smile was genuine and slightly rueful. "Busted. See, you know me better than you think you do. Okay, no pressure. But it will really hurt his winter revenues." When Tracy glared, Kim's grin widened and she said, "Okay, I'll stop now."

As Tracy rose, Kim stood as well. The two women hugged. "I've got to get home and change," Tracy said. "I've got an evening class."

"Think about it, will you?"

"Like I have a choice. You know I love you and wish all three of you"—she patted her sister's stomach—"everything good."

Dave Markov sat in his small office in the Catskill Lake Resort, going over the reservation list for Kim Ryan's Creative Loving Weekend. Fifty-one of the fifty-two available rooms were booked, a great showing. All four meeting rooms were laid out for the lectures, product displays, and demonstrations that would be held throughout the weekend. God, who could have imagined when this all started that there was so much money in talking about sex. He'd even been considering asking Kim whether she could increase the number of weekends she held each year. Sure, he had lots of other meetings scheduled, but he would eagerly make room for more of Kim's lucrative weekends.

Six years earlier, at his mother's insistence his stepfather had turned control of the aging, off-the-beaten-track, two-hundred-room resort hotel to him, rather than shutting down the Catskill Lake Resort completely. Dave had had great plans and had immediately begun taking courses and reading books on hotel management. He'd show the old man and make the resort the showplace of the area. He took every cent he and the bank could provide and remodeled the three aging buildings.

Slowly, however, he'd had to accept the fact that, although the setting was picture-postcard perfect and the area secluded and intimate, being remote had its disadvantages. Too far from ski areas to attract snow-sport enthusiasts, the Catskill Lake Resort got none of the guaranteed winter traffic on which other resorts depended. Finally he accepted the fact that during the depth of the winter his resort just had to shut down. Since the setting was spectacular during the other three seasons, he was getting quite a few tourists, and because of his careful management, the return business was brisk. In those early years the resort had held its own. Barely. His stepfather had gloated, telling him at frequent intervals that he'd never be a "hotel man" and would never make a go of the inn.

Then, after eighteen mediocre months Dave had been approached by a statewide square dance group looking for a place for a summer gathering and he had jumped at the opportunity. The weekend had been an unqualified success. He and the organizers had combined forces to create a comfortable atmosphere, with spacious and convenient rooms for dancing and teaching and efficient yet intimate hotel rooms for the out-of-town participants. Almost thirty couples had attended and had been delighted at the location and facilities. The following year, at Dave's suggestion, they set aside one room for businesses so they could peddle everything from Western and square dance clothing and jewelry to books, records, and teaching tapes. For the first time the organization had made money and vowed to return every year.

With the success of the first square dance weekend, Dave began to solicit various groups looking for places for weekend and eventually week-long meetings. Now he hosted four chocolate weekends a year, along with quarterly ballroom dance, model airplane, and radio-controlled car festivals. He arranged a sixties weekend, and when that was highly profitable, he added a fifties and a seventies weekend; now the three semi-annual events were fully booked several months in advance. Several large corporations also conducted their annual retreats at the Catskill Lake Resort.

He took advantage of people's love of fall foliage and arranged leaf season tours, then recruited local science teachers for spring and summer nature festivals. He played up the nature theme with bird-watcher weekends and overnight stays to observe meteor showers, complete with experts to explain the science of it all. He'd even used the nature theme in his decor, with prints and paintings of animals and birds everywhere. A local collector had lent him a collection of antique weather vanes and bird houses, which were displayed in the lobby. Now even his stepfather had taken notice of his success and had extended grudging praise. He also admired the fact that no event had ever been canceled, a great risk in the hotel business.

None of the events, however, was as lucrative as Kim's hot sex weekends. Since attendance was limited to about fifty couples and the demand was tremendous, the weekends were booked a year in advance and he was able to charge a bit more than for other groups. Income from booking the booth space was a great addition to his bottom line as well.

When the phone rang, Dave distractedly picked it up. Recognizing the response to his greeting, he put down the papers he had been reading, leaned back in his desk chair, and propped one cowboy-booted foot on the opposite knee. "Kim, it's great to hear from you. How's everything?"

"Everything's fabulous," Kim said. "The weekend booking is finally complete. I'll fax you the corrected roster tomorrow and you can finish assigning rooms."

"No problem. We're all ready for you. Diana's been in touch

and her stock will arrive on Friday afternoon." Diana's Lingerie Shop, a local intimate apparel boutique, had booked one of the smaller meeting rooms for display and sale of her most upscale and outrageous stock and a small guest room for trying items on.

"Great. I look forward to seeing her again. She's one of my favorite people."

Dave pictured the charming, yet outrageous senior citizen who had joined the Creative Loving Weekend two years earlier. She did a brisk business in all types of sexy underthings, from teddies and peignoirs to crotchless panties and corsets. About sixty pounds overweight, Diana was able to encourage even the most self-conscious woman to indulge her love of silk and lace and buy items from her line of lingerie in plus sizes. Last winter she had added an assortment of satin boxers and thongs for men.

Dave tapped a pencil on the folder on his desk. "I also spoke to Matt of the Adult Toy Box. He wants an entire room for himself this weekend so I've arranged for him to have the guest suite nearest the main meeting room."

"That's great. Have we enough vendors to fill the remainder of the space? It looks really tacky to have empty areas."

"No problem. We'll even be a bit crowded." Dave ran his slender fingers through his curly, jet black hair, trying in vain to get it off his forehead. "Oh, and the hot tub's fixed."

"Wonderful. I'd hate to have to tell the folks that they can't fool around in the pool or the hot tub after hours. It's one of their favorite spots to make out."

"I know." He sighed. "I've always dreamed of getting you in there with me."

Kim's laugh echoed through the phone wires. "You are an outrageous flirt."

"And the problem with that is—?"

"None. As long as everyone, including you, me, and Elliot, understands that you've never been serious."

A confirmed bachelor, Dave had enjoyed a long-term and totally innocent flirtation with Kim, which warmed and complimented them both but which neither would ever dream of acting on.

There was a noticeable pause. "Dave," Kim said, "I do have to give you a heads-up on something and you're not going to like it."

Dave could hear the serious tone of Kim's voice and became alert immediately. He took his foot down and leaned his elbows on the desk. "Shoot."

"I'm pregnant."

Immediately delighted for his longtime friend, he almost shouted, "Holy shit. That's fabulous," then added in a slightly wistful tone, "Elliot's a lucky man."

"That's what I keep telling him. Anyway, here's the problem. I'm having twins and the doctor has termed it a high-risk pregnancy."

Dave shifted the phone to his other hand and rubbed the back of his neck. "Twins. No kidding. Are you all right?"

"Never better."

Shit, Dave thought. What the hell did her pregnancy really mean? "I hope you don't have to cancel or shorten the weekend."

"No. This next weekend's fine, but the January one might have to go."

Damn. This was the worst time for that kind of news. With the help of a hefty bank loan, based in part of the success of the sexuality weekends, Dave had just added twelve private cabins on the back of the property. Damn. To make matters worse, in the back of his head, he could see his stepfather laughing at him. Cancellation!

"I'm thrilled about the twins," he said, "but needless to say, not about the January weekend." That was the last event before the resort closed until the middle of March. "What will make the decision for you? Will it depend on how you're feeling? Is there anything I can do to make it easier for you?" He forced down a tinge of panic. Slow down, he told himself. It's not a tragedy. Is it?

"I wish you could, but my doctor's adamant. Complete bed rest by November so my doing anything as strenuous as the weekend is out. I'm hoping, however, to convince my sister to take my place."

Sister? "I didn't know you even had a sister. If she's as hot as you are, she should be a smash."

"That's the problem. She's not, at least not now. She used to be like me, I guess, but for the past few years she's been out of circulation. Bad marriage and, I think, a total lack of self-confidence. Beneath it all, I know she can do it, but just because I know it doesn't mean I can convince her of it. She's going to come with me on the twentieth so maybe you can help show her how really easy it can be."

"I'll sure try." In more ways than one, he thought.

"She can bunk in with me, I suppose," Kim said, "but if you've got an extra room, that might be better."

"I've got a few left so that shouldn't be a problem and I'll be sure to make her comfortable." Dave had never had a problem with women that he couldn't solve with his charm, good looks, and sense of humor, and he was sure that Kim's sister would prove no exception. He idly polished the toe of one embossed boot on the back of the leg of his jeans. If he had anything to say about it, this sex weekend would prove a revelation to Kim's sister and she'd decide to host the next weekend, even if it was only to see him. Piece of cake. He'd have to play his cards very carefully, however. Very carefully.

As she started for home Tracy realized she was starving, but then being nervous always made her hungry. She joined the line for a local drive-through, and while she waited for the woman in front of her to order for the brood of children that filled her van, Tracy thought about Kim's offer. Rubbing her hand on the steering wheel of her Toyota, she tried to picture herself leading a discussion about bondage or sex toys. Sure. Right! Wouldn't Andrew have a laugh at that one.

"Making love to you is like fucking a beached whale," he had screamed that last afternoon, stark naked with his engorged cock in his hand, the palm of his other on her friend Sharon's breast. "I couldn't get a response out of you if I were the greatest lover in the world. You've got no passion in your soul, Tracy. No fuckin' passion at all."

That awful day her afternoon class had been canceled suddenly due to a bomb scare and she had gladly rushed home to prepare a special dinner for her husband. No take-out tonight. Opening the front door, she had heard muffled noises from the end of the hallway. Curious, she had wandered toward the doorway to their bedroom, only to see the cliché tableau: her best friend and her husband of almost three years. They had been unaware of her presence as they writhed on the bed, Sharon's hands on Andrew's erection, his fingers working in her vagina. "God, you're so hot, baby," he moaned. "I can't wait to fuck your beautiful brains out."

Sharon's giggle filled Tracy's ears. "It's not my brains you want to fuck. How bad do you want me, Drew?"

Drew? He'd always insisted to her that his name was Andrew and he didn't like diminutives.

Andrew bucked his hips, sliding his engorged penis through Sharon's fist. "Can't you tell, baby?" As Tracy stared, too horrified to react, Andrew leaned over and bit Sharon's nipple, so much larger than hers, then suckled noisily. What seemed like hours later, he crawled upward. "Suck me, baby," he growled, then thrust his swollen, purple cock into her mouth. In and out he pushed as Tracy's throat closed and she almost gagged with the memory of the only night he'd put his penis in her mouth.

Sharon's fingers dug into Andrew's buttocks as she took his entire length between her lips, moaning with obvious pleasure, her crotch thrusting against Andrew's thigh. When he finally pulled back, his erection was glistening with her saliva and he was panting. "Such a good little cock-sucker," he said, then he crawled to the foot of the bed and buried his face in her groin. Tracy watched Sharon's hips ram upward as Andrew worked between her spread thighs.

"Andrew," Tracy finally squeaked. "What's going on? I don't understand."

Two faces snapped around and spotted Tracy standing in the doorway. While Sharon turned away, her face bright red, Andrew merely said, "Grow up, baby. What's there to understand? You have to know that you're a frigid bitch so even you must have realized that I have to satisfy my needs elsewhere. You can't even give passable head. Sharon's far from the first woman who I've fucked in this bed, and all have been a thousand times better than you. I've got needs and you're hardly worth the effort most of the time."

Andrew turned Sharon's face toward him and kissed her deeply. "You can't even get me off most of the time." His laugh was harsh and grating. "Maybe there's hope for you, though. Why don't you take some notes, professor?" He made the word *professor* sound like a curse. "I'm sure even you are capable of learning. Frigidity is probably curable given enough practice." He glared at her. "Wanna join us?"

For several seconds Tracy just stood there watching as her husband climbed on top of her erstwhile friend, lewdly rubbed his cock, then rammed it home. "No fuckin' passion." For a moment more she stared at Andrew's ass muscles as he continued pumping, his hand kneading Sharon's breast. "You gettin' this, babe?" he yelled, his voice following her as she ran: out of the house, out of Seattle, and back home to New York.

The divorce had been easy, with no children and few assets to worry about. She had said little to either her mother or her sister about her reasons for returning or for the divorce. She had taught college courses in creative writing and extemporaneous speaking in Washington State, so when she got back to New York, she got a temporary job as a secretary while she approached a former professor and friend who recommended her for a one-year visiting professor slot at the local community college. The following year she accepted a permanent position on a tenure track.

As the woman in the van drove forward, Tracy pulled up to the speaker, ordered a burger, fries, and a soda, quickly paid, and picked up her food. She parked, unwrapped the burger, and took a big bite. There's no way I can run Kim's weekend, she thought as she chewed. No way. And yet, how can I let Kim down? We need the money for Mom and she needs to support the new babies. Elliot can't do it alone, at least not easily.

Tracy smiled as she munched a french fry. Babies. Twins. God, she wanted children. Andrew had been against the idea and had worn a condom every time they made love. Suddenly she saw that last afternoon clearly. He hadn't been wearing a condom, she realized. Not with cute little cock-sucking Sharon. He didn't care whether Sharon got pregnant or whether they passed some disease around. Funny, she thought. Now I'm grateful for those condoms. If he was fucking around, at least he didn't bring any "presents" home to me, and a baby would have made everything so much more complicated.

Tracy got through her early evening public speaking class on autopilot, then spent several hours the following morning in her office dealing with the problems of many of the students in her classes. Although she wasn't an official advisor, she had somehow quickly become a mentor for several dozen of her students. Incoming freshmen needed advice on dealing with being away from home and she had talked quite a few through their first few weeks alone. Sophomores came to her with dating problems, fraternity and sorority issues, and juniors and seniors asked for help with career planning. Everyone needed guidance on dealing with difficult professors.

Maybe Kim was right and giving advice wasn't so difficult. But sexual advice?"

Chapter

2

Sometime during the second night, Tracy got up and wandered into the living room of her tiny apartment. She'd been over and over it all and had gotten nowhere. She settled on her faded sofa with a pad and pencil, determined to sort everything out. She drew a line down the center of the page then headed the left-hand column *Do it* and the right-hand one *Don't do it*. Beneath the *Do it* heading, she wrote, *Money, Help Kim, Help the Twins, Help Elliot.* She stopped writing and accepted the fact that she was trying to make the left-hand list longer and trying not to get to the second column.

She took a deep breath and, with her heart pounding, wrote *Frigid* in the right-hand column. She stared at the word, the feelings harsher seeing it glare at her in black and white. Well, pencil on a yellow paper, she told herself, trying to ease her terror.

Okay, Tracy, let's be honest here. You had a few relationships before Andrew, and although there was no great love, there was some good sex. Okay, I never really lived with anyone but there were some weekends away from home with boyfriends, right? Weren't those good?

Yeah, she continued, but did any of those guys come back

for more? Maybe it had taken a weekend away to convince them that she wasn't any good at sex. Wasn't it good with Andrew at first? she asked herself. If she were being honest, it had been good but certainly not great. No fireworks. At its best it had been comfortable but not earth-shattering. Whose fault had that been?

She looked down at the word *Frigid* on her pad, then wrote *Curious* under the words *Help Elliot*. She was curious about a lot of things. She read novels with sexy scenes, and now that she was trying to be brutally honest, she had always wondered whether real people participated in activities like that. Could she?

Beneath *Curious*, she wrote the word *Orgasm*. If she believed all the sexy novels she'd read over the years, she had never had one, well, not a real feeling-the-earth-move, fireworks one. Was it because she was frigid? She had picked up a magazine in the beauty parlor several months ago when she had to wait for a haircut. There was an article on frigidity headlined on the cover, and with sweat prickling her underarms, she had turned to the first page. "Almost no one is truly frigid." Was that really true or was she the "almost" that proved the rule? Had Andrew been wrong? He must have felt guilty as hell, and embarrassed at having gotten caught. Maybe he had just lashed out at her. Their sex hadn't been wonderful. She stopped herself. Be honest! Toward the end their sex had been lousy, but was it her fault? Andrew's? Was it just that they hadn't been compatible?

Her pencil hovered over the *Don't do it* column, then she wrote, *What do I know about anal sex and stuff like that?* I even gag at oral sex. After a while she set the pad and pencil on the sofa beside her and eventually, with her head on the back of the cushion, fell asleep.

The following morning she decided on a plan that might help her sort out all her conflicting feelings. Kim was right about one thing at least. She could go to the weekend and just listen. Sit in a corner and absorb. Maybe then she'd have a better idea of what to do about January. No way was she going to put herself out there as some kind of sexual expert unless she felt she could do it, and do it well. And that was that, money or no money.

That afternoon Tracy called Kim. After exchanging pleasantries, and listening to Kim gush about the babies, Tracy pressed the tension from her shoulders and said, "I've been thinking about the weekend. I still don't think I'll be able to take over for you, but I have no classes on Fridays so I thought I'd go with you and see what it's all about."

Without a second's pause, Kim squealed, "Oh, Trace, I'm so happy. I know you'll understand so much more once you've seen what goes on. How about coming over next Tuesday? Elliot has to work late and we can have dinner, just us girls, and I can give you a better idea of what the weekend's all about."

Now that she had decided, Tracy realized that she didn't want to take the chance that some offhand remark of Kim's might make her want to change her mind. "I've got a late afternoon class and anyway we can talk on the way up there." That way she'd remain committed. She smiled. Maybe she should *be* committed.

"Okay, whatever you think. This is going to open your eyes," Kim said.

"I'm sure it will," Tracy said softly.

As Kim hung up the phone, Elliot walked into the bedroom, where his wife was stretched out on the bed. Five feet nine inches tall with thinning brown hair and a thickening waistline, Elliot was three years older than his wife. His slightly pudgy face softened as he glanced at his wife's abdomen. Kim knew that to him, the twins wouldn't be real until she looked like she'd swallowed a watermelon and he could feel the babies move. "Who was that?" he asked.

"Tracy. She's agreed to come to the weekend."

Elliot sat on the edge of the bed. "That's great news. She should really enjoy it, and maybe if she loosens up a bit, she'd be willing to fill in for you in January."

"*Loosens up* is a mild term for it," Kim said, shaking her head. "She wasn't always uptight the way she is now and I have no clue what's up. Since she came back from Washington, she's been a different person." And until recently I haven't been eager to help. She shut her mind to that thought.

"I didn't know her before she moved to the coast. I gather she was freer, looser before."

"Freer. That's a great word for the way she was before Andrew. She was open, available somehow." Kim shook her head slowly. "Somehow that person she married did something to her. She says the divorce was amicable, but I can tell. He fucked with her head somehow." And mine. God, he was such a shit!

Elliot nudged his wife over on the bed and stretched out beside her. "Don't play shrink, babe. It'll just get you into trouble. You've been quite open to me about your immediate dislike of Andrew. Don't let your feelings cloud your objectivity."

Kim sighed. Someday she'd tell him the entire story. "I know, but I'm not objective. Tracy's my sister. I try so hard not to treat her like one of the women who write to me for help, but I keep wanting to shake her and get her to tell me what that bastard did to her."

"You don't know that he had anything to do with anything," he said calmly. "She might just have mellowed."

"She's not mellow. She's closed up tight. She doesn't date, she doesn't have any real friends, and she's been back almost two years. All she seems to do is teach, work with her students, and read. She's a hermit with no social life and no sex. It stinks to high heaven."

"Okay, so what can you do about it?"

"I have high hopes for this weekend. Maybe if she mingles with couples with great sex lives, she'll get the bug." Kim turned and lay her head on her husband's shoulder. "Great sex makes life worth living."

"Maybe she's not the type to indulge in casual or kinky sex. Maybe she needs a stable, permanent relationship like ours."

Kim reached out and wrapped her arms around her husband's waist. "Oh, Elliot, I do love you and we have the best relationship. But there's really nothing wrong with casual sex as long as both parties know the ground rules."

"We started with casual sex and look where it got us." He patted her stomach. "Sex isn't everything. As you always say, good sex isn't a cure for a bad relationship, or in her case, no relationship at all."

Kim laughed. "There's nothing worse than having my own words thrown back at me."

"However," Elliot said with a comic leer, "don't knock good sex." He tangled his fingers in his wife's hair, pulled her head back, nibbled on her lips, then bit her earlobe.

Feeling all the wonderful, familiar sensations, Kim cupped the back of Elliot's head and pulled his face to hers. "Never," she whispered, her voice already growing hoarse. "For a thousand reasons, I'd never knock good sex."

Early in the afternoon of the following Friday, Kim and Tracy pulled into a parking space beside a small restaurant about a half an hour from the Catskill Lake Resort. So Elliot could have the use of their only car for the weekend, he had dropped Kim off at Tracy's apartment, which was midway between Kim's place and the resort. The hour they had been driving had passed quickly, with chatter about their joint history, world affairs, books, TV shows, and a thousand other bits of small talk. They had carefully avoided talking about the weekend. Kim had suggested that they stop for lunch since she'd probably be involved with preparations once they arrived at their destination and she had told Tracy that she wanted one last quiet moment.

The mid-September day was magnificent, clear and cool with white puffy clouds occasionally obscuring the bright sunlight. The ride up the highway had been spectacular, with tall evergreens and still-green deciduous trees interspersed with a few golden aspen and occasional scarlet, orange, and flame yellow sugar maples. "Fall is the most fabulous season," Tracy said, climbing from behind the wheel of her eight-year-old Toyota. She stared at one huge maple in which the leaves at the ends of the branches had turned, but the ones closest to the trunk were still brilliant green. "I think the mix of the green and the reds and golds is so beautiful." She inhaled, enjoying the slight snap in the air.

"I just love this time of year, too," Kim said, rubbing the small of her back. Although she was showing only slightly, Tracy had noticed that her sister's entire body seemed a bit off balance.

"Are you feeling okay?" Tracy asked. Since Kim had told her sister about the fact that she was a high-risk pregnancy, Tracy had been concerned, yet trying not to hover.

"Thanks for caring so much, Trace. I'm actually feeling really good." She rubbed the small of her back again. "Except for my back."

Tracy draped an arm over her sister's shoulders as they walked toward the entrance to the diner. "The timing of this weekend is working out pretty well. It's late enough that you're not even queasy anymore, yet soon enough that you're not really showing. Are you going to tell people at the workshop about the babies?"

"I don't think so," Kim said, pulling the heavy door open. "Since we don't know anything about the next weekend, I think I'll leave well enough alone."

Tracy waggled two fingers at the hostess and then followed the woman to the back of the dining room. They sat and were handed huge plastic-coated menus. "Don't be chintzy, sis," Kim said, motioning to the menu. "Remember that Uncle Sam picks up half of everything."

"Half? You pay that much in taxes?" Tracy asked.

"Between federal, self-employment, and New York State tax, yeah. As an independent contractor, it really sucks. Every quarter I open my wallet and the Unc takes pretty much whatever he wants."

"It can't be that bad," Tracy said, laughing.

Kim's answer was merely to raise an eyebrow.

Once the waitress had taken their orders, Tracy asked, "You said before that you wouldn't tell people about the babies because of your doubts about the next weekend. What does this weekend have to do with the next one?"

"We've avoided talking about this weekend for over an hour. Are you sure you want to discuss it now? You seemed to want to do it all cold."

"I'm getting more and more curious, so if you don't mind, I'd love to ask a few questions."

"I don't mind at all. Shoot."

"What about this weekend affecting the next one?"

"In the last year or so I've begun to get quite a few repeaters," Kim said.

"You mean folks pay that much to go again? Why would anyone want to learn about kinky sex more than once? There's not that much to know, is there?"

"There's a lot to know, but it's not just that." Kim's smile was a bit bemused. "Trace, this weekend is many things to the attendees. For some it's a chance to learn about, as you put it, kinky sex, and to play if they want in complete privacy. For others it's a chance to get away from the kids and spend two full days concentrating on each other. A few are looking for kindred spirits to play with and some come for the shopping, to add new toys to their collection and try them out in an atmosphere of acceptance."

"You mentioned vendors when we first talked. Isn't saying that you're coming to a creative sex weekend to shop like telling folks you're buying *Playboy* for the articles?"

Kim giggled as she said, "Not at all. Most people buy something if only to remember the weekend."

"Tell me about the first one," Tracy suggested.

Kim gazed off into space as she said, "I hosted the first of these weekends three years ago. I placed a few ads to run beside my columns and expected to have maybe a dozen couples. I was shocked when I received reservations from thirty-three."

The conversation was interrupted by the waitress, who placed a grilled cheese sandwich and a Coke in front of Tracy and a tuna salad platter and a glass of ice water on the Formica-topped table for Kim. She placed a dish of well-done french fries between the two women. When they were alone again, Tracy said, "Thirty-three couples? From just a few ads?"

"I was astounded, I can tell you, but Miranda had quite a following even then. When I thought about what I had undertaken, I was terrified. I had spent hours and hours going over what I could talk about but facing the actuality of it all was daunting. I leave a lot of free time, of course, for playing with all the ideas we discuss, quiet walks so couples can just 'be together,' and in the evenings there's a guy who plays quiet dance music on a keyboard. I also set aside as much time as I can for short one-on-one meetings with individuals and couples who want some personal advice.

"That first weekend the whole thing scared the hell out of

me but Dave was a rock. He'd been doing theme weekends for quite a while and made a lot of suggestions. He's the one who thought that I could get companies to set up booths or rooms to sell stuff."

"Sex toys and kinky lingerie?" Tracy asked, taking a bite of her sandwich.

"Don't knock it, babe. Dave and I share nice hefty space fees and the shop owners do a really brisk business. This weekend I have a lingerie shop and a toy company, who each get their own room. The book, magazine, and video store shares a large room with a gift-type shop with aromatherapy candles, bath oils, and such and a bakery and confectionary."

"Cakes?"

"Silly gift ideas. They have penis-shaped lollipops, cakes, and cupcakes with dirty pictures on top. Things like that. Dave has made great contacts for me. He's got an amazingly entrepreneurial mind."

"He sounds like quite a guy."

"He is. Between us, we've made this one of his most lucrative of his theme happenings."

"What else does he do?"

Kim told Tracy about the varied nature of the weekends that the Catskill Lake Resort hosted. "He also does a leaf-watching weekend in late September and early October each year, with guided walks, nature bus tours, and big fires with marshmallows. That's why we picked this weekend, just before the leaf-loving tourists flock into the area." She took a forkful of cole slaw then poured a pool of ketchup on the french fry plate. She shook her head slowly. "I know the doctor told me to watch the fried food, but I'm so hungry all the time."

"Maybe because you're eating for three," Tracy said.

"I know, but as the doctor said, two of those three are really, really, really tiny."

Tracy giggled, then sipped her soda. "I think I like your obstetrician. If you don't mind, let's get back to the repeaters. Why? They can take weekend vacations anywhere, I assume. Why would they come to your weekend for a second time? It's not cheap, after all."

"It must have been my fifth or sixth weekend when I got my first repeaters, and I was as mystified as you are. I remember them so well. Juan and Linda Ortiz. In their forties, with three teenage kids. I ran into them in the lobby that Saturday afternoon and I asked why they came back. She was a pisser. 'It's the atmosphere. Here I can be open about things I've always been really closed about. It's you, Kim. You encourage me to let loose.' She poked her husband. 'And he just loves the "me" who emerges.' I guess that about says it."

"That's quite a compliment, sis," Tracy said, dipping a french fry into the ketchup. "It also reinforces that fact that I could never do it."

"We promised each other before we left this morning that we wouldn't talk about the future and I'm going to hold you to that. We can discuss everything on the way home. For now, just roll with it. No decisions or negative thinking."

Nodding, Tracy said, "Okay, sis. I'm rolling."

Forty minutes later, Tracy turned off the highway onto Catskill Lake Road. Signs with whimsical weather vanes all pointed toward the resort. As she rounded a bend, Tracy caught her first glimpse of the old resort hotel.

The three four-story buildings, each white clapboard with forest green shutters and trim, formed a U. Each building was surrounded by a deep porch adorned with white rocking chairs and hanging pots of bright red ivy geraniums, their leaves still green despite the increasingly cold nights. Cedars and pines intermixed with colorful maples and sycamores cuddled close to all three buildings. Remains of brightly colored gardens, some of the less hardy flowers already frost-killed, surrounded graveled walkways. She parked in the large lot and just looked at the hotel. "The place looks wonderful. How did you find it?"

"Before our wedding, someone gave Elliot and me a brochure and this hotel looked so comfortable that we decided to honeymoon here. Midsummer is particularly lovely, and although we had lots of ideas for day trips, we ended up sitting by the pool most of the time."

"When you came out of your room."

Tracy was amazed to see Kim blush slightly. "True. Anyway, when I got the idea for the weekends, I had no doubt. This place was perfect and I wouldn't settle for anywhere else."

A few hundred yards from the open side of the U was tree-lined Catskill Lake. The field between it and the hotel was covered with dozens of large Canada geese and several varieties of ducks, all pulling up bills full of grass. Several swans floated idly on the water's mirror-smooth surface. In a fenced-in area beside one building, three people were target shooting with bows and arrows, and Tracy could hear the squeals of the courageous souls in the outdoor pool.

What startled Tracy most about the resort were the bird feeders and birdhouses. They were everywhere, hanging from every available tree limb, suspended from curved wrought iron poles, and nailed to the top of wooden supports sunk into the well-manicured lawns. Birds of all kinds sat on perches, nibbling at the seed offerings. Chickadees, titmouses, blue jays, and English sparrows attacked sunflower seed feeders; woodpeckers climbed over the mesh around peanut holders; and gold- and house-finches nibbled daintily on thistle seed. A pair of cardinals and some white-throated sparrows wandered beneath one of the feeders, pecking for anything another bird had thrown overboard. Tracy pictured the one small feeder she had put on the tree outside her front door and the bird book that sat on the table beside her window. "I've never seen so many feeders. I've got one at home and I could sit and watch the birds all day."

"They're fabulous. Dave's got them everywhere. They're a delight to all the children, and many of the adults, too. He attracts birds and birders alike. They do a hawk census twice a year here during their migration."

Tracy watched a pair of loudly chattering squirrels chase each other up the trunk of a huge oak that shaded one side of the central building. "Just wonderful." Reluctantly, she got out of the car and opened the trunk.

When Kim reached out for her suitcase, Tracy held it back. "Don't baby me," Kim said. "It'll make me crazy. Please, Trace, treat me as if I weren't pregnant. Please."

Tracy handed Kim her suitcase and pulled her own out. As they started toward the main entrance, the door opened and a tall man walked toward them. "Dave," Kim called.

As they approached each other, Tracy got a chance to study Dave Markov. Tall and well built, Dave was a nice-looking man without being handsome. His face was angular with a trace of five o'clock shadow shading a prominent jaw line with a deep Kirk Douglas-type cleft in his chin. His hair was very dark and he wore it long, curling over his ears and his collar. His eyes were deep blue, topped by heavy black brows. As he drew closer, Tracy admired his long black lashes.

"Kim," Dave said, his voice warm and welcoming. "It's wonderful to see you again. You look ravishing, as always." As Tracy watched, Dave hugged her sister and kissed her full on the mouth.

I wonder whether they've ever made it, she thought, then mentally slapped herself.

Dave turned his electric smile toward her. "You must be Tracy." With his arm around Kim's waist, hugging her close, he extended his other hand. "Welcome. I'm delighted to meet you."

Tracy took the proffered hand, admiring his strong grip and slightly roughened skin. "I'm really glad to be here. What a setting. Your hotel is magnificent."

"Thanks. I guess I'm like a proud father. Admire my child and I'm yours forever." He unwound his arm from around Kim's waist, grabbed their suitcases, then led them into the cavernous, yet comfortable lobby.

Tracy's first impression was of carefully crafted space designed to look homey, with brightly colored overstuffed chairs and sofas that begged to be cuddled in. Braided rugs and white ginger jar lamps were set off by ferns, snake plants, and philodendrons that, in turn, softened the rugged lines of the hand-carved wooden tables and chairs arranged to encourage game and card playing. Exposed beams crossed the high ceilings, which set off wood-paneled walls with white trim around the windows and doors. There were two TV sets in separate seating areas, each tuned to a different afternoon talk show. Several women sat around each, animatedly discussing the problems of the participants. Animal and bird prints covered the paneled walls along with dozens of weather vanes and birdhouses.

Dave guided them to the long desk, behind which were two young women, busy with phones. "Meg, Annelise, these are Kim and Tracy Ryan. Set them up, will you?"

"Actually it's Tracy McBride. Ryan is Kim's married name."

"Of course. I'm really sorry." Dave looked chagrined. "I don't usually make faux pas like that."

"No problem."

While they had been talking, Meg had created two card keys and scribbled the room number on an envelope for each. "I'll need you each to sign in, of course, but here are your keys. Your rooms are ready whenever you are."

"Rooms?" Tracy said. "I thought Kim and I could share. I don't want to put anyone out or cause you extra expense."

"Don't be silly," Dave said. "You will each need some privacy during the hectic lunacy. I had an extra room and it's no trouble at all."

"Thanks, Dave," Tracy said. "That's very thoughtful."

"Get settled and I'll see you both later," Dave suggested, then stepped behind the check-in desk to help with a large group of people who had just arrived.

After they had signed register cards, Kim and Tracy headed for the breezeway to the adults-only building. "He's really cute, isn't he?" Kim said *sotto voce* as they walked.

"I guess," Tracy responded, "if you like the macho type."

"Macho? Funny, I don't see that in him at all. He's really a great guy and a good friend."

"Does he ever make it with the folks who attend your workshops?" Tracy asked, desperately trying to ascertain whether he was a threat to her sister's marriage. Babies or no babies, Kim was an attractive woman and might be tempted by a guy like Dave.

Kim faced her sister at the foot of a flight of stairs. "This weekend isn't an orgy, Trace. These couples come here to get closer to each other, not to pick up complications."

"I understand that, but you said that occasionally some of the couples do"—she struggled for the right words—"play together. I just wondered whether he's ever a third."

Kim started up the stairs. "I've really no idea. I've never seen any indication of anything like that, but God knows, he's attractive enough."

"Do you find him sexy?" Tracy asked.

Kim stopped at the second-floor landing, puffing slightly, and put down her suitcase. She turned to face her sister and gazed at her intently. "I can still read your mind, Trace, and no, I'm not tempted by Dave Markov. Elliot and I are monogamous and I wouldn't dream of changing that."

Tracy heaved a silent sigh of relief. "Sorry, sis. That wasn't worthy of me."

"No, it wasn't." Then Kim winked. "Actually, if I were ever to fall off the monogamy wagon, I could do lots worse than Dave. He's got a really sexy mouth and bedroom eyes."

Tracy looked blankly at her sister. "He has?"

"God, Trace, you've been out of circulation much too long. Maybe this weekend will improve your sex life, too." Kim walked down a long interior hallway toward her room, with her sister following.

"My sex life is fine just as it is," Tracy said to her sister's back.

"Your sex life is nonexistent and has been ever since you got back from the West Coast."

"You know nothing about my sex life," Tracy said, as she glanced at her envelope, then at the room numbers.

"Okay, so you've got a great sex life. I've just never seen any sign of it."

"Lay off, sis," Tracy said, finding her room and setting her suitcase down beside the door.

"Sorry. You're right. It's none of my business." Kim looked at her envelope. "I'm down at the end of the hall. Why don't you unpack whatever you need to and meet me in the lobby in fifteen minutes? I have to check on a lot of stupid details, and while I do, I can show you around the facilities so you can get to know how they're all set up."

Half an hour later, Dave closed the door behind him and dropped into his office chair. Kim's sister was going to prove to be an interesting project. The two women looked alike superficially, but their body language and dress separated them.

Where Kim wore her jeans tastefully snug and her light yellow shirt with the top two buttons open, Tracy wore her jeans one size too large with a loose turtleneck sweater bloused over the waistline, hiding whatever shape she had. Where Kim wore her medium brown hair softly curled around her face, Tracy merely pulled hers back into a ponytail. Kim wore chunky gold earrings and her sister wore small pearl studs. Where Kim looked him in the eye, direct and maybe a bit flirtatious, Tracy's eyes avoided his. When Kim had reached for him to say a friendly hello, Tracy had stepped back. It was just a tiny step but Dave had seen it.

Bringing her out of her shell should prove an intriguing project, he thought, and a necessary one if he was to keep the Creative Loving Weekends going. If anyone could teach a woman about sexuality, it was him. He tried to picture Tracy with her hair loose instead of in its tight ponytail, her eyes misted and dark with passion, her chest heaving, her body open to him. Yes, indeed, an interesting project, one he'd begin after the first session of Kim's workshop. He had little doubt that the sensual atmosphere that Kim created would soften even her prickly sister.

Chapter

3

For more than an hour, Kim showed Tracy around the resort, from the room filled with electronic games and pinball machines to the small gym with mirrored walls, which contained a treadmill and several pieces of exercise equipment. Tracy saw the indoor pool and spa in their building, which had access restricted to those staying in that section of the hotel only. There was, of course, a similar indoor facility in each of the other buildings and an outdoor pool complex complete with a separate twelve-foot-deep diving pool, a kiddie pool with gentle sprinkler, and a sixteen-person hot tub.

When Kim went back to her room to take her doctor-ordered midafternoon nap, Tracy took a book, found a comfortable chair in a quiet sitting area at the end of their hallway, and read for quite a while, trying to tamp down her anxiety.

At seven-thirty that evening, after a quiet dinner with her sister, Tracy settled into a softly padded white metal chair behind a long white table at the rear of a large meeting room. The room, which appeared able to hold about a hundred people, was quickly filling with couples of all ages, shapes, sizes, and colors. There was a woman in a wheelchair and a man with his lower leg in a cast, a pair of crutches resting against the table beside him.

The oldest couple appeared to be in their seventies, a sweet-looking woman with marshmallow hair and a man with a mane of iron gray hair and a florid complexion. Although Tracy realized that their looks must be deceiving, the youngest couple looked to be about twelve, holding hands and whispering to each other, giggling occasionally as they, like most others, surveyed the other attendees. A huge black man stood in a back corner looking uneasy as his partner tried to wave him into the chair beside her and he kept shaking his head. Several of the seated men squirmed in their seats. As she gazed, she realized that, for the most part, the women looked comfortable while the men were slightly uneasy.

Most people were dressed casually, in jeans or slacks with shirts, sweaters, and sweatshirts of all types, but a few men had sport jackets on and a few women wore silk blouses or shirts with sequins and dress slacks. Tracy had debated for a while as to what clothes to bring with her so she'd brought an assortment. Since she might be introduced to someone as Kim's sister, this evening she wanted to set the right tone, stylish yet quiet and calm, so she had settled on a moss green turtleneck sweater with slightly baggy, well-washed, used-to-be-blue jeans. She wore little makeup, and her only jewelry were her pearl studs and her functional Timex watch. She toed her feet from her sneakers and hooked her sock-covered insteps over the railing of her chair. Kim, dressed in a marigold yellow man-tailored shirt with straight-cut jeans and ankle boots, stood in the front of the room chatting with several couples. Tracy marveled at how relaxed her sister looked, smiling and laughing, shaking hands with each of the people in turn.

She became aware of movement beside her and turned to see Dave Markov standing over her. "Hi," he said, handing her a glass of white wine and setting one for himself on the table beside her. Tracy had noticed a setup at the side of the room with sodas, beer, and open bottles of white and red wine but she hadn't helped herself. "To get folks relaxed," Dave said, looking around. "Watching Kim work the crowd? It's amazing how she manages to put people at ease. She's quite a woman."

"Yes, she is." She gazed at Dave as he folded himself into his chair, and she recalled Kim's comments on his sexy mouth and bedroom eyes. Although her sister had assured her several times that he was no threat to Kim's marriage, there still was a tiny niggling doubt in Tracy's mind. She had to admit that he was attractive. He had a way of looking at you, not around you, while you spoke, as though your words were the most important he had ever heard. There was something intense and focused about him. She wouldn't blame her sister if she had been interested at one time.

Dave sipped his wine. "I think her pregnancy has made her even prettier."

"You know about the babies?"

"She called me to warn me that the next weekend might be a nonevent." He sighed. "It will be quite a loss, and there will be lots of disappointed people. I've already got reservations for all the available rooms, and there's a waiting list."

"So soon? It's not for four months."

"I know. Kim's weekends fill up a year in advance. She told me you probably weren't interested in running it for her. How come?"

"That's really between Kim and me," Tracy said, then deliberately concentrated her attention on the front of the room.

"Sorry. I didn't mean to be nosy."

The couples Kim had been talking with took seats and she perched on the edge of the large table at the front of the room. "Good evening, everyone." The room quieted. Tracy had been teaching public speaking long enough to appreciate

Kim's immediate command of the audience. Not only her voice but her body language and eye contact made her the immediate center of attention. "I've met many of you already but I'd like to start at the beginning and tell you a little about me and about how this weekend is going to proceed. First, let me introduce myself. My name is Kim Ryan, alias Miranda, and I've been running these Creative Loving Weekends for over three years. Some of you out there"—Kim glanced around the room—"are familiar faces. For you, welcome back. For the rest of you, welcome."

Tracy tried to see her sister as her audience might see her, poised and confident, yet with an aura of ease and acceptance. She was totally comfortable with what she was doing in a way that Tracy knew she could never hope to be. Another reason for her not to even think about attempting the weekend, money or no money.

Kim continued, "I want to make this very clear right up front. I'm not a sex therapist or a counselor of any kind. I've no 'professional' credentials at all. I'm just someone who's been there, done that. I'm married to a wonderful man and have been for about five years. Our relationship is everything I could want and"—she winked and it appeared as if she were talking personally to each person in the audience—"the sex is terrific.

"I started dating when I was in my teens and had several long-term relationships, but until Elliot, none of them became permanent. When it's right, it's right, and we both knew it. Before that, I had indulged in a lot of one-night stands, many of which were fun, some of which were disasters. I spent a lot of my life ignorant, trying to find out what all the shouting was about. I think I've learned at least some of the answers—well, maybe I merely know most of the questions."

There was a titter from the audience. Tracy glanced at Dave, who seemed enthralled with Kim's speech, even though he'd probably heard it many times.

"About four years ago, I was working as a stringer for a local newspaper in my hometown when the woman who wrote the advice column took some of her own advice, reached for the brass ring, married a guy from California, and quit on the spot. With only a day until deadline, and the column unfinished, the editor asked me whether I'd fill in for that week only, until he hired someone else. Well, I'm still writing it. When I began, I thought I knew it all and could answer, if not all, then most of the questions troubled people sent me. I'd always had lots of common sense, and since I'd been married for a year at that point, I figured I could handle it. Actually, if the truth were known, over the years I've learned as much as I've taught.

"On what basis do I answer questions? I use my experience, lots of reference books, and a great deal of merely observing humanity. As most of you know, I run a very active website, too, through which I can ask my visitors for help with finding information and request answers to opinion questions. I ask everyone I write to and those who read my column to remember one important principle, and I'll ask that of you for this weekend. It's your life. You have to make decisions yourself and take responsibility for them. I can only give you my take on things and, I hope, occasionally suggest a different way of approaching a problem.

"Everything's colored by my own feelings about things, so if at any time this weekend I go somewhere you don't want to go, don't go there. It's just that simple. I take no offense if, during a forum, you get up and leave. If it's not your thing, find something that is. However, don't judge others. Remember that one man's meat . . . Hmmm." As the audience burst into laughter at Kim's double entendre, she merely shrugged and grinned. Tracy guessed that she'd made that joke several times in the past but it still sounded as fresh as it must have been the first time.

Tracy leaned back in her chair and thought about the point that her sister was making. Good advice, she thought. Kim's so sane. I'll try not to judge, especially when I don't understand.

Kim took a sip of water from the glass beside her on the table, then continued. "Now, about the weekend. We're here to have fun. That's the most important lesson I can teach, about the weekend and about your sex life in general. Have fun. I have only a few rules. I know some of you have children and have to keep in touch with your baby-sitters. Please call them periodically, so they don't have to call you. If you have a cell phone, turn it off, or if you just can't bring yourself to be completely out of touch, please put it on vibrate so it doesn't disturb us. If it rings and you have to answer, take it outside. As for business calls—tell them you've got total amnesia and can't answer any business questions or deal with anything professional until Sunday afternoon. Or maybe Tuesday, or Christmas. Somehow you have to carve out your own personal time, time to be with your partner. Time you two can focus on each other. Not the business, not the kids or the crabgrass.

"You've noticed the wine, beer, and sodas on the table over there." She pointed. "Since no one's driving anywhere tonight, please help yourself and be generous. Except for hard liquor, drinks are complimentary. If you want a cocktail or other liquor-type drinks, we're on the honor system. Please sign the list with your name and room number. Alcohol is available so you will all be relaxed but it's not for you to get drunk, so imbibe as you like but within limits. Too much often makes men willing but sometimes unable, women eager yet possibly preoccupied, and both of you careless. No one in here wants to do something he or she will regret in the morning. Or not even remember." There were a few giggles.

"This wonderful hotel has been hosting our weekends for several years and we're occupying almost all of the rooms in this building. There are folks in the two other buildings who aren't in our group, so if you see people wandering the grounds, or whatever, remember that they might not be into Creative Loving. Try not to embarrass anyone." A few in the audience giggled. "The pool and hot tub in this building are for our use only and will be available around the clock." She winked. "Even for midnight skinny-dipping if you're so inclined. There's no lifeguard so please don't go in alone, and you'll need your room key to get through the door. Just remember that you might have company.

"Your rooms aren't soundproof but I'd like you to pretend that they are. Make noisy love if you like. As a matter of fact, I encourage it. Just try to keep the shouting down to moderate shrieks, and if you hear something next door, ignore it. With that in mind, please don't murder your partner this weekend. No one will pay any attention to the screaming."

Kim calmly waited until the laughter abated while Tracy gazed at her, amazed at her sister's ability to set everyone, including herself, at ease with such potentially embarrassing topics. Tracy was even becoming comfortable with the idea of a kinky sex weekend. For everyone else, of course.

"All the TVs in your rooms have been unplugged. That doesn't mean you can't plug them back in, but don't use them as an excuse not to talk to each other. This is a couples weekend and that means spending time interacting, not staring at the tube. The dining room has a section especially for us, separated from the rest of the diners by several movable partitions. It's set up mostly with tables for two. If you want to be with another kindred couple, fine. Find a larger table or move two tables together. Just remember that the focus of everything this weekend is the two of you."

Without necessarily realizing what they were doing, several couples slid closer and clasped each other's hands. Tracy knew that, when judging an audience's reaction to a presentation, body language said a lot. In this room the body language was all about loving and closeness.

"Here's how the weekend will work," Kim continued. "First, you have a schedule of the forums in your brochure. If you can't find yours, there will always be a stack in each meeting room. Not every workshop will necessarily be to your taste so pick and choose. Are you interested in fantasies, dirty talking, erotic writing to share ideas with your partner, oral sex, anal sex, masturbation? Maybe you're ready to explore bondage or pain as part of pleasure. I've added a new forum this weekend on kissing and foreplay in general, which will take place right after this, followed by the one on masturbation. I'm sure you'll find something to enjoy and maybe you'll learn something about sex, about your partner, and even about yourself.

"As you might have seen, there are rooms set up by companies trying to sell you stuff. There's a room for toys, one for a company that sells sexy and silly lingerie for both sexes, there's a bookshop and an X-rated movie rental company. And before you ask, yes, every room has a VCR, so again, just plug it in. Browse and buy if you're so inclined or just wander and get aroused by what you see. I don't specifically endorse any product and everyone's taste is different. Just remember, the key word is fun. Oh, and new this weekend is a display and sale set up by an erotic bakery, so if you've always wanted to eat pussy and your partner isn't so inclined, buy a chocolate one."

Tracy winced at the vulgar language and there was a buzz of nervous laughter in the room. "Yes, I said pussy. Folks, it's just a word. Maybe it's one you've never used, but you all certainly know what it means. Before I ran my first weekend, I had to think carefully about what words might offend and what to call body parts. I considered always using the words *penis* and *vagina*, but to me they're much too clinical for discussions of, say, dirty talking and storytelling. I'm sorry if I offend you, but sometimes it just feels right to use those Anglo-Saxon four-letter words. So, hold on to your hats." She stood up and walked the length of the front of the room as she said, "Fuck. Suck. Tits. Pussy. Cock. Dick.

"Phew. Better now?"

The room erupted in laughter and most of the audience seemed to relax again. "I hope you go away from here on Sunday afternoon with at least one new idea or activity that you and your partner can enjoy playing with for a long time to come. Maybe it's just a new way to communicate or an appreciation of kissing. Maybe it's sharing erotic stories, playing with toys as part of foreplay, or whispering sweet and dirty somethings into each other's ears.

"Maybe you'll merely spend an entire weekend devoted to each other, so you'll learn how wonderful it can be when you decide to concentrate on good sex together." Kim looked around at her audience. "Oh, and one more thing. Some of you might be wondering about the couples who are here for their second time, or more for that matter. This weekend is devoted to great sex. It's a perfect way to get away and concentrate on each other, a way to invigorate your sex life by adding new ideas, a place to be selfish. Enjoy!!!" She walked to the center of the front table.

"Just in case you think I'm going to do all the work, I have some assignments for you. First, raise your antenna and get in contact with your partner. Try to read body language, expressions, tiny hints of what he or she might be trying to tell you yet not have the words. Frequently it's difficult, if not impossible, to talk about things you'd like to try so turn up and tune in. Then spend every forum and every discussion holding hands."

Tracy saw several couples reach for each other's hands as Kim continued, "If you hear something that curls your toes, squeeze your partner's hand. Don't talk, just squeeze. That's your cue, partner, to consider what your lover has just said without words. Is she saying that she'd like to try bondage, or buy a vibrator, or masturbate while you watch? Is he trying to tell you that he'd like to watch you strip for him, or see you in some outrageous lingerie? Would he or she like to try oral or anal sex?

"Your second assignment is for every time you make love. I want you to tell your partner when he or she does something that really curls your toes." When the audience stirred, she said, "Yes, with words. It can be as simple as moaning 'Good' at the appropriate minute or as complex as 'I love it when you touch my breasts.' Difficult to put things into words? It will get easier, I promise."

Several heads nodded. "After you've both done that at least half a dozen times, move on to 'I love it like that but it would be even better if you'd . . .' That's a nonpejorative way of asking for something you'd like without hurting your partner's feelings. 'I love it when your fingers are inside me, but it would be even better if you'd move more slowly,' or 'I love it when you nibble on my nipples but I wish you'd bite a little harder,' or 'Squeeze my cock more tightly.' I think you get the idea."

Tracy was surprised at the nonthreatening methods of communication her sister had focused on. She really understands this stuff, Tracy thought. "Okay, here's one last nonverbal method of communication I think you might try. When you get home, I want you to write about your ideal night of sex. It might be making love on a beach or tied to the bed. Open your mind and be as creative as you can. Make up a story or write a first-person account. However you want to, do it. Then exchange stories and separate."

There was a buzz in the audience and lots of nodding heads. What a fabulous idea, Tracy thought, a great way to lower the risk of mentioning something to your partner.

Kim walked toward the back of the room. "One last thing. Let me introduce two people to you. First, my sister Tracy. She's going to be helping, and learning, just as we all will be. Stand up, Tracy."

Tracy rose about a foot off her chair as everyone in the room turned to look at her. She'd intended to remain in the shadows but it seemed that Kim wasn't going to let her.

Kim moved behind Dave's chair and pulled him to a standing position. "This guy here is Dave Markov. He's the owner, manager, and coordinator here, and as such, he's in charge of everything, from TVs that don't work to special meals. Ask him for whatever you need and he'll see to it that you get it. Mostly. He's a gem and we're lucky to have him. From a personal standpoint, without him, this weekend wouldn't happen."

Kim returned to the front of the room. "Okay, that's all the generalities from me for now. I've probably forgotten something but it will all be clear as the weekend rolls on. There's a whiteboard outside on which I'll write notes, possible time changes and such. I'll also try to make myself available for brief private discussions with those of you who wish on a first-come, first-serve basis and there will be a sign-up sheet there, too. For right now, let's take a fifteen-minute break and then we'll begin with the forum on foreplay, followed by one on masturbation. For those who want to attend either or both, they'll be right here and there's information about those and all of the forums in your brochure. For the rest of you, have fun and I'll see you when you want me."

Tracy sat quietly as Dave got up to leave. "I assume you're staying for the forums." When Tracy nodded, Dave said, "I'll see you later, but for now I've got a hotel to run."

"Right," Tracy said distractedly. "See you later." After two forums on how to be sexy.

* * *

It was after ten o'clock when Dave reentered the main meeting room and saw Tracy sitting alone in the chair she'd been occupying when he'd left her two hours before. She looked . . . well, the best way he could describe it was shell-shocked. He sat down beside her and, moving slowly, asked, "Where's your sister?"

"She's off to bed. The doctor's got her on a pretty tight leash."

He almost laughed out loud at the expression on Tracy's face. She looked like a virgin at a hooker convention. Getting her to open up enough to run the winter weekend was going to be fun. "You've got that deer-in-the-headlights look. Are you okay?"

Tracy hesitated, then said, "I'm not really sure."

"How were the forums?"

"That's why I'm not really sure. They were not what I expected at all." When Dave didn't comment, Tracy continued, "People talked about things."

Hot, exciting things, he hoped. "What did you expect?"

"I guess I thought Kim would lecture and everyone else would listen. It wasn't that way at all. Lots of people talked. People who didn't know each other from Adam discussed how they liked to be kissed and how and when they masturbated."

Dave watched her blanch as she realized what she had said. He took her hand, for now in an almost brotherly fashion. "This is a weekend for people who are pretty open-minded. Did everyone have something to say?"

"No, not everyone, of course, but I would say more than half of the people had something to say, or asked an intimate question. I know more now about my sister's sex life than I ever did or ever wanted to." She squirmed in her chair. "And Elliot's, too."

"I guess that would make it a bit awkward. It's probably

easier to talk to strangers about stuff like that than to learn the intimate details about people you know."

As Tracy sat, shaking her head, Dave thought about his next move. He had finished everything he needed to around the resort and now he wanted to see what he could do about his main project: getting Tracy into bed. "Have you seen the sales rooms yet?"

"No. Kim was going to show me around after dinner but she ran into a couple who were here for the fourth time. By the time they had finished catching up, it was time for the kickoff session."

"Great. Let me." He glanced at his watch. "It's almost ten-thirty but most of the rooms should still be open." He stood, then helped Tracy up with a hand beneath her elbow. As if it were natural, he guided her toward the door with a hand in the small of her back.

Tracy's mind was spinning. So many people had been so open about sex, particularly during the forum on masturbation. She was shocked but, she had to admit, also titillated. When she and Andrew had been together, she had touched herself occasionally, usually because Andrew had left her unsatisfied and she had never climaxed. Of course, that hadn't been his fault.

Dave led her into the Onondaga Room, just beside the main meeting room. Tables were covered with displays of sex toys, and a number of couples wandered, touching, giggling, and putting several intended purchases into small plastic shopping baskets. Tracy walked from table to table, simply staring at the assortment of products for sale. Dildos and vibrators of every type, color, and size, lubricants and massage oils. There was a box containing something called Ben Wa balls and one for anal beads, whatever they were.

"Meet Matt Morrison," Dave said, introducing her to a tall, angular-featured man in his mid-thirties. "This is Kim's sister, Tracy."

"Nice to meet you," Matt said, shaking her hand.

"Matt's store, the Adult Toy Box, is all the way down in the city, but he's been coming up here for Kim's weekends for more than two years."

"And it's really worth the effort," he said, looking around at the dozen or so shoppers. "Kim heats them up and I provide the firewood."

"Excuse me," a thirty-something woman said. "Could you help us with something?"

"Business calls," Matt said to Dave and Tracy, then followed the woman to the far side of the room.

"Matt's toy collection is pretty extensive," Dave said, wandering between tables filled with merchandise. "If he doesn't have what you want, he has dozens of catalogs and can order just about anything." He pointed to the small sales table at the front of the room. "He's really good at this. He stocks batteries of all sizes and even extension cords. Every store stocks condoms, of course, and he has them in all colors, shapes, and sizes. He's even put together assortment packs so folks can experiment."

As she looked around, Tracy's mind was boggled. She knew sex toys existed, of course, but the variety of items for sale was astounding. Dave stopped just ahead of her, picked up a medium-sized, pale tan dildo, and stroked the surface, his long fingers wrapping sensuously around the shaft. "Ever try one of these?"

Tracy could feel her face heat, and her tongue was unable to articulate a syllable. She shook her head.

As though unaware of her discomfort, Dave continued, "These are made of a new plastic with a really lifelike surface. No more cold, rigid plastic, although I gather many women like the icy feel." He picked up another dildo. "This one can be filled with either hot or cold water. You should try it sometime."

Tracy stared at the dildos. She'd never owned one, but if she was being honest, she was now becoming curious. She could feel the prickle between her legs. Move on, Dave, please! she screamed silently. Finally he put the dildo down and moved into another area of the room.

Oh, God, Tracy thought as she followed him. This is too much. She stared at a table covered with bondage gear: handcuffs, chains, padlocks, lengths of rope, and studded dog collars. She reached for something labeled a spreader bar then pulled her hand back. All this equipment had her breathing rapidly and her heart pounding. Her underwear suddenly felt too tight. Farther down the table was a display of whips and paddles. Tracy felt almost woozy. Shock? Desire? She didn't wait to find out.

Without conscious thought, she hustled toward the door with Dave right behind her. "I'm sorry Diana's already closed up for the evening," he said, indicating the door to the Seneca room. "You'll meet her tomorrow. She's a character and I know you'll love her."

Tracy tried to moisten her lips. "What does she sell?" she asked, her voice cracking just a bit.

"The most delicious and outrageous lingerie you've ever seen."

"Oh," Tracy said, picturing a *Playboy* centerfold in a black peignoir.

"Listen," Dave said, bringing her back to the present, "let's wander over to the bar and get a drink. You look like you could use one."

Several minutes later, seated at a small booth in the back of the Saratoga Bar, Dave sipped a beer. The room consisted of two sections—a long bar with adjoining booths, the seats covered in deep burgundy leather-look plastic and the tables topped with highly polished wood; and a larger room with tables and chairs, a man playing a keyboard, and a small dance floor. Tracy's glass sat in front of her untouched. "Want to tell me about it?" Dave said.

"Tell you about what?" Tracy said, grabbing her glass and taking a gulp of her beer to wet her straw-dry mouth.

"Let's be honest here. I might not be the most perceptive man around, but it's pretty obvious that this whole thing upsets you. I would have thought that, with Kim for a sister, you'd be pretty open about all this."

"I'm not like Kim." Not at all.

"I have to admit that Kim told me a bit about you, that you had been married and aren't anymore. I'm a pretty good listener."

"I don't know what you're talking about."

"Did your husband have anything to do with this?" Tracy's eyes began to fill with unshed tears, all her emotions painfully close to the surface. Dave reached across the table and took her hand, holding it tightly when she tried to withdraw. "Tell me."

"I can't," Tracy said, a tear now trickling down her cheek.

"You can pretend I'm a bartender, someone you'll never have to see again. I promise I won't tell anything." He squeezed her hand. "Please. It might help, and from the looks of you right now, it couldn't get any worse."

Using her other hand, Tracy pulled a napkin from the holder on the table and swiped at her tears. "Maybe not, but my thoughts are all mine. I'm not a good sharer."

"Okay then, let me guess. Hubby wasn't good in bed and he told you it was your fault."

Did it show? Was everything in her mind written in bold letters across her forehead? Hearing Dave say it like that made Tracy want to hide. He was much too perceptive so she said nothing.

"It's not unusual, you know, for a man to blame his inadequacies on his partner." While Tracy stared at the bubbles in her beer, Dave continued, "Your ex made love to you, and when you felt nothing, he told you that you must be frigid."

She could hear Andrew's voice. Frigid bitch. The shudder echoed through her entire body.

"Shit, I hate being right." Dave stared at his beer glass, then lifted her chin so he could look directly into her eyes. "Listen, and listen good. I'm not Kim, but I'm a pretty smart guy. That frigid line is the oldest one in the world, used by guys who haven't got the faintest idea how to make love to a woman."

He was really a nice man. Too smart for his own good, but really nice. She wiped her eyes and said, "Thanks for trying to reassure me." The picture of Andrew and Sharon flashed through her mind. They didn't seem to have any trouble doing it.

"Let me see how much more I can guess. He kissed you but you felt nothing. Then he squeezed your breasts and maybe pinched your nipples. By then he was hard so he rubbed your clitoris, complaining that you weren't wet yet. So he poured some lube into his palm, rubbed it on his cock, and pushed inside."

Her eyes widened and she whispered, "How did you know?"

"Pretty close?"

Her voice was so soft that he barely heard her. "Yes."

"He fucked you for a while, then he came, rolled over, and fell asleep."

"How . . . ?"

"It's such a cliché but it's a cliché because there are lots of men like that. Did you ever get excited?"

"Sometimes, but by the time I did, he was asleep."

"So you went to sleep angry and frustrated."

Suddenly, as if beyond her control, the rest of the story came pouring out. "Eventually, I found him making love to my best friend in our bed. Without a condom. He told me that he needed something real since making love to me was like fucking a beached whale."

Dave stared into Tracy's tear-filled eyes. "Don't call what you two did making love. It wasn't. Making love is a mutual exploration, with pleasures on both sides. Giving pleasure can be just as wonderful as getting pleasure."

"Right," Tracy said, a nasty edge to her voice. "Giving pleasure. Right."

Dave's expression turned darker. He looked almost angry. At her? At Andrew? "There's more. Tell me all of it," he coaxed and it didn't occur to Tracy not to.

She pulled her hand from his and took a long swallow of her beer. "He once said I could make up for everything if I really wanted to give him pleasure. It was awful."

"Go on."

Tracy stared at her glass, unable to meet Dave's eyes, but somehow also unable to stop herself from continuing. "He wanted me to, you know, put my mouth on him. I tried, but he told me I obviously didn't know how to do it so he held my hair and rammed himself into my throat." She remembered it all, the smell of his heated crotch, the taste of his thrusting penis, the pain of his fist pulling at her hair, the sound of his hoarse breathing. And his roar.

Dave's frown was almost scary. "He came in your mouth?"

She could almost feel his final thrust and his semen filling her mouth and dribbling down her chin. "First I gagged and he screamed that I couldn't even do something that simple right. Then I vomited right there all over the bed."

"Of course you did."

Tracy's head jerked up and her eyes widened. "What do you mean, of course I did?"

"Had I been in that situation, first I would have thrown up, on him if I could arrange it, and then I would have belted him. I guess you didn't belt him."

A wisp of a smile crossed Tracy's face. "I wanted to, but I thought it was his right to ask me to do that."

"You mean he had the right to orally rape you?" Was that what it was? "Did he ask whether you wanted him to do that?" When she remained silent, he continued, "If you didn't give your consent, it was rape, pure and simple."

Tracy wanted to believe everything Dave was saying, but it wasn't that simple at all. Dave placed his hands on the table, palms up, then looked at Tracy. "Trust me?"

Somehow she trusted him, if only a bit. Slowly, she placed her hands in Dave's. "It's only Friday night. I want you to think about this. I think you're a sexy, sensual woman buried beneath a load of horseshit fed to her by a husband who didn't know his ass from a hole in the ground about making love. Before this weekend is over, I hope you can discover how wrong he was. Think about it." He took a last drink of his beer and stood up. "Think about it."

Chapter

4

An hour later, Tracy sat in a rocking chair on the wide side porch of the main building. Cuddled in the yellow flowered quilt she had brought down from her bed, she sat pondering the night. The crisp fall air smelled of wood smoke, and the white light from the full September moon washed the color from lawn and lake beyond.

Her mind was filled with the events of the past few hours. First there were all the sexy things her sister and Dave seemed so comfortable with. Dildos, bondage, dirty words, nothing seemed to faze either of them. As a matter of fact, very little seemed to faze anyone attending the weekend. Was she the only one left with some feeling of privacy about sex? Was it really privacy or was she just a prude?

And Dave. When she first met him, he had seemed nice and easy, a friendly sort of man. Now he seemed erotic, dangerous, like one of those heroes in the romance novels she enjoyed. How were they usually described? Animal-like grace. Deep, piercing eyes. It would never have occurred to Tracy to apply these phrases to a real person before—and now? Bedroom eyes and a sexy mouth, Kim had said. She sat back in the rocker thinking about Dave's incredibly masculine hands. How would they feel on her body? Was she really as frigid as her husband had told her she was?

She pressed her chilled fingertips against the cooling cup of coffee she had brought out with her from the pot in the lobby. She closed her eyes and considered all that Dave had said to her in the bar. If only she could believe it.

As if she had conjured him, she heard him say, "I love sitting out here late at night. It's so peaceful. Since we haven't had the first hard frost yet, there are still a few crickets and cicadas left."

Resisting the urge to smooth her hair, Tracy closed her eyes and concentrated on the music of the insects that she hadn't been aware of before. "I'm sorry if I'm disturbing you," Dave continued. "May I join you?"

Actually you are disturbing me, she wanted to scream, more than you can possibly understand. You're messing with my head. You're not safe. "Of course."

"I'm sorry if anything I said earlier upset you. I didn't mean any harm."

She smiled and hoped it showed in her voice. "I know that. It's just that this weekend is unsettling me in ways you can't possibly imagine. I'm not sure whether I should have come."

"You can always leave. It's not a long drive so you can take the car and head home. You can pick Kim up on Sunday or I can drive her back."

God, he was so reasonable. She should go home. Back to being a slightly reclusive, sexually repressed college professor. That would be chickening out, she thought. Running away. No, she'd stay. Somehow knowing that she could leave took some of the pressure off. "It's okay," she said, hoping she wasn't making a big mistake. It was one thing to think she was abnormal and quite another to have her face rubbed in it. "I think maybe I need to do this." She heaved a sigh. "I don't know."

"May I make a suggestion? I've attended lots of Kim's forums and I think I know what she would say. Try to relax, then have another drink, light some of the candles in your room, turn on some soft music, and soak in a hot bubble bath. You know what to do while you're there, don't you?"

She had indeed heard Kim say it just a few hours before. Masturbate. She couldn't say the word out loud, but she knew that masturbation was supposed to be the answer to so many questions about sexuality. Discover the secrets of your own body so you can teach your lover. Everything Kim had said earlier had made sense at the time. Now it was just too scary. "Thanks for the suggestion." Keeping the quilt wrapped around her, Tracy stood up and grabbed her coffee cup. "Good night, Dave."

He stood up and took the mug from her. "I'll take care of that." Then he raised her face with the knuckle of his index finger and kissed her lightly on the mouth. "Think about things. I know that there's a hot, sexy woman inside there," he said, tapping her breastbone through the quilt. "This weekend might just prove to be a revelation."

Without another word, Tracy walked inside and up the stairs to her room.

Tracy's room was small and comfortable. Practical hotel furniture with a light birch finish, several ginger jar lamps that gave off lots of light, and a double brass reading light with off-white shades over the queen-sized bed. The prints on the wall depicted huge single flowers, a lily on one wall and a chrysanthemum on another. The drapes, which matched the quilt, were tan and covered with huge yellow flowers, and the industrial carpet was green and tan tweed. The room was spotlessly clean and smelled of the potpourri in a small dish on the dresser.

Reflexively Tracy folded the quilt and turned on the small

bedside radio. She shook her head slowly as dreamy jazz filled the room—with lots of clarinets and saxophones. Did the last couple who had this room enjoy the music, or did the maids have orders to tune the radios to a sexy listening station? Somehow she wouldn't put it past Dave to think of that sort of thing. His last words rang in her head. This weekend might just prove to be a revelation.

She slowly pulled off her sneakers, socks, and jeans. Her shirt followed. The mirror over the dresser was large enough that she could see herself down to her knees. Andrew had said that she had no passion, but she did have a love of sexy lingerie. Didn't that prove anything? Wasn't he wrong about that part of her? She gazed at herself. Tonight she wore a peach satin bra and panty set, with ivory lace over most of her breasts and mound. Slowly she removed the bra, and taking a deep breath, she examined her body. Not too bad, she thought. Yes, a bit of a tummy, and at thirty-five she admitted to some droop in her breasts. It could be worse.

She didn't work out and she lamented that her abs weren't smooth and taut like the ones in the infomercials on TV, but all in all, her body wasn't bad. She wondered what Dave would think of her, then deliberately pushed that thought from her mind. She placed her hands on the sides of her ribs, then slid them up until they cupped her breasts.

Her gaze fell on the candles on the dresser, and almost reluctantly she paused, then she lit two candles and turned off the other lights in the room. In the flickering light of the candles, she returned to the mirror and again studied her body, thinking about Andrew. What had he seen when he looked at her? Had she changed from the woman he married to the one he cheated on?

Had they ever spent a romantic evening with soft-summer-night music and candles? Had he ever really looked at her? Was Dave right when he said that Andrew had been a lousy lover?

She thought about their lovemaking sessions, which had dwindled to only one a week toward the end. Was that why he had been forced to go elsewhere? Had she driven him away? She had to admit to herself that she had been the one who had delayed it as long as possible, until he didn't try very often. Particularly during the final year of their marriage, Tracy had tried to think up excuses to avoid the humiliation of his attentions. First, she had laid down the law that they couldn't make love when she had her period and she had occasionally denied that she was finished so she could avoid him for an extra day. Sometimes she had even complained of the cliché headache. She had started wearing cotton pajamas instead of nightgowns, and when Andrew came home late from work, she would feign sleep when he climbed into bed. Working late. Had she just been naive? Had he been with Sharon? Or someone else?

It had been her fault that they had made love so seldom. No, when they did have intercourse, it hadn't been making love. He'd move over next to her and give her *the look*. She'd try to smile, and when she didn't demur, he'd say something like, "No headache? No period? Great. Let's do it!" While kissing her perfunctorily, he'd open her pajama top and knead her breasts. He would inevitably say, 'I love your tits,' and he would suckle and pinch until he was hard. Then he'd pull her pajama pants down and slip his hand down her belly and between her legs. "I don't know what's wrong with you," he'd say. "You're not even wet." He'd spit into his palm, lubricate his hard penis, and push it into her, just as Dave had described.

Sometimes she actually enjoyed his lovemaking and found herself getting aroused. She'd hold him and wind her legs around his waist, pressing her mound up against his erection. He'd push and pull until his back arched quickly and he made a small gurgling sound. He'd collapse on top of her until he caught his breath, roll over, and almost immediately fall asleep, leaving her dissatisfied and furious. But furious at whom? Thinking back, she knew she'd been angry at herself for her inadequacies. But had she been angry at the right person?

She heard her sister's words at the foreplay forum. "My definition of a quickie is a sexual encounter in which one of the participants isn't satisfied, sexually or emotionally."

"What do you mean 'emotionally satisfied'?" one woman asked. "Don't you mean when one person doesn't come?"

"Of course," Kim had answered, "orgasm is an integral part of good sex, but sometimes I find I don't need to achieve physical climax. Frequently the pleasure of my husband's orgasm is pleasure enough for me. I feel fulfilled and no longer aroused. That's what I mean by emotionally satisfied. But," she continued with a grin, "an orgasm is a fabulous way to top off a sexual encounter."

Orgasm. That was what this was all about, wasn't it? Okay, Kim had said that orgasm wasn't everything. It was the journey, not the destination. Well, Tracy's journey had seldom been anything but painful and her orgasms all but nonexistent.

She pulled off her panties. Actually, if all the fanfare was right, she'd never had even one orgasm. With a sigh, she walked into the bathroom and turned on the water in the big Jacuzzi tub. She unplugged the radio and moved it to the side of the sink. If she was going to relax, she had to have music. She vividly remembered the silence in the bedroom she shared with Andrew. The whir of the clock radio and Andrew's heavy breathing were the only sounds she heard while they made love.

Tracy wandered back into the bedroom and got a beer from the small refrigerator, another of Dave's amenities. As she twisted off the cap, she heard Andrew's voice. "Have a drink, why don't you? Maybe that will loosen you up."

As the sound of the water running in the tub and the dreamy music filled the air, she tried not to be angry with her ex-husband. She had thought she was in love with him in the beginning. Looking back with as much objectivity as she could muster, she had to wonder whether she had ever cared about him.

Back in the bathroom, Tracy grabbed a bottle of bath gel and poured it beneath the taps. For several minutes she watched the bubbles rise, then when the tub was full, she turned off the taps and climbed in. On a shelf within easy reach was a collection of sponges, loofahs, and thick, soft terry facecloths. She chose a pink soap from the snifter of small pastel shell-shapes and lathered her hands. Experimentally she rubbed her breasts and felt her nipples tighten. Masturbate. The word echoed and reverberated. Torn between the fear that she could never be truly aroused and her curiosity, she rubbed the soap over the washcloth until she raised a thick lather.

The tub was large enough that, as she lay back, only her shoulders, upper chest, and nipples projected from the warm bubbles. Slowly she rubbed the cloth over her collarbones and down to her breasts. What was she feeling? she asked herself. Was she becoming aroused? She wanted to be excited, wanted to believe that she could experience an orgasm. What had Kim said earlier that evening when she discussed what she called The Orgasm Myth? She thought back.

"Kim," a nicely dressed woman with soft red hair had said hesitantly when Kim asked for questions, "you say that every woman can achieve orgasm, but aren't there women who are truly frigid, incapable of coming?"

"Yes," Kim had answered, "there probably are, but women who've never had an orgasm fall into many categories, and very few of them are incapable of climax. Some have achieved orgasm, but for them, it wasn't gigantic, just small spasms easily missed in the activity of lovemaking.

"Others have never truly reached climax. Most frequently that's because they have never been with a man who knew the right things to do to fully arouse their partner. Someone once said that a man flames like a match and a woman heats like an iron."

A few people in the audience nodded. "It takes a man several nanoseconds to become aroused, while a woman can take upwards of twenty minutes to get high enough to climax, and it takes the right stimulation. Many men have no clue how to do that."

"Hold it," an older man toward the rear of the room said. "You seem to be blaming the guy. I, for one, wasn't born knowing. Most women I've been with seem to expect that we're going to make all the moves, and know exactly what to do. If we don't, it's our fault."

"Let's get a few things straight," Kim said. "First of all, let's forget the idea of fault. We're here to learn, not to assign blame. Ladies, answer this question. How does a man learn exactly what pleases a woman? We've discussed the fact that all women are different. Some like one kind of stimulation, others want something quite different. When you go into a new relationship, you assume that your partner will know exactly what to do and where to touch when. How is he supposed to know that?"

"He's the man," a female voice called out. "Isn't that his job?" Tracy tried to see which woman had spoken but she was out of her line of sight.

There was a flurry of giggles but Kim took the question seriously. "Are you saying that he should go out and practice on lots of different women until he's got a list of possibilities, then come back to you and try them all out?"

"Of course not," the same voice said. "That's ridiculous."

"It certainly is. So how's he supposed to know?"

"He just is."

"Right," a man said. From the tone of his voice, she thought the man was her partner. "That's what she really expects, that I'll just know."

As a clamor arose, Kim held her hands up and the room quieted. "Okay, we've gotten to the root of one of the greatest myths of sexual relationships. That he'll just know, like the men in those popular romance novels we all like to read. He touches, she melts, and then they both come. Well, ladies, men don't 'just know.' Sure there are lots of things that women have in common and most men know what those are. Kiss, touch nipples, rub clits, but how hard should he kiss? Should he caress your nipples or pull and twist a bit? Should he rub hard or stroke lightly? Should his touches be the same all the way through or do your desires change? No man can possibly know exactly what turns you on from moment to moment unless you teach him or you learn together through open communication."

Did Andrew have any clue what turned her on? Tracy wondered, watching Kim and the couples in the room. Did she?

"Ladies," Kim continued, "here's a question for you. I don't want you to answer, just think about it. And no knee-jerk reactions, please. What kind of touches curl your toes? When you're close to orgasm, exactly what movement, stroke, caress, squeeze, thrust will push you over the edge?" Kim stood silently at the front of the room for several moments. As Tracy considered the question, she realized that she didn't have the faintest idea what might push her over the edge, since she'd never been near it.

"I'm sure some of you can answer that question quite easily," Kim said, "and your answers will differ greatly. Some would mention a long, hard push or a bite on the neck, others a clitoral rub, and still others a slap on the behind. But I'll bet that there are some of you who haven't a clue. And if you don't know, how can your partner?"

Tracy's eyes widened. Kim was right. She looked around and saw that several women's heads were nodding slowly. "I don't want you to think that orgasm is the be-all and end-all of sex," Kim continued. "It isn't, by a long shot, and over the rest of the weekend we'll explore the joys of the journey rather than the destination. Let's not forget, however, that orgasms are important, too. Okay, so the question now becomes, How can you find out what curls your toes? And the answer is masturbation."

Again the room buzzed with cross-conversations, which Kim allowed to continue for a few moments then silenced with a raise of her hands. "Some of you have heard all this before, but at the risk of boring you, I'll repeat myself. Masturbation is the single most important way for you to learn about your body. No man was born knowing and even the most experienced man needs guidance from his partner to help him find out exactly what to do. That's your responsibility, ladies. And by the way, it's his responsibility to teach you about himself in return. Before you can teach, however, you first have to know. So masturbate."

She perched on the edge of the table at the front of the room. "Touch yourself. It's really okay. It's your body and you're entitled to touch it if you want to, no matter what your mother told you about how bad it is. Let me fess up. The way I learned was in the bathtub when I was in my early teens. I was lying there reading a hot section of a novel and suddenly I realized that parts of my body were reacting. My breasts were supersensitive, my nipples were all scrunched up, and my vagina was feeling swollen and slippery in a way that had nothing to do with the water I was sitting in. I touched and rubbed the parts that felt good as I read"—she smiled, obviously at the memory—"and as I reread that section, something suddenly happened. I was not too well educated but I guessed that I had just had an orgasm. I spent a lot of time in the tub that winter."

Tracy pictured the bathroom in their small house in Westchester and Kim in the tub as the room erupted into somewhat nervous laughter. Over the noise, Kim asked, "Anyone want to comment on that?"

"It works," a woman's voice said softly. "I don't want to go into details but I was here last year. Tim and I had some problems and I had hoped that Miranda—Kim—could help. Well, she did." Tracy located the speaker, a slight Asian woman with long, straight black hair sitting on the far side of the room.

The man sitting next to her looked surprised and embarrassed as he said, "Is that what changed everything?" The woman gave him a jab in the side with her elbow and everyone laughed.

"Point made," Kim said.

Now Tracy lay in the tub thinking about her sister's explorations. Curious, she conjured up the scene in *Gone with the Wind* when Rhett carried a kicking Scarlett up the staircase at Tara. She'd watched that section of the movie more than a dozen times, replaying the DVD until she was sure it would break. Now she again imagined what happened when they got to the bedroom, him subduing her with kisses and expert strokes. She pictured him pulling off his robe, his engorged cock sticking straight out from his groin.

As she created the scene in her mind, she rubbed her breasts with the soapy cloth, then pulled and twisted her nipples. She was surprised by the dart of pleasure that streaked from her breast through her belly to her groin. Eyes closed, candle scent filling her nostrils, strains of a sensuous clarinet in her ears, she dreamed of Rhett's caresses while her hand haltingly slipped to her pubic hair. "God, you're so hot," Rhett said in her mind. "Your body aches for me and you hate yourself for that. You need me, yet you don't want to."

Need, Tracy thought. I don't need, really. I'm just curious. She slid her fingers through her coarse hair to the part of her that wanted to be touched. She slipped her fingertips through her folds and found them slippery, lubricated. Andrew had always complained about a lack of lubrication but was that because she'd seldom been excited? She touched, explored. In the back of her mind she wanted to slip her fingers into the channel but it seemed so scary, so she concentrated on her clitoris, now swollen and sensitive.

She touched her clit lightly, then rubbed and slid up and down either side of it, enjoying the heated sensations. She pictured Clark Gable, then David Hasselhoff in his skimpy red bathing trunks, standing in the surf, pulling down his suit, his cock hard, his arms beckoning her. George Clooney in green scrubs, then without them. She wanted and she felt empty somehow.

She looked around the tub and spotted the empty bottle from the bubble bath, a cylinder slightly thicker around than her thumb. She picked it up and lowered it beneath the water. Could she do it? Did she have the right? Did she have the right not to?

As she rubbed her clitoris with one hand, she pressed the slender bottle against her thickened inner lips and pushed. The bottle had penetrated only about an inch when she felt the first stirrings of her body's reaction: her belly tightening and vaginal muscles squeezing.

"Oh, God," she whispered, continuing to rub and pull and push the bottle. The spasms deepened and suddenly her body was out of her control. Her breath caught in her throat, her pulse pounded, her fingers moved in their own rhythm.

The feelings lasted several moments, then slowly subsided. "Holy cow," she said aloud. Had she ever climaxed before? Not that she remembered, and she would have remembered something as explosive as that. Replete, she lay in the tub for several minutes, then lazily climbed out, dried off, and fell into bed.

She awoke the following morning aroused. She had slept soundly but her sleep had ended with an erotic dream, the exact nature of which she couldn't quite remember. However, it left her breathing rapid and her vagina wet and swollen, her muscles twitching. When she touched her breasts, which were naked because for the first time in many years she had fallen asleep nude, she quickly discovered that they were aching to be touched, and she obliged. Experimentally she rubbed the erect tips and felt the same shaft of pleasure she had experienced the previous evening. With more courage she reached down and touched the places she had found in the tub. The spasms that engulfed her were sudden and violent and occurred without any penetration.

Stunned by the rapidity of it all, she slowly came down and a wide smile crossed her face. All but giggling, she rose and dressed. Two ideas warred in her mind. The first was that she had a new toy, her own body, and she could play with it whenever she wanted. But in addition was the realization that she wasn't frigid. It had been Andrew's fault. Okay, not exclusively, but it hadn't been her burden to shoulder alone. They could have worked on it, but Andrew had been more interested in blaming her and she had been too ignorant to realize that it could, and should, change. How sad. Maybe they could have worked it out eventually, but he had never given her the chance. Oh well, she thought as she headed down the hallway toward breakfast, it was his loss.

As she entered the dining room, she saw Kim, seated at a table for four, talking to a black couple who appeared to be in their late twenties. When her sister saw her, she waved her over. "Tracy, this is Alicia and Ty Bennet. This is their third time here."

Tracy slid into the empty seat. "Nice to meet you."

"Our pleasure," Alicia said. "You're a lucky lady to have Kim for a sister. She's the best." She was tiny, with soft toast-

colored skin and rows of tiny braids tied in a ponytail that
hung almost to her waist.

"They're two of my staunchest cheerleaders," Kim said.
"Why don't you tell Tracy why you're here again? This is her
first time."

"It's pretty simple," Ty said. He was tall and slender with a
shaved head and a tattoo of an American flag on his forearm.
"We've got three kids. Actually we're pretty sure that Wayne,
our youngest, was conceived here two years ago." He winked
at his wife and squeezed her hand. "Anyway, Alicia is on the
pill now so that won't happen again. Three children is enough."

Tracy smiled, imagining these two delightful people as parents.

"That was the reason we came here the first time," Alicia
continued, her deep brown eyes filled with her obvious love
for her husband. "Our parents sent us here as a fifth anniversary present. Marcus was three and Vanessa was fourteen
months. We were at our wit's end. Two small kids and no time
or energy for each other. My mom was, and still is, a reader of
Miranda's column. There was a letter from a couple pretty
much like us, and Miranda's advice was to get away from the
kids for a night or, better still, a weekend. So my folks got together with Ty's folks and they not only funded the weekend
but took care of the kids as well."

"No small present," Ty said, "but we came home new people, having discovered how to be Man and Woman occasionally instead of just Mommy and Daddy. Now a weekend with
Miranda is their present to us each year."

"For a moment," Alicia said, "when they suggested coming
here for a second time, we told them no. They insisted, and although it sounds selfish, we came to our senses and snapped
up the offer. It's a weekend just for us, and boy, do we need it."

Kim squeezed their hands. "I'm making them the poster
children for being selfish once in a while."

The couple stood. "We're going to take a walk before the first forum." Ty extended his hand. "Nice meeting you, Tracy."

Ty's hand was warm and soft. "Nice meeting you, too," Tracy said, "and I'm sure I'll be seeing you again before tomorrow."

Alicia groaned. "I don't want to think about going back home. I'm concentrating on this weekend and being with Ty. Let's hear it for selfishness." She squeezed Kim's shoulder. "Thanks for being you."

As the couple walked away, Tracy said, "I don't understand. There are so many places they could go for less money and they don't seem to need your guidance. Why do they come here year after year?"

"I think it's the atmosphere. Sexual, sensual, permissive. Here every couple is allowed to be whatever they choose to be, including selfish if that's what's best for them."

"It must be nice to get reactions like that," Tracy said.

"It's wonderful but it's not the only great feedback I get. As you'll see tomorrow, I post my e-mail address and give every couple who prefers it a stamped envelope addressed to me. I suggest that they wait a month, then write and tell me what they got the most and the least out of. I get the most wonderfully rewarding letters."

"Do you ever get negative letters?" Tracy asked, wondering how she would deal with it.

"I do, and they used to hurt. Now I use them to lengthen or shorten forums, or leave some out altogether. Elliot keeps my head on straight. He says that I'm never as bad as the bad letters and I'm never as good as the good ones."

"Speaking about forums, I had a thought," Tracy said. "That bit you do during the intro about nonverbal communication. Maybe you could turn it into a full forum. Your ideas are wonderful and I can't help thinking about Andrew and me, and whether some of that might have helped us."

"I put it in the intro because I want to be sure everyone hears it."

"How about a session attached to the introductory one, with ideas from the audience, too?"

Kim was quiet for a moment, then nodded. "You might be right. I never thought about it but many of the letters mention that those techniques started a dialog that eventually moved out of the bedroom and into other areas as well." She nodded slowly. "Great idea, Trace. Thanks. Of course, that's assuming that there is another weekend."

As Tracy held up her hand to close that topic, she watched Kim look her over and her cheeks colored. She had rummaged in her suitcase that morning and had found a rust-colored turtleneck and had tucked it into the waistband of her jeans. She had put on a bit of blush and lipstick that morning and taken care with her hair, using two barrettes to pull it back and away from her face. "You look particularly good this morning, Trace."

"I feel pretty good," she said, grinning.

"There's a twinkle in your eye. I won't ask where it's coming from."

"Good," Tracy said, then rose to attack the buffet. She helped herself to fluffy scrambled eggs, crisp bacon, and a small soft roll. As she was pouring herself a glass of orange juice, she heard a voice behind her.

"Good morning," Dave said, his breath warm just behind her ear. "You look very pretty this morning."

"Thanks," she said, glad she had taken extra care with her appearance. She turned and looked him over. His jeans were black and tight across his thighs and he wore an oatmeal-colored Aran Isle sweater with the sleeves pushed up over his lightly furred forearms. His cowboy boots were highly polished. "You look pretty good yourself."

Where had that come from? she wondered. Flirtatiousness?

Her? What changes an orgasm had wrought. Well, two orgasms actually. She felt herself grin and turned back to the buffet. As she picked up her plate and glass, Dave asked, "Can I pour you some coffee?"

"Thanks," she said, motioning to her glass and the roll that was threatening to fall off her plate. "I'd appreciate that. I'm not managing too well." And Dave would need managing if she weren't to get in way over her head.

"Sugar? Cream?"

"Black please."

As Dave watched Tracy head for the table where her sister sat, he thought, This is going to be even easier than I expected. Beneath it all, she's heating up and I'm certainly going to be there when she comes to a boil. He dropped Tracy's coffee off at her table, then left to tend to hotel business. He had been successful in the past by letting the first possibility of intimacy go by, so even if he hadn't had a reason to leave Tracy with only her imagination, he would have. He would bet that her imagination was working overtime.

Chapter

5

Between breakfast and dinner, Tracy sat through four forums and learned more than she had ever imagined about oral sex, anal sex, toys, games and role playing, and sex and the Internet. After dinner she was due to attend a forum on the one aspect of sex she least understood: power and control. Tracy sat in a corner of the dining room and realized that she had been in a state of mild arousal for the entire day. All this talk about sex and her discoveries of the previous evening had kept her skin tingling, her nipples erect, and her vaginal tissues swollen and damp.

She looked around at the couples seated at quiet tables for two in the Creative Loving section of the dining room. Most were talking softly, gazing lovingly into each other's eyes, and holding hands. A few larger tables were occupied by two couples, talking together and laughing. As she sipped her after-dinner coffee, Tracy saw Dave enter the room. Her palms immediately became sweaty, her pulse accelerated. After the brief words they had exchanged that morning, her imagination had been working overtime. Was her newfound ability to achieve orgasm real or was it just a product of masturbation? Did it mean she really wasn't frigid? Could a man arouse her the way she seemed to be able to arouse herself? Was Dave a man she could experiment with?

She watched his gaze flash around the room, obviously checking on all the tiny things he coordinated to make the Catskill Lake Resort the comfortable yet efficient hotel it was. Could he also be looking for her? She dried her palms on the thighs of her jeans and tried to put a neutral expression on her face.

When his eyes caught hers, he nodded slightly and started in her direction. There must be so much to do to keep the resort running, she thought, and that would be a good conversational gambit, something to keep any discussions on a superficial level until she understood exactly what she wanted.

"Hi, Tracy," Dave said. "May I join you?"

"Sure," Tracy said.

He slid into the chair that her sister had occupied until a few moments before. "Where's Kim?"

"She grabbed a quick bite, met with a few couples in short one-on-one sessions, then went to lie down before the evening forum. By the way, thanks for finding such a lovely room for me on such short notice."

"It is, isn't it. That's one of my favorites, with a great view of the lake."

Tracy had sat for almost a half an hour before dinner just gazing out her window at the lake and the trees beyond. The foliage, the water fowl, the mirror-flat surface of the water, all combined to create an idyllic scene that she could have stared at for hours. She also recalled having had fleeting visions of herself and Dave skinny-dipping in the cooling water. Switching mental gears, she said, "It must be quite a job keeping this place running so smoothly." There, she thought, a safe topic.

"It is, but the smoothness is superficial. Beneath, this place is filled with a zillion minor annoyances and more than a few major problems."

"Really?" Tracy said. "Like what?"

"We had a small plumbing problem in one corner of Building 2, and that put three rooms out of commission and two of the cabins have no heat. Fortunately I'm not overbooked, but if I don't have everything fixed by next weekend, I'm going to be in a mess."

"Is next weekend a big one? What's going on?"

"It's the first weekend of leaf season and I'm just about fully booked. In addition to the wandering tourist, I've got several nature groups and about two dozen members of a local birding society."

"That's great." Reflexively she added, "Is there anything I can do to help?"

"Not at all. With luck and my crackerjack handyman, it will all work out." Dave took her hand across the table. "Thanks for asking."

There was an electricity in his grasp that Tracy wasn't sure she wanted to feel just yet. Had it always been there or was it a product of her new awareness? Taking control of her thoughts, she said, "You said that two of your cabins have no heat. I haven't seen them yet and they sound deliciously rustic."

"You look like you're finished with dinner. How about I give you the quickie tour?" Without waiting for an answer, he arose, pulling her hand gently until she also stood. His palm on the small of her back, he guided her out a side door and down a pine needle-covered walkway. With the sun setting, tall evergreens cast long shadows but the path was well if subtly lit.

Tracy took in a deep breath of snapping crisp mountain air and, since she wore only a blue pin-striped cotton shirt, hugged her forearms against her body for warmth. "Sorry,"

Dave said, whipping off his tweed jacket. "I forget that others aren't used to how cool it becomes once it gets close to twilight." As he wrapped the jacket around her, she was aware of his body heat trapped in the wool and his clean masculine smell caught in the fabric. "It's just a short walk." He draped his arm over her shoulders. Tracy tried not to read too much into his friendly gesture but the heat of him caused an immediate reaction in her nipples.

As they rounded a curve in the path, a magnificent vista opened before them. The sun was almost at the horizon, casting long golden fingers across the water's surface. Tall pines and maples were backlit, forming deep black silhouettes. As they stood, a puff of wind created tiny ripples and caused a light rustling in already dying leaves. A small boat rocked beside the resort's dock, and a flock of Canada geese flew overhead in a tight vee, their honks reverberating through the stillness. As they disappeared behind the trees and stillness returned, Tracy whispered, "What a wonderful spot."

"It's one of my favorite places on the grounds," Dave said softly. He moved behind her and cuddled her against him. "In the spring there's all the new green, and on a summer afternoon you can watch swimmers dive off the float. This whole area," he said, gesturing over her shoulder to a flat section of the lawn sprinkled with whitewashed rocks, "is all spring bulbs, hyacinths, daffodils, and tulips. Part of me wants to put a few benches here, but then it won't be as private somehow."

Tracy gazed at the scene. "It's wonderful. And so quiet."

They stood for several minutes, then she felt him shiver. "I've got your jacket and you must be cold. Why don't you show me the cabins?"

They walked another hundred feet to a secluded area about an eighth of a mile from the main buildings. Twelve small, neat cabins with heavy wooden exterior beams and sand-colored walls were scattered beneath the trees. "They're perfect," Tracy exclaimed.

Dave's grin showed his white teeth in the gathering twilight. "I had them built last spring. There are twelve, and until last weekend when a heating unit went, they've always been fully booked. People love the idea of living out in the woods, with all the conveniences of the main house just a short walk away."

"What happens when it rains? Isn't that a problem?"

"I worried about that a little, too, when I built them, but each cabin comes equipped with a few big umbrellas and an assortment of brightly colored ponchos for the kids. We get more than our share of power outages, too, but there are flashlights and lots of candles. People seem to enjoy—what did you call it?—rustic."

"I think they're wonderful." How many times had she said the same thing? Wonderful. Couldn't she think of any other words? Had her brain turned to oatmeal? She forced her brain to focus despite the intimacy of standing here in the twilight with Dave. "Can I see one of the ones that isn't occupied?"

Dave led her to one darkened cabin, took a master key from his pocket, and opened the door. As he flipped on the light, she took in a quick breath. The living room was small, with a stone fireplace and a fully stocked wood box. The air inside was cold, an obvious testament to the heating problem. The furniture was mostly wood, with russet and forest green cushions and thick multicolored braided rugs covering highly polished wood floors.

"You've got great taste," she said, as she crossed the living room and poked into the two small bedrooms and the modern bathroom with its double tub. "This is perfect for a family with kids or two couples, or just two people who want some extra privacy."

"Exactly what I had in mind." When she returned to where he stood, Dave grasped the lapels of the jacket she still wore and gently pulled her close. "Exactly," he said softly. Gazing into Tracy's eyes, he lowered his mouth until he was just a breath away.

Tracy braced herself. It had been obvious that he was interested in her and she had known this was coming. Did she want him to kiss her? Why the hell not? she asked herself. Why not see what happens? When she didn't pull away, she watched the corners of his mouth curve upward slightly.

She tipped her head back and closed her eyes and was surprised when he didn't kiss her. Instead, he said, "Something's very different. You've changed since yesterday."

Her eyes snapped open, her disappointment almost palpable. She focused on what he had said. He was right. Yesterday she wouldn't have dreamed of standing in a dimly lit cabin in the woods, hoping to be kissed by a man she'd known for just over a day. Something had changed in the flash of an eye, with the movement of her hand beneath the water of her bathtub. Was that change real? She wanted to find out. "Does it matter?"

"I guess not." Then his lips met hers, soft and warm, asking, not demanding. Relief flooded through her. He did want her; at least he wanted to kiss her. She gave herself over to the kiss, and as she melted, she felt her heart pound and her knees weaken. It's too fast, she told her body. I need to understand more. Soon, her body answered. It will be soon.

He didn't pursue the kiss, and as their lips parted, he released the front of her jacket. "You know what I'd like to do? I'd like to light a fire and lie with you in front of it. I'd like to kiss you, and make love to you. I'd love to see your naked body, illuminated only by firelight, your hair spread over my arms, your eyes heavy-lidded with passion."

Trembling from both need and terror, she flattened her

hands against his chest. "This is happening a little too fast for me," she whispered.

"I know. I was just fantasizing." He backed away. "Anyway, it's almost time for this evening's forum and the Saturday night one is quite something."

"I know," Tracy said, moving away from him. "Sexual Control and Power Games."

"I'd like to meet you afterward for a drink."

She considered his request. She knew she was playing way out of her league, but she wanted to test her wings. "That would be nice, but I don't know exactly when the forum will end."

"Don't worry. I'll find you." He placed a quick kiss on her lips, then walked her back to the main house.

As she made her way through the hallways toward the main meeting room, she began to wonder why Dave had made that pass. After all, she wasn't particularly attractive and she certainly wasn't sexy, so why had he kissed her? As a substitute for her sister? Nah, she thought. She wasn't at all like Kim, and she didn't really believe they had a thing going, even in Dave's mind. So the question plagued her. Why?

Dave dropped into the swivel chair behind his desk. Idly he thumbed through a stack of preregistration forms for the next two peak-of-foliage-color weekends and the classic car gathering to follow, then set them down again. He had nothing much to do until the evening forum was over, and although he could sit with her, he wanted to give Tracy time to dream. With any luck she'd be at a slow simmer by the time he picked her up. God, she was something. There was a hot little number beneath the frozen exterior, and he was just the one to thaw her out. It had been quite a while since he'd had to work this hard for a woman, but he was definitely enjoying it.

The kiss had been an obvious first step and the timing had been perfect: setting sun, scent of pine. Atmosphere! And she had gone along with it. Even better. What, he wondered, had happened the previous evening that had changed the mousy Miss Tracy of Friday afternoon into the experimental Saturday evening woman who had let him kiss her. Remembering their conversation on the porch the previous evening, he pictured her touching herself and climaxing. That must have been it. She's discovered the power of an orgasm and she's playing with the ideas that follow. He wondered about her reaction to bondage and power games. God, he'd love to play with her. He closed his eyes, tipped his chair as far back as it would go, and put his booted feet on the desk.

Maybe they'd make a bet on something with the winner getting an hour of the loser's absolute servitude. She'd lose, of course, and she'd pay her debt willingly. What would he do? After her reaction to the toys he'd shown her the previous evening, maybe he'd present her with a vibrator and ask her to put on a show for him. He let his mind create the scene.

"You belong to me, you know. You have to do exactly what I say."

She gazed at him with acceptance and trust. "What should I do?"

"First, you need to be undressed. Jeans first." She quickly removed them and tossed them aside. "Now take your shirt off, and do it slowly so I can watch. And I want complete silence so I can concentrate."

He saw her color rise, but she nodded, then slipped one button at a time through its buttonhole until her blouse hung open from her shoulders. "Off," he said, and she allowed the cloth to fall to the floor. She was gorgeous, in a flesh-colored bra that was more lace than fabric and panties that formed only a tiny patch over her pubic hair.

He had already inserted batteries in a long, slender, flesh-colored toy, and when he flipped the switch, the vibrator began to hum. "Massage your tits with it," he said, handing it to her.

He deliberately used the most abrasive words he could, knowing that it embarrassed and excited her.

Her hand shaking slightly, Tracy took the wand and touched it to her flesh. Immediately Dave could see her nipples tighten and her hips move. Minutes later, when she lowered the vibrator, he snapped, "I didn't tell you that you could stop." He hesitated. "But maybe you're right. Maybe it's time to move it to your pussy."

Looking at the floor, Tracy slowly moved the wand toward her mound. "Look at me," he said.

She slowly looked up and stared into his eyes. He returned her stare, then lowered his eyes to the vibrating wand, now slowly moving toward her crotch. "Spread your feet apart," he said and she did. "Show me."

"What?" she asked.

"Show me what makes you hottest. Touch the vibrator to all those places that your fingers know so well."

"But—"

"No talking. Show me."

Seemingly reluctant, she touched the tip of the wand to the crotch of her panties. Dave watched her knees almost buckle. "Have you ever felt anything like that before?"

When she shook her head, Dave's grin widened. God, he loved teaching her everything. "Good. Move it around until you find the best places. Press hard if it feels good that way, or touch yourself very lightly. Learn about your pussy."

His eyes didn't leave the toy as she moved it around. Finally he glanced up and watched her eyes close. "Please," she whispered, her entire body trembling.

"Please what?"

"I can't stand up anymore."

He took her hand. "Come inside." He quickly removed her bra and her soaked panties, then stretched her out on his bed. "Now, continue."

As he watched her back arch, he pulled off his clothes. Crouching between her legs, he took the toy from her and rammed his cock into her sopping channel. Holding totally still, he handed her the vibrator and said, "Touch yourself while I'm inside you. I want to feel you come."

When the toy touched her pubis, he could feel the vibrations on his cock but he wanted to feel more. "Are you close?"

"God, yes," she answered.

"Then let it go. I want it."

She touched the wand to her clit and he felt the tiny spasms grow in strength until his cock was being squeezed along its entire length. When she began to writhe, he pressed his hands against her hipbones to keep her still, reveling in the feel of her climax. As she called out his name, he released his hold and let his body go. With only a few thrusts he came.

He returned to reality grinning. He dropped his feet from his desk, sat up straight, and wriggled his hips to make his powerful erection fit more comfortably in his jeans. It would happen. He'd make it happen.

An hour and a half later he stood outside the Cayuga Room as the evening's forum ended. Several couples walked out hand in hand, exchanging excited glances. Others made their way into the Seneca Room, where Diana had her lingerie shop, or the Onondaga Room, where he and Tracy had wandered through the adult toys the previous evening. Still others looked embarrassed, but Dave could bet that many of them had been intrigued as well. Power was a heady and very erotic drug.

As the room emptied, Dave walked inside and approached Kim and Tracy, talking quietly at the front. When Kim saw him, she said, beaming, "Things are going great. How's it all doing from your end?"

He bussed her cheek. "Everyone seems to be really happy with everything. Not a complaint in sight."

Kim's jaw opened in a face-splitting yawn. "That's just as it should be," she said, "but I'm going to drop from exhaustion any moment." She hugged her sister, then Dave. "Guys, I'm heading for a long phone call with Elliot and then sleep. See you at breakfast."

As he watched Kim's retreating shape, Dave said, "What did you think of the forum?"

Tracy blew out a long breath. "It's really heavy stuff, many topics I'd never given a thought to. I listened to the reasons that someone might want to be in control or be controlled, but I don't really get it."

"Don't knock it if you haven't tried it." Deciding to drop the subject for the moment, Dave placed his hand on the nape of Tracy's neck and guided her from the room. He'd decided to touch her as often as he could, knowing it would keep her off balance. She felt really good, too, her skin soft and warm. He threaded his fingers through her hair and lightly massaged her scalp. "I'd like you to meet Diana. She's a real character and I know you two will hit it off."

With Dave's hand in her hair, Tracy walked toward the Seneca Room. Her mind was whirling with all the new information she'd gotten from the most recent forum. Controlling and being controlled were such foreign concepts to her, but she also had to admit that all the sexual talk had her excited and curious about so many things.

As they entered, the room was buzzing with couples whispering softly. Racks of peignoirs, camisoles, teddys, and bra and panty sets stood along the walls. Torso manikins were attired in tight corsets, crotchless panties, and bras with the nipple areas removed. One wore a black leather bathing suit-type thing, arrayed with chains and laced up the front with a red leather strip that fastened at the top with a tiny padlock. Another table was covered with menswear, including leather pouches, thong jockstraps, and satin boxers. Tracy spied a male torso manikin that sported a pair of tight gray bikini briefs with a design on the front that looked like the face of an elephant. When she realized that the man's penis fit into what looked like a trunk, she broke out laughing.

"Would you believe I've sold seven of those?" a voice behind her said. "Most to women as gag gifts, but one in extra large to a man who was going to 'surprise' his wife. By the way, the manikin wasn't anatomically correct so I stuffed the elephant's trunk with a big piece of polish sausage. I tried a hot dog but it didn't give the right effect."

Still laughing, Tracy turned and saw a very overweight woman, probably in her sixties, wearing a black spandex corset that barely covered her ample flesh, with black fishnet stockings attached to the garters, three-inch-high black spike heels, and a sheer black robe. Her makeup, while obvious, wasn't overdone, and her smile could light up several states. Tracy could only stare. "The hot dog was just too skinny," the woman continued. "No one wants to think a guy has a wiener for a weeny."

"Tracy," Dave said, hugging the woman and giving her a deep kiss on the mouth, "this is Diana. I'm sure you think that your sister is the star of the weekend, but we all know this is Diana's show." He released the older woman. "Diana, this is Tracy McBride, Kim's sister."

"So you're Kim's sister," the older woman said. "I'm so glad to meet you. I've heard a lot about you."

Tracy realized she had stopped breathing so she took in a large gulp of air. "Thanks," she said. "It's nice to meet you."

"You look like a woman who's into lacy underthings," Diana said. "What can I show you?"

Tracy thought about the pale seafoam green lace set she was wearing. Just a lucky guess on Diana's part? As Tracy's mind raced for something to say, the older woman noticed that a thirtyish couple had selected a few items, so she excused herself and walked over to help them with their purchases. "She's quite a character," Dave said, "but she sure sells merchandise."

"The outfit?"

"She dresses in a different selection of her larger-size line each session, and it seems to encourage women who would have never thought of wearing things like that to give it a try."

Diana wandered back, obviously having heard their last remarks. "It's a shame that so many women are hung up on size, so I give them a look at me. After they get over the shock, they begin to seriously reconsider. So many men want to buy things for their wives and I've usually got pictures of myself in the lingerie that I can include with the purchase to make their ladies feel better. I make a good demonstration project, and most women think they look slimmer than I do so they give it a shot."

Tracy couldn't stop grinning. "You certainly are a great advertisement for what you sell. I'm ashamed of everything I ever thought about larger-sized ladies in sexy outfits like the stuff you're wearing. I can even imagine you in some of those black leather outfits."

"I had an idea a few weeks ago," Diana said to Dave. "I thought that next time, I'd bring a few costume-type things. Maybe a cat burglar outfit, a pirate costume, or a prison guard. What do you think?"

Dave looked thoughtful. "I think it's a great idea. Maybe we could get someone to write up some scenarios for people to use."

"You mean for role playing?" Tracy asked. "Stories they could act out?"

"Sure," Dave said. "How about packaging an entire role-playing kit, with a story or screenplay, costumes, props, and things like that? You might also get together with Matt and create a beginner's bondage kit."

"Fabulous," Diana said, her gaze distant, the wheels obviously already turning in her mind. "Let me see what I can come up with for next time."

"If there is a next time," Tracy said, as they walked toward the bar.

"If there is a next time."

If Dave had anything to do with it, there would be.

They found a quiet table toward the back of the bar and Dave ordered a beer for each of them from a waitress dressed in black jeans and a bright red man-tailored shirt. From the other section of the bar, strains of music from a keyboard softened the atmosphere. "This hotel is so big," Tracy said, keeping the conversation neutral.

"Actually, it's far from the largest one around. I've got about two hundred rooms. Some of the lodges near the big ski areas have over a thousand."

Tracy let out a long breath. "Kim told me you specialize in theme weekends like hers."

"There aren't any weekends like Kim's," Dave said, "but yes, I do offer a lot of events with themes."

"Are they hard to set up? There are so many things to coordinate."

"After you've done it a few times, it gets easier. They are all pretty much the same, each with a different centerpiece. For the most part, they're just get-togethers for people who share a common interest."

Keep it impersonal. "What was the weirdest one you ever had?"

"I don't know about weird," Dave said, sipping his beer, "but the most earsplitting was a polka weekend. Although they got a building to themselves, things got pretty loud. They had three rooms in that wing with polka bands playing until the wee small hours. Fortunately no one called the cops, but when they wanted to reserve the building for the following year, I insisted on no music before noon or after one A.M."

"Are there any groups you won't book?"

Dave took a pretzel from the bowl in the center of the table. "I've nixed any type of rock or rap festival, although we're really too small for groups like that to be interested anyway. I do an annual jazz thing, but I learned quickly. Like the polka group, the music is limited and they're pretty good about it all. We only had to call the cops once, after which they settled down."

"Any others you've said no to?"

Dave scrunched his face. "Animals. No animals. My first and last was a group of herpetologists who held an amphibian and reptile show and sale. They lost three very expensive snakes. Sadly, one was never found and one froze to death when he escaped through an open vent."

"The third?" Tracy asked.

"We found that one in a guest's room. The screams led us right to it. So now, no animals."

Laughing, Tracy said, "You still have a nature motif and lots of birds."

"Outside. All the birds are outside." She could see him lightly grit his teeth. "Even that's a problem. It's a full-time project to keep the grounds free of duck, swan, and goose doo. I really love animals of all kinds, you understand, and I hate to turn down a paying customer." He sipped his beer. "I'd love to host an annual cocker spaniel get-together, for example, but you understand that I have thousands of square feet of carpet to protect."

"Of course," she said, feeling totally relaxed despite the sight of Dave's sexy blue eyes across the table.

They talked for an hour, about his job and hers, TV shows and movies they both enjoyed, and the current problems in the Middle East. The conversation was lively and thoroughly entertaining. Dave was a really charming man, Tracy decided. Eventually, however, she stifled a yawn and glanced at her watch. "It's almost midnight, and I'm going to turn into a pumpkin."

"Come on," Dave said, rising. "I'll walk you to your room."

I'll walk you to your room. Tracy almost groaned. She could picture the awkward scene at her door. To kiss or not to kiss. She felt like she was seventeen again. "You don't have to do that," she said. "I'm sure you have better things to do with your time."

Dave merely cocked his head slightly to one side. Okay, she thought, corny line. Still discussing an op-ed column they had both read in the *New York Times* the previous weekend, they walked to Tracy's second-floor room. She inserted her card key into the lock, and when the mechanism clicked, she pushed the door open. "Thanks for a wonderful evening," Tracy said past the lump in her throat.

"Thank you," Dave said, his eyes suddenly hot. "Does it have to end?"

"Yes," Tracy said, wondering how hard he might push and wondering as well whether she wanted him to. "I think it does."

"Of course," he said, leaning down and pressing his lips against hers. The kiss was gentle at first, but deepened when she didn't pull away. As his arms circled her shoulders, his tongue asked for entry, and she gave it. When the kiss heated still more, she felt her heart pound and her breathing rasp in her ears. Reflexively she arched her back, pressing her pelvis against his groin. His palms cupped her face and his thumbs caressed her cheeks and played havoc with her senses.

His desire for her was obvious, but she realized that she

wasn't quite ready to jump into the deep end of the pool. And Dave was certainly the deep end. She flattened her hands against his chest and pushed gently.

The kiss ended, leaving her staggered. How could she have believed she was frigid? "Good night," she said, needing time. "Good night, Tracy. I'll see you at breakfast."

Tracy undressed and put on an ivory silk nightgown. The lace over her breasts abraded their sensitive tips, pebbling her tight nipples. Stretching out on top of the quilted bedspread, she thought about Dave. He wasn't handsome exactly, but God, was he sexy. Why hadn't she seen it when they first met? Well, she saw it now. And he had great hands. She remembered the sight of his long, blunt, callused fingers wrapped around his beer glass and the feel of them on her face. Now that she knew where to touch herself, she created scenes in which Dave took her, sometimes gently, sometimes forcefully, and rubbed her nipples and her mound. As she dreamed about pirate costumes and prison guards, she pushed herself higher and higher until, with a small moan, she climaxed.

Later she pulled the quilt over herself and fell asleep.

Chapter

6

Dave didn't appear at breakfast, and Tracy was surprised at the depth of her disappointment. She found that she was becoming more and more intrigued. She had no idea whether he would have any interest in pursuing their flirtation beyond the weekend, but somehow she hoped he would. As she sipped her coffee at a small table in the corner of the dining room, she saw Kim approach the buffet table, surrounded by three couples.

Until this weekend, Kim had always been Tracy's big sister, to be emulated and resented in equal measure, as all little sisters loved and hated their older siblings. Her mother, who had raised the two girls after their father's death, had been as evenhanded as she could, and looking back, Tracy admired her mother's supreme effort to treat the sisters as individuals. However, with a six-year age difference, there wasn't any way that Tracy hadn't been annoyed when she had a strict bedtime and Kim had a loosely enforced curfew. Kim drove Tracy to middle school, waving at her high school friends while quietly grumbling about "little sisters." During Kim's teenage years, she had been Tracy's unpaid baby-sitter. While she languished at home, Kim had chatted on the phone to her friends about how awful it was to be trapped with the dwarf, as she called Tracy in those years.

Remembering, Tracy understood and forced the remaining bad feelings back into the deepest part of her mind. Now she looked at her sister, almost idolized by those attending the workshop. She was the expert, the guru. If Tracy agreed to run the January weekend, she would be thought of the same way, an awesome responsibility. Even with her new understanding, small as it was, there was no way. No way.

The rest of the morning went well. Kim held the roundup session, answering questions, giving last-minute advice, with special suggestions for newlyweds, couples adjusting to having children, empty nesters, and seniors. She handed out envelopes for feedback, and all the couples promised to write.

Perched on the edge of the front table, she summed it all up. "Folks, I wish you happiness and great sex." Like Charlton Heston in *The Ten Commandments*, Kim raised her hands and spread her arms. In a deep voice, she slowly intoned, "Go forth and fuck like bunnies." There was a burst of laughter, then a prolonged round of applause.

With Tracy trailing behind, Kim spoke to many of the couples, then checked on the business end of the weekend with the various vendors. "We did fabulously," she said, when the two women finally got a moment to sit in the almost empty lobby with cups of herb tea. "This was the most successful weekend we've ever done."

A warm hand landed on Tracy's shoulder from behind. "It was sensational," Dave said, "as always, of course, but this one was better than any in the past. By the way, two couples who came together to stay only over Friday night and hadn't signed up for your workshops gave me credit cards this morning. They had listened clandestinely from the hallway, and shopped in both Matt's and Diana's. They also said they loved the pastries. They extended their stay an extra night and felt it only fair that they pay the incremental charge for the workshop part of the weekend."

"That's quite a compliment," Kim said, in a whoosh of breath, her eyes wide. "That means we had fifty-six paying couples." With a wide smile she said, "Not bad. Not bad at all."

Dave circled around and dropped into the wood and burgundy-upholstered chair beside Tracy. He was wearing black corduroy slacks and a green plaid flannel shirt with the cuffs turned back. "The most we've had before was forty-eight. You're a wonder, Kim." He looked at Tracy. "Have you reconsidered running the workshop in January?"

"I don't think I can," she said.

"I won't push you," Kim said, "but I sense a *but* at the end of that sentence. Give yourself just a bit more time." She turned to Dave. "When do you have to know?"

"I guess I need at least six weeks' notice. I would love to book something else into that time slot, but I don't think there's any other group looking. If I get any requests for that weekend, I'll let you know."

"What will you do if we cancel?" Tracy asked.

"I'll probably close early. I was planning to end the season on the fifteenth of January, but if you don't use that weekend, I might just close around the fifth. I'll have to see what reservations I have when we get closer. I usually run at a loss through much of the winter and it's probably cheaper to shut the place down. I won't open again until sometime mid-March, after the worst of the snow. We do a grand reopening spring nature weekend."

"We missed you this morning," Kim said. Tracy could have kissed her sister for both changing the subject and asking the question she couldn't.

"Sorry. I had to get a heating guy in to look at the two cabins I told you about, and the only time he had was Sunday morning."

"Will he get them fixed?" Tracy asked. "You said that you had them all rented for next weekend."

Dave smiled, seeming flattered and delighted that she had remembered such a seemingly insignificant detail. "Fortunately it seems to be a minor wiring problem and should be fixable by the middle of the week."

"That's good news," Tracy said softly, settling back into her chair. It wouldn't pay to seem too interested. She dropped her gaze to Dave's hands. He absently stroked his long, blunt fingers along the nap of the fabric of his slacks. Back and forth, back and forth, until Tracy's skin tingled. Did he have any idea what his fingers were doing to her?

"What time are you two leaving?"

Kim answered quickly, "I have a few more things to finish up and then I want to get home. Frankly I'm totally trashed and I want to see Elliot, of course." A small, slightly embarrassed smile crossed Kim's face.

"I understand," Dave said. "All this sex talk has made you want to jump Elliot's bones."

Chuckling, Kim said, "You've got the idea. I'll probably only be an hour or so, and then we can get out of here. Tracy and I can stop for a late lunch, then Elliot can pick me up at Tracy's. I'll be home in time for my midafternoon nap." She winked so that it was obvious exactly what would happen before the nap.

"Why don't you ladies join me for lunch?" Dave asked.

"Thanks, Dave," Kim said, "but I think I'd like to get going as early as I can."

"Where do you live, Tracy?" he asked.

"I'm about halfway between here and Kim's."

"Tracy drove?"

Kim nodded. "I'm afraid so, so I have to drag her away."

"How about this?" Dave said. "Kim, you can drop the car at Tracy's and Elliot can pick you up there. That way Tracy can stay and have lunch with me." He turned his electric blue eyes toward Tracy. "It might not be too peaceful since there are usually problems when everyone checks out, but I'd like to get to know you better. Maybe there are questions about the layout of the weekend that I can answer for you and I can drive you home later. Maybe I can get the kitchen staff to pack us a picnic. It's too lovely a day to waste."

The day was magnificent, almost summer-like temperatures with a cerulean blue sky, puffs of fluffy white clouds, and a soft breeze. "I don't know." Tracy looked at Kim.

"Great idea," Kim said. "That way I won't feel as guilty about dragging you home so early."

Was it tempting fate? Tracy wondered. Play with fire and you get burned and Dave was definitely fire. However . . . She took a deep breath. "I'd love to if it's not too much trouble to drive me back."

"Wonderful," Dave said.

Dave found himself delighted by the idea of lunch and a leisurely drive through the September afternoon with Tracy. Originally he had intended to seduce her, or at least give her the impression of seduction to bolster her self-image and attempt to entice her to chair the January weekend. Now he found that he was intrigued by the woman herself. He had seen the changes in her in just two days. Her hair was more stylishly arranged, this morning in a short French braid. She wore a cotton shirt the color of ripe apricots tucked into her jeans, and there was pink in her cheeks that told of the use of a little makeup. When he noticed the mark on her belt where she must always fasten it, he realized that she had pulled it a notch tighter today. It was a heady feeling to watch a simple caterpillar turn into something more. A butterfly? Maybe not, but certainly something more, and he was partly responsible. He loved the idea of opening her up like a special gift. How to convince her to let him? That was the burning question.

Two hours later Tracy and Dave sat on a thick plaid wool blanket only about ten feet from the lake. The small secluded area just a few hundred feet from the hotel was surrounded on three sides by thick vegetation which muffled the slight breeze. Fortunately, the air was just cool enough to balance the heat of the September sun. Tracy let her head hang back and enjoyed the sunshine on her face. Although they were just a little way from the main building, it was as though they were alone.

Their lunch had been simple—turkey sandwiches and wedges of cheddar, fresh local tomatoes, and crisp macintosh apples polished to a high shine. Dave had brought bottled water and wine. Tracy had opted for the water but now accepted a plastic glass of Pinot Grigio.

Dave reached into the picnic basket and brought out a bag of stale bread. "Come on," he said, reaching for her hand and pulling her to her feet. As they walked to the edge of the lake, a dozen ducks squawked loudly as they paddled for the shore.

Dave handed Tracy a large hunk of stale bread and she broke off small pieces and threw them toward the water. "You must come here often," she said. "The ducks see you and scurry over."

"Not as often as I'd like, but I try." He took a deep breath. "I just love it here. I remember first coming here with my parents when I was a kid. They always brought bread so we could feed the ducks." Several large black-and-white geese flew in and landed on the lake about twenty feet from the shore, their long black necks and white throat patches gleaming in the sun. "Now the Canada geese have all but taken over." He tossed a handful of bread bits onto the ground and they watched the fowl lumber onto the land.

"They're so graceful in the water but a bit awkward on land," Tracy said, to fill the silence.

"We all have our elements. I know you're not totally comfortable in Kim's sexual one, but I think you'd do just fine."

Tracy turned so Dave couldn't see her blush. "I know you want me to do the weekend for your own reasons." Without letting him interrupt, she continued, "It's just difficult for me to even consider passing myself off as some sexual expert. I've never done many of the things Kim talks about."

"Do you think she has?"

"Of course," Tracy said, yet suddenly wondering whether Kim had actually tried bondage or anal sex. When Dave didn't immediately say anything, Tracy said, "I listened to everything she said. She was talking from experience."

"Her own or that of her letter writers? Don't jump down my throat for suggesting that she's not telling the total truth, but I've met Elliot, and although he's a wonderful guy, he doesn't strike me as the adventurous type. Of course, if Kim's taught me anything, it's that you never know."

Although, since her return from the West Coast, they hadn't spent much time together, Tracy loved Elliot like a brother. The three of them had been to dinner several times, and they had spent afternoons with Kim and Tracy's mother. He was down to earth, and maybe just a bit stuffy. Was he the type to tie her sister to the bed and tease her for hours?

Dave continued, a small smile playing across his face. "Can you see him in a leather thong, playing Robin Hood to Kim's Maid Marian?"

A vision of Elliot, paunch and all, in a leather thong leaped into her brain and she couldn't help the giggle that bubbled out. "Actually I have a little trouble picturing Kim in that scenario, too."

"So maybe some of what she talks about comes from her imagination."

"It feels so genuine that I never considered that maybe she hadn't done it at all." Why was this all so difficult? She tore off a chunk of bread, crumbled it in her hands, and tossed it to the hoard of hungry water fowl.

"I could teach you," Dave said, so softly that Tracy almost didn't hear his words.

She turned and stared at his profile, watching the breeze ruffle his long, softly curling hair. "What would you teach me?" she whispered.

She watched Dave feeding the birds, staring out over the sparkling water. "I'm not new to sex," he said, his voice rough. "I find you attractive and, well, frankly you turn me on. You know there are layers of agendas here and I won't try to kid you. I want you to run that weekend. But just as much, I want you in my bed."

Tracy's throat closed and her hands shook. She heard Andrew yelling about her lack of passion.

"I know you have issues," Dave said, turning to her. "I think maybe we can get past them."

Tracy almost couldn't get the words past the lump in her throat. "My ex-husband—"

"I know," Dave interrupted. "He worked you over real good. Can you just forget that he ever existed? Begin anew? With me?"

"I don't know."

"Let me tell you this. I'm not making a declaration of undying love. I think we could be friends and I'd like to see you again. Frankly, I'd like to make love to you and teach you how sexy you are."

Tracy felt tears pool in her eyes. "What if I'm not?"

"Why don't you let me worry about that?"

"That's a stock phrase. How can I not worry about whether I'm frigid?"

"You're not," he said, dropping the bag of bread chunks and grabbing her shoulders. "Would a woman who's frigid react like this?" His kiss was hard, filled with pent-up desire. His tongue demanded entry to her mouth and she slowly parted her lips. He plundered, taking, pulling strange new emotions from her.

She felt her insides liquify, and as if of their own volition, her arms slid around his neck to hold herself up. Her body trembled. Suddenly, the kiss changed. It became soft, asking rather than demanding, drawing out instead of pulling from her. His hands roamed her back, his hard chest pressed against her breasts. His fingers tangled in her hair as he changed the angle of the kiss to get still closer.

She was awash in sensations, colors swirled behind her closed eyelids. Heat pooled, then rushed through her body. She could feel her tissues swell and moisten. In the tiny section of her mind still capable of coherent thought, she heard Dave ask whether she still thought that she was truly frigid. His voice drowned Andrew's out.

Then he backed away and he seemed as shaken as she was. "No love," he said. "No commitments. Just a lesson in passion."

Slowly Tracy began to breathe again. Unable to speak, she merely stared at Dave.

Dave found he was totally shaken by the kiss and it took all his willpower not to throw her onto the blanket and fill her with his need. He had intended to lure Tracy into an affair of sorts, sex lessons with no emotional entanglements. He'd had lots of such relationships, passion, arousal, with no involvement. He could do that with Tracy. He could and he would. He would keep it simple, uncomplicated.

Dave had always kept his relationships simple. Except for Marlene. They'd been dating for about three months when she started making plans for their future. He'd enjoyed talking about the wedding and, of course, the honeymoon, in bed after wild lovemaking. They'd just slipped into becoming engaged and planned to be married on the first anniversary of their meeting. About two months before the wedding, he'd begun to wonder whether they were confusing lust and love. Did he love her? He hadn't a clue.

When he'd voiced his doubts, Marlene had laughed them off. "Everyone gets cold feet," she'd said, but it wasn't just cold feet. Over the ensuing weeks he'd become more and more sure that the whole thing was wrong. Marlene was in love with being in love. She reveled in the wedding plans, spending hours making guests lists and seating charts, worrying about whether to have cheese puffs or shrimp. When he tried to talk to her, she laughed it off.

Finally, a week before the wedding, he got her attention by saying, "I don't want to get married."

"Don't be silly. The wedding's next Saturday."

"I won't be there."

"Of course you will." She'd patted his arm. "We love each other and we'll have a great life."

As she continued to natter on about their future, he felt the panic rise. He was in a box with no way out and it was strangling him. He began to sweat and couldn't catch his breath. "I can't do this. I just can't do this." He'd walked out and not answered his phone calls for almost a month.

He knew he'd hurt her and he wanted to apologize but what could he say? He was guilty of leading her on, not disabusing her of her notions of forever. For months he'd been unable to get his guilt out of his mind. Now, almost six years later, he hardly thought about it, except for moments like now.

"Think about it and let's have dinner Wednesday evening. We can talk. Maybe later we can do more than just talk. Maybe you'll decide to let me teach you what a sexual woman you are, but it will be your decision." He kissed the tip of her nose. "I'll try to influence you, of course."

He watched Tracy close her eyes, then nod slightly. "Dinner at least," she said, her voice catching in her throat. "Maybe just dinner."

"I'll settle for that," Dave said. "If I have to."

If he knew anything, he knew that settling wouldn't be necessary.

Dave's beeper sounded, and as he stared at the screen, he cursed then told Tracy that he had to return to the hotel. "It's about two o'clock now. Shall we plan to be on the road by three? That should give me enough time to settle what I need to here."

"That sounds fine," she said. "I'll meet you in the lobby." They packed up the remains of their picnic, and taking the basket, Dave left Tracy to ponder.

After he was gone, she sat on the grass, her back against a large rock outcrop. What the hell was going on with her? Here was a man, a very attractive, sexy man, who wanted to show her what she had been missing in bed. Was that so terrible? She had always thought that sex was about love and commitment but maybe sex was, as this weekend had pointed out, about fun. Many of the couples who attended the weekend were just out for a good time. Were they all devoted to each other forever? Could you have good sex with only fun in mind?

There had to be caring, not necessarily about the future, but about each other at that moment, sharing something that was supposed to be so wonderful. She'd had more sexual excitement this weekend than she'd had in all of her marriage. Why couldn't it go on just like that? She liked Dave and he obviously liked her. Couldn't that be enough?

They met in the lobby just after three and the drive to Tracy's apartment took only about forty minutes. They chatted about inconsequential things, not touching on the issue burning in her mind. Maybe by now he'd changed his mind. They'd gotten caught up in the sensuality of the moment and the invitation had just popped out of his mouth. He didn't really mean any of it. He'd stop in the parking lot, let her out of the car, and drive off. She began to dread it.

They arrived at the house in which Tracy had her small apartment, and Dave got out of his four-wheel-drive SUV. As Tracy climbed down, Dave grabbed her suitcase and placed a palm in the small of her back, the heat burning through her shirt and jacket. He's always touching me. Is it deliberate? Does he know what his touch does to me? Of course he does.

She led him to her door and he set her case down. "Thanks for driving me home," she said, trying desperately to get past this incredibly awkward moment. She fished her keys from her purse with a shaking hand, and as she tried to push the key into the lock, she dropped the entire mass.

"You're terrified," Dave said gently, as he picked up her keys. "I don't ever mean to frighten you." He tipped her face back and kissed her softly. "What's wrong?"

"Nothing," she said, pulling away. "I'm just tired. It's been a long weekend and I have a class first thing tomorrow morning."

He tugged at her braid. "It isn't nothing, but I won't press. What time Wednesday works for you?"

"Wednesday?" she croaked.

"We have a date, don't we?" he said, looking puzzled.

He's got no idea how difficult this is for me, she realized. "I guess we do." She wanted him to do all the things he had promised, yet she hadn't the courage to hope that he could.

His smile was wide, showing white teeth. "You thought it was all talk and that exposed to the real world away from the lake and the sensuality of the weekend, I wouldn't want to go through with it, didn't you?"

Reluctantly Tracy nodded and Dave continued, "I want you," he said, his hand beneath her chin preventing her from looking away. "And I'll have you, if you're willing." He put his finger over her lips to keep her from speaking. "You have my phone number if you truly want to call it off."

"What if it's just dinner?"

"Then it's just dinner." He paused, then added, "And I'll be very disappointed."

Tracy called Kim on Monday afternoon, and although they talked for more than half an hour, she found herself unwilling to tell her sister about her date with Dave. When Kim asked what she thought of him, Tracy only said that she was impressed and thought that he was a really nice man.

"Yeah, he's quite a guy," Kim said. "Elliot and I both like him tremendously."

She remembered the discussion of Elliot in a leather thong and bit her tongue to keep from laughing. "He has nothing but nice things to say about both of you, too."

"You know I don't want to pressure you, but how about coming over sometime and reading some of Miranda's columns? I could answer any questions and it might give you a different slant on everything."

Dave would give her a very different slant, she thought. "I'd like that." After her evening with Dave, at which point she'd know what she was going to do. She hoped she would.

"Let's say the end of the week. I've got no classes Friday. Lunch?"

She could hear additional warmth in Kim's voice. "Wonderful. I'll call you Thursday evening and we'll agree on details."

When she realized how much she was looking forward to their lunch, Tracy was delighted by the sisters' newfound closeness. "Great. See you Friday." Friday. As she hung up the phone, Tracy realized that for her, the week's focus was Wednesday. It was as though there were a giant roadblock and somehow she couldn't really think past it. Friday seemed a lifetime away.

Tuesday dragged. Wednesday morning she taught her creative writing class, then saw students in conference for several hours. As she talked with them about job placement, she marveled at her ability to compartmentalize her thoughts. Although she functioned as she always had, Dave's face was never out of her mind. Dinner. Just dinner. Right?

He had arranged to pick her up at six, and by five-thirty she was dressed in khaki slacks and a soft black V-necked sweater. At five-forty, however, she was dressed in jeans with a butter yellow tailored blouse, and by five-fifty she wore the khaki slacks with a forest green flannel shirt. As the doorbell rang, she tugged off the shirt and dragged the original black sweater back on. She slipped into white sneakers over white socks, while calling, "Just a minute." She had had her hair softly permed, and glancing in the mirror, she fluffed it around her face. Did she look like a woman who was about to be seduced? Just dinner.

"Coming," she called, then winced at her inadvertent double entendre. Nothing was simple and straightforward anymore. Breathless, she yanked the door open. "Hi," she said, then watched as his eyes roamed her body. She'd bought new slacks at Wal-mart, one size smaller than usual, and they hugged her body snugly. The deep V of the sweater allowed a peek into her cleavage.

"You look great," Dave said. He was dressed in jeans, with an ivory turtleneck beneath a brown plaid shirt. His brown leather Western boots were highly polished, and he wore a matching leather belt with a turquoise and silver buckle.

She managed a nervous smile. "You don't look bad yourself."

"Let's get out of here," Dave said, "before you faint or I attack your lily-white body."

Her shoulders relaxed a bit as she slipped on a lightweight black jacket. It was going to be all right. They drove to a small Chinese restaurant that Tracy recommended, and ordered hot and sour soup, egg rolls, and spare ribs, promising the waiter that they would order their main courses later. They talked about their respective weeks, the weather, a really bad made-for-TV movie they had both seen recently, struggling to keep the conversation light. Anytime there was a lull, Tracy's mind worked overtime to find another innocuous topic.

Their soup arrived and they ate in silence, Tracy barely able to swallow. Finally, Dave said, "Can we drop the smoke screen?"

"Excuse me?"

"You're making nonstressful conversation to ward off the topic that's on both of our minds." He reached across the table and took her hand. His eyes boring into hers, he said softly, "I want you."

"I know," she whispered. She sat back as the waiter removed their soup bowls and placed plates of ribs and egg rolls in the middle of the table, then added side plates for each of them.

When the waiter asked, "Are you ready to order now?" Dave waved him off.

Taking Tracy's hand again, Dave said, "I don't want to scare you, as I know I do, but maybe it's best to get this all out in the open. Here's what I've been dreaming of since Sunday. I take you home after dinner and I slowly undress you, kissing and licking every inch of your soft, white skin." When she tried to pull her hand back, he held on tightly and continued. "I bite your nipples and nibble at the inside of your elbow."

When she continued to stare at her plate, he said, "Look at me. Please."

She slowly raised her head and gazed into his eyes. "I touch and stroke you everywhere until you're writhing on the bed, wanting and needing what you know I can give you. You want me to fill you, and I want to. In the middle of every night since we met, I close my eyes and I can almost feel my hard cock slide into your wet body. It makes me so hard it hurts." He paused, then asked, "Have you thought about it, too?"

She couldn't lie. "Yes." And she had masturbated to her private fantasy every night.

"So why are we here?"

"Because I'm really terrified. I'm afraid that . . ."

When she didn't continue, he said, "Tell me. Please tell me."

"In my dreams I can respond to you." She almost couldn't get the words past the lump in her throat. "In reality I'm afraid that there's nothing inside of me. No heat. No nothing."

"That's bullshit and you know it."

"That's the real problem. I don't know it." She could barely swallow.

"Then let's get out of here and let me show you who you really are." Without giving her a chance to respond, he motioned to the waiter for the check. They were silent while he paid and, as he signed the credit card receipt and added a substantial tip, the waiter handed him a doggie bag and said, "Maybe you'll need food later."

Tracy flushed bright red. Were they so obvious? What the hell. He wanted to show her, and could knowing be worse than the way she felt right now? Could the reality really be more devastating than all the doubts? They slipped on their jackets and climbed back into Dave's car for the short drive back to Tracy's apartment.

Chapter

7

Like something out of a romantic movie, Dave closed the door behind him, leaned against it, and pulled Tracy tightly against him. His lips found hers and teased, tempted, and tormented. "Like my dreams. You taste like my dreams." He didn't give her time to breathe, time to think. He pulled her jacket off, then his, his lips never leaving hers, rendering her unable to do anything but react. No, she admitted in the still coherent part of her brain. She could stop him if she wanted to. She didn't.

He kissed her neck, then nipped at the muscle at the top of her shoulder. His hands found the bottom of her sweater and then the skin beneath. "God, I've thought about little but this," he growled, his hands and lips never still. He turned them until her back was pressed against the door, seemingly unable to wait to have her. His knee pressed between hers, and then he suddenly stopped and pulled away. "No," he sighed. "Not like this."

Deeply disappointed at his abrupt departure, she moaned and he grinned. "Oh, we'll do it but not in the middle of the floor like two animals." He took a deep breath and let it out slowly. "Do you still doubt yourself?"

She shook her head, overwhelmed by the depth of her reactions to him. Her pulse pounded and she leaned slightly toward him. "No," she whispered, then shook her head again. "A little, maybe."

His laugh was deep and rich. "I understand." He picked up their jackets and dropped them onto the sofa. "You won't soon." He took her in his arms again, kissed her, then growled, "Which way?"

She didn't pretend to misunderstand and motioned him toward her bedroom, smiling to herself. In anticipation of the evening, she had vacuumed and changed the sheets. When they entered the bedroom, Dave said, "I want to go slowly, show you all the wonderful things you've been missing, but I'm not sure I can." He took her hand and placed it on the front of his jeans. She could clearly feel the evidence of his excitement. She squeezed slightly and heard him groan as he grabbed her wrist and pulled her hand away. "None of that or I won't last two minutes." He heaved another cleansing breath. "This night is for you." He kissed her again deeply, touching not only her mouth but her very soul.

Tracy felt his hands roam her back, then cup the cheeks of her buttocks to bring her body closer. Again she felt the hard ridge beneath his pants, this time against her mound. She allowed her head to fall back and Dave quickly moved his kisses to her throat and neck. Everywhere his lips touched seared, turning her blood to molten lava. The sound of his harsh breathing mingled with hers, both nearly inaudible over the pounding of her heart.

His lips moved down the center of her chest above the deep neck of her sweater. Had she selected it to make this easier? Maybe, she admitted. "You smell so wonderful," he whispered, "and you taste wonderful and you feel wonderful."

When she reached for him, he gently guided her hands to her sides. "I told you, this is only for you."

"But—"

"For you." When he was content that she wasn't going to move, he placed his palms against her jaw and kissed her again. It was so selfish, she thought, letting him make love to her without participating, but if it was what he wanted . . .

He grabbed the hem of her sweater and yanked it off over her head. When she saw his eyes as he looked at her, she was glad she had picked her most provocative undies, a black demi-bra with red embroidered roses over each nipple. "My God, woman," he said, his voice hoarse, his words uneven, "I feel like I've unwrapped a wanton hussy." She wanted to say something clever but his hands found her breasts and she could no longer think.

He cupped her, then slipped his fingers beneath the satiny material, and when he squeezed her nipples, she shuddered. He swiftly removed her slacks and footwear then lifted her onto the center of the double bed. On his knees, he followed, just gazing at her bra and matching black bikini panties with an embroidered rose over her pubis. He grinned. "Diana would be proud of you. Those are designed to drive a man crazy." He removed all his clothes except his briefs then, with a leer, stroked his erection with the palm of his hand. "They succeed."

Obviously unable to wait, he unhooked her bra and removed her panties as well. Naked, she lay on the bed, watching his eyes for any sign that anything about her turned him off. There was none. Then his briefs were gone and she watched him unroll a condom over his erection.

Incredibly impatient, it seemed like hours until his mouth was on her nipple and his hand slid through her pubic hair into her soaked center. He explored her folds, and when he finally found her clit, he rubbed it with his thumb while his fingers delved into her channel.

Maybe her recent masturbation had honed her body's responses, or maybe it was there all along to a man who understood, but she felt the heat blossom low in her belly. Her head pressed into the bed in her attempt to press her mound more firmly against his talented fingers. "You'll teach me exactly what you like," he said, "but for now . . ." He filled her with three fingers and stroked her clit with his other hand. Shards of electric heat knifed through her, settling deep between her legs. It was there, and she only had to reach for it. "Yes, baby," he purred. "Take it."

Higher and higher she climbed until her entire being was concentrated around his hands. Hard strokes, then light caresses, probing and teasing her, urging her to grab for the ultimate ecstasy. Then she did. With a moan, she came, hard spasms of pleasure pressing against his fingers. Wave after wave crashed over her. Then he was inside her, his cock filling her completely, and she felt the tide begin again. Again! Again! He thrust into her until she screamed from the pleasure of it. His loud yell joined hers as he climaxed, his back arched, his hard thighs banging against hers. Panting, almost unable to breathe, she collapsed. Dave cradled her tightly against him and she dozed.

Sometime later she awoke to the sound of the front door closing. He was gone! The bed where he had been lying was still warm from his body, but he was gone. Although her clothing littered the room, his clothes were nowhere to be found. Tears filled her eyes until she was afraid she would choke on them. She thought it had been so good. She was a failure after all. Something had gone terribly wrong and it was all her fault.

Then his face was at the bedroom door. "Are you as hungry as I am?" he asked.

It took a moment to gain her bearings. "Hungry?"

He must have seen the look on her face and he quickly crossed the room, settled on the side of the bed, and took her in his arms. "Oh, baby. I'm sorry. I went to the car to get the leftover Chinese food."

"Sorry," she said, tears flowing freely down her cheeks.

"No, I'm sorry. You were sleeping so peacefully and I thought, when you woke, you'd be as hungry as I am." He hugged her tightly and his arms felt so safe, so right.

She sat up and smiled weakly. "I woke up and you were gone. I heard the front door and I thought . . ." God, don't let me be clingy. It's not that kind of thing between Dave and me.

"I can imagine what you thought and it must have scared you to death. Let's just let it pass." He grinned at her. "Now, ribs or egg rolls?"

She took a deep shuddering breath, then realized her stomach was growling. "Both," she said, her heart as light as it had ever been.

After Chinese food, they were both still hungry so she rummaged through her refrigerator and put together the ingredients for a simple omelet. After they had cleaned the dishes, Dave said, "Hungry?"

"We just ate," Tracy answered, puzzled.

He licked his lips and tipped his head to one side. "Who's talking about food?"

They made love again, and again she climaxed. When they lay together beneath her quilt, he asked, "Are you feeling better about things?"

She thought for a moment. "Yes, I think I am."

"You know," Dave said, "I feel sorry for your ex-husband. He never found out what a hot little number you really are." He cradled her more tightly. "This is a nice place you have here. Your bedroom is like your lingerie."

What a strange comment, she thought as she looked

around. The room was simple, with ivory walls, simple miniblinds covered by sheer curtains, a floral quilt with matching sheets. Nothing special.

Dave continued, "It's sensual somehow. Like the scented candles. Next time we'll wait long enough to light them. And the prints on the walls. Flowers in full bloom, nothing held back. The quilt is satin, cool and slick, and the lights have wonderful, multicolored, Tiffany-type shades. It all says sensual, almost erotic."

"I didn't intend that at all. It's sort of embarrassing."

"It shouldn't be. It's you, and whether you were conscious of doing it or not, that's what your bedroom says."

"How do you know all that?"

"Remember I had to decorate an entire hotel. I read a dozen books on interiors and the messages they send." Not self-conscious about his nudity, Dave slipped from the bed and headed for the door to the small bathroom.

Tracy tried to stifle a giggle. "What does my bathroom say?"

He opened the door and burst out laughing. Tracy had filled the bathroom with Mickey Mouse: shower curtain, towels, soaps, together with a large Mickey print on the wall. "It says you're a combination of so many things. It will be my pleasure to unravel you."

As the door closed behind Dave, Tracy reveled in her pleasure. The sex had been great. Orgasmic. She giggled at her joke. It certainly sounded as if Dave was interested in continuing their relationship, whatever that was. What was their relationship? It was hot, erotic, and yet comfortable somehow. Not love, not yet even deep friendship. Just fun. Hot, sexy fun.

An hour later, Dave was dressed and ready to leave. "I wish I could stay," he said, pulling on his jacket, "but I have to go. I have a hotel to run in the morning." He kissed her. "I can't get away over weekends. It's my busiest time, and I don't want to wait until the middle of next week to see you again. Can you come up? Maybe Saturday evening?"

Grinning, Tracy said, "I'd love to."

For the first time Dave looked unsure. "I'd love for you to stay over, but if you do, everyone on the staff will know it immediately. How would you feel about that?"

"I don't know yet," she said.

"Come up Saturday and we'll go to a wonderful little place I know of. Then afterwards . . . It's like when we were teenagers when we still lived at home and had to find a place to be alone." His eyes lit up. "One of the cabins isn't rented for this coming weekend. We can go there and be away from the eyes of my staff."

"I'll be there around six. Does that work?"

He kissed her until her brain was totally fuzzed. "That's only a few days from now, not too long to wait."

He released her, and when the door closed behind him, she dropped onto the sofa. She was blown away by what had happened to her in the past several hours. Her entire picture of herself had shifted. The lovemaking had been fabulous, and Dave had obviously enjoyed it as much as she had. After what she had learned over the weekend, she considered that Dave might want more than the plain vanilla sex they had had, but he had promised to teach her. Actually, if she remembered correctly, he had promised to let her teach him. How could she do that? What did she have to teach him? She'd never received or performed something as ordinary as oral sex. At least, she hadn't enjoyed it. She remembered being in the front seat of some guy's car. She had dated him in college and they'd driven to some quiet spot. Lots of necking, then he'd unzipped his pants and pressed her face into his crotch. It had been all she could do not to retch. Then there had been the episode with Andrew. What if she could never do that? And anal sex?

She stretched. Nonproductive thinking. She'd had a fabulous evening and now she was overthinking, worrying about too many *what-ifs*. "Just enjoy what was and stop the rest, right now!" Following her own advice, she turned off the lights, climbed into bed, and slept dreamlessly.

Although she couldn't follow her sound advice all the time, she focused on the pleasure. Friday, she and Kim met for lunch at a small Italian restaurant halfway between their apartments. Kim had given her a thick envelope with several dozen of Miranda's columns. Now they were seated at a small table with a blue checked tablecloth and paper place mats, and each ordered spaghetti, Tracy's with white clam sauce, and Kim's with meat sauce. While they nibbled on salads, and talked about nothing much, Tracy wondered how to ask her sister the question burning in her mind.

"Earth to Tracy," Kim said. "Are you receiving?"

"I'm sorry, sis," Tracy said, realizing she hadn't heard Kim's last few sentences.

"I asked you about Dave. Did you enjoy your lunch with him?"

"Lunch?" They had had dinner.

"Last Sunday. Remember?"

"Sure. Right. It was great."

"Something's going on, Trace. Give."

Tracy couldn't help but grin. "We had dinner together Wednesday evening. He drove down and we had Chinese." Twice.

Kim looked at her sister for a moment, then said, "You can't kid me. There was more than dinner. Right?"

Tracy felt color flood her cheeks. "Much more."

"Bravo! That's great. Was it good? Did the earth move?"

Her grin widened. "I think it registered eight point three on the Richter scale."

Kim jumped up and hugged her sister. "I'm so glad. You

two deserve good things. When are you going to see him again?"

"I'm driving up to the hotel on Saturday." She straightened the napkin in her lap. "It's really scary. I feel like I'm out on a very thin limb."

Kim looked puzzled. "Why? He's a nice guy and I know he wouldn't hurt you. Is this serious?"

"You mean between us? Not at all. That's the strangest part. We agreed that this is just sex." She grinned again. "Great sex, but just sex. No love stuff, no entanglements."

"You're two grown-ups. What's wrong with that?"

"I don't know. It just feels funny. Sex is supposed to be about commitment."

"Horse pucky. Sex is supposed to be about sex. For good sex, you need some level of caring about each other, but more than that, what happens happens."

Tracy's mood shifted. "I've been thinking about the weekend and I have a question that I don't know how to ask."

"Trace, just ask. I'll answer if I can."

"Have you done all the things you talk about in your forums?"

Kim burst out laughing. "Not all. Elliot is more creative than you might imagine, but he's not at all into whips and such."

Tracy remembered her conversation with Dave. She still couldn't imagine Elliot in a thong. Kim leaned closer. "I did get my behind slapped during sex with an old boyfriend and I have to admit at that moment it felt really hot."

Tracy was so far into this bizarre conversation that she pressed on. "Anal sex?"

Kim paused, a hesitation Tracy wondered about, but then she said, "Elliot and I tried it a few times and it didn't turn either of us on." She studied her sister. "I've learned a lot from my readers. In addition to my columns, I can give you lots of letters from people who do the most unusual things, then write me to ask whether they're normal."

"Are they?"

"Who's to say what's normal. If two consenting adults want to play in some unusual way and they get pleasure from it, why not? Getting back to your question, in the forums I never say I've done everything. I tell them what I can, then say what others have said."

"You mean you make the stuff up?"

"Not really. It all seems really logical and I say what makes sense to me. About everything. I talk about sexual dysfunction but I've never experienced it, either from me or my partner. Yet I can talk about it. Is that what's worrying you about the weekend?"

"I suppose. Until Wednesday I carried a lot of baggage but I've gotten rid of some of it. With Dave's help."

"Dave strikes me as a man with a lot of experience. He's probably *been there*, *done that* with lots of things. Relax and ride with it."

"Well, give me a few weeks, and if things go well, I might just do that weekend after all."

Tracy arrived at the Catskill Lake Resort at six the following evening and found Dave involved in a dispute between two guests. It took almost fifteen minutes to get things settled, fifteen minutes of hungry gazes at each other, pounding hearts and rapid breathing, sweating palms and aroused flesh. When he finally approached her in the lobby, he suggested a local restaurant. "Are you hungry?" he asked.

Admitting to him and to herself, she said, "Not for food."

Arm in arm, they almost trotted to the same cabin that she had seen the previous weekend and hurried inside. Dave had a fire already laid and lit it with an extra-long match. Then he yanked the bedding from the bed and spread it on the floor in front of the leaping flames. "Come here," he said, his voice already hoarse. "Tonight you're going to teach me what you like."

Tracy had already knelt beside him, but at his words, she froze. "I don't think I can."

"You can, believe me." He unbuttoned her navy and red striped silk blouse and pulled it off. "Let's start here." He kissed her collarbone, then the side of her neck. "Which do you like better?"

"I like them both," Tracy said.

"Not a good answer," he said. "You have to choose or I will assume you don't like either."

She smiled slightly, then said, "My neck."

"Good girl." He nibbled up and down the side of her neck, nipping at the tendon at the side. "Now this." He kissed her deeply, then grabbed the back of her hair and pulled, kissing her throat. "Which?"

"I don't know? I like everything you do."

Dave shook his head. "Cop-out answers are not allowed. Do you mind when I pull your hair a little bit?"

"No," she said, suddenly shy. It was as if she were admitting something a little dirty.

"Good." He pulled her hair slightly harder until her back bowed. Then he bit the soft skin just above her red satin bra. "And that? Is that good?"

"Yes," she said, her voice raspy.

Still holding her hair, he slipped her bra straps from her shoulders and exposed one full breast. "And this?" He suckled at her nipple, and when she moaned, he said, "That tells me all I need to know." Soon they were naked and his mouth was on her belly. "How about this?" He stroked her inner thigh, then pulled her pubic hair lightly. "Is that good?"

"Yes," she said, barely able to control her voice.

"Then this will be better." His mouth slid down until it was between her legs.

"Why are you doing that?" Tracy said, tightening as she remembered how disgusting Andrew had said it was. She had a flash of Andrew between Sharon's thighs. Maybe she was the one who was disgusting. She squirmed, trying to get away.

"I'm doing this because I want to. Does it bother you?"

"Andrew . . ."

Harshly, Dave said, "I'm not your ex-husband and I don't do things I don't enjoy." She felt him lick the soft flesh of her upper thigh, then he ran his tongue along the creases at the tops of her thighs. "Is this so terrible?" he asked.

Tracy waited for him to pull away but he continued to tickle her most intimate places. Slowly she let her muscles relax until his tongue found her swollen lips.

He cupped her buttocks and lifted her more firmly against his mouth. "Tell me it's good. Moan and pant for me."

When his tongue found her clit, she groaned loudly. "Oh, my God," she said, her body writhing. She felt herself open to him, all the fears disappearing into the whirling colors of her pleasure.

"Tell me not to stop."

"God."

He pulled back. "If it's good, tell me not to stop. Tell me."

"Don't stop. Oh please, don't stop."

He didn't. His tongue lashed at her clit, then he licked long strokes along her slit. When his fingers stabbed inside her and he sucked on her nub, she thought she would fly apart into a million shards. There was an ancient rhythm to what he was doing and she could barely hold still. "Faster?" he asked, then demonstrated. "Or more slowly, like this." His fingers barely entered her, then inch by inch burrowed inside as his tongue slowly licked. "Tell me."

"Slow. I like it slow."

"Show me." He took her hand and placed it on her mound. "Show me how you like it best."

She couldn't. Her fingers had gotten very adept at bringing herself to climax but she couldn't do it while he watched. As she remained silent, he teased her, touching lightly, and blowing cool air on her hot flesh. He held her wrist tightly so her hand rested on her wet, swollen skin. "Show me or I'll keep you here, right on the edge." He increased the speed of his strokes, then slowed again. "Show me."

As if of its own volition, her fingers found her clit and she rubbed. With his fingers inside her, she felt orgasm build. Then his fingers stilled. "I want to feel you come," he said. "Do it."

And she came, spasms clenching his fingers. "God, I can feel your muscles as you come," he said. "It's so wonderful."

"I want you inside me," she said, amazed at what she was able to ask for. He quickly put on a condom and thrust inside her, filling her completely. She wrapped her legs around his waist and pulled him, arching her back and thrusting with her hips to increase the sensations. It took only a few strokes for him to come, and as he did, she felt another orgasm build. Sadly, he had come just a few moments too soon. "Do it," he said, panting, his softening cock still inside her.

"What?" she said, slightly puzzled. Did he know she was slightly unsatisfied?

"You know. You want it. You need it. Take it."

"I'm fine," she lied.

"No, you're not. You need more." When she hesitated, he said, "I want to do it for you. Take my hand and show me what you need. Teach me how to do it just right."

Teach him? She could, and he was right, she did need it. Until recently she hadn't had an orgasm; now she craved the completion. Hesitantly, she took his wrist and put his hand on her clit. Then she guided his fingers to her sopping flesh and used his knuckle to stroke until, with a shout, she came again.

When they had caught their breath, he said, "You learn quickly, sexy lady. You're fabulous. That was sensational."

She couldn't control her grin. "Yes, it certainly was."

Chapter

8

The following Tuesday, after her morning class, Tracy drove the half an hour to the Willow Grove Nursing Home to visit her mother. As always, the older woman was sitting in her wheelchair on a sunny, glassed-in porch, gazing at the wide lawn beyond. Tracy leaned over and kissed the older woman on the cheek. Despite her Alzheimer's disease, Ruth looked to be in good health, her complexion smooth and relatively unwrinkled, her steel gray hair blunt cut and held at the back of her neck with a gold barrette. Tracy always noticed her nails, carefully trimmed and scrupulously clean. "Hello, Mom. How are you today?" Today she wore a soft pink fleece robe with navy blue pajamas beneath.

Ruth continued to smile without any recognition. "How are you feeling today?" Tracy asked, not expecting an answer. "It's a beautiful day, isn't it?" Silence.

"Ruth's doing quite well today," a bosomy uniformed woman fussing over another older lady said. Her frizzy black hair was tamed with several combs and her deep, black eyes twinkled. Her uniform consisted of a shocking pink scrub top with maroon cotton pants. Willow Grove specialized in hot colors, from the employees' uniforms to the hallway walls, hung with surreal paintings, mainly splashes of hot colors on white backgrounds. A bright red-and-blue parrot squawked from his cage in one corner of the porch.

"I'm glad, Marge," Tracy said, recognizing one of the warm, caring aides who populated Willow Grove.

"Oh, yes, she certainly is. Missus Ruth had a wonderful breakfast and ate all her soft-boiled egg." Tracy loved the melody of the Caribbean in Marge's voice, and she pronounced her mother's name "Root." The woman walked over and patted Ruth's hand, then tucked a granny square afghan snugly around her legs. "It was fine, wasn't it, darlin'?"

Ruth made eye contact with the woman and her smile broadened. As she always did, Tracy blessed Willow Grove and the care with which it selected its staff. Every attendant seemed to be genuinely concerned with the well-being of the residents, something that had been missing in most of the other places she and Kim had visited.

"I had a wonderful weekend, Mom," Tracy said, as Marge crossed the room to sit with an older man who had just settled into a slatted plastic chair. She lowered her voice and pulled over a chair so she could sit beside her mother. "It was one of Kim's Creative Loving Weekends, and I met so many delightful people." Tracy spent the next few minutes telling the vacant woman about Diana and Matt, then about Dave. "He's a very attractive man and we're sort of seeing each other."

Sort of seeing each other. What a wimpy phrase. He was all she could think about. She had relived their night of wild, uninhibited sex several times. As she thought about it, she realized that, between Dave and Kim, she understood so much more than she had only a week before. She might just be able to run the January weekend. She'd never be as knowledgeable as her sister, but she would work hard and do her best. Kim would be of tremendous help, too. Her entire body tingled as she thought about how Dave would help as well. Let's hear it for a complete education.

Tracy had been silent for several minutes as she gazed at her mother. Ruth was a tremendous incentive, too. Looking around, she realized that she would probably have forced herself to run the weekend if only to keep her mother in Willow Grove, but now it seemed so much more possible. She talked at Ruth for another half an hour, then stood up and kissed her on the cheek. "I'll see you next week, Mom. I love you."

"I love you," Ruth whispered, her eyes still focused on the lawn outside the window.

Startled, Tracy crouched and put her face where her mother couldn't avoid her eyes. Ruth gazed at her forehead, then lowered her eyes to meet her daughter's gaze. Her smile broadened. "Thank you," she said.

"For what?"

Marge wandered over. "She only says three things, Tracy. 'I love you,' 'Please,' and 'Thank you,' and she says them pretty randomly. I don't think she makes any real connection to the outside world anymore. Don't be sad, though." As Marge continued, Tracy stood up and Ruth's gaze returned to the window, her expression calm and relaxed. "Wherever Ruth is, she's happy."

"Yes, I guess she is." With her eyes moist, Tracy left.

Tracy arranged to have dinner with Kim a few days later. Elliot was going to be working late so the sisters had several hours to relax together.

Over a dinner of franks and beans, the two women talked about the twins and little else. Tracy wanted to tell Kim about the weekend, but she wanted to enjoy her secret for a few minutes longer and Kim hadn't asked.

After pouring cups of decaf coffee, Kim said, "Trace, I'm afraid I blew you off a while ago when you asked me whether I had done everything I talked about at the forums."

Puzzled, Tracy said, "I didn't think that at all. You were honest with me, weren't you?"

"Yes, and no. We were pretty close before you married Andrew."

Confounded by the non sequitur, Tracy said, "I know, but we lost touch when I moved."

"It wasn't your moving that came between us, Trace. I was embarrassed and I pretty much dropped you."

"Embarrassed? I don't understand."

"There's quite a bit I need to say, so hang on and let me talk for a few minutes. Remember the barbecue Mom threw the summer before you were married? It was a few months before I met Elliot and I had been unceremoniously dumped by a guy I had been with for almost a year."

"Josh. I remember him well." She lowered her voice. "Personally I thought he was a bit stuffy for you."

With a rueful smile, Kim said, "Frankly, as I think back on him, you were right. He was . . . Well, that's past history and not what I wanted to talk about. At the barbecue Andrew came on to me."

Tracy's eyebrows shot up but she said nothing.

"Trace," Kim said, reaching across the small kitchen table, then pulling her hand back, "I let him. I was feeling really shitty about myself and he was an attractive younger man. He kept touching me and whispering erotic words in my ear. He made me feel desired and I needed that at the time." Tracy had never seen her sister look so miserable. "When he suggested that we slip out for a few minutes, I agreed. Trace, we ended up in my bedroom."

Although she was shocked at what her sister had just said, Tracy saw tears in her sister's eyes. "And?" she said softly.

"I was in my mid-thirties and I should have known better, should have been stronger, but I wasn't. We stripped really quickly and he opened the window, supposedly so that we would have some cool air. Thinking back, I'm sure he wanted to be able to hear the sounds of the party, while we . . . It wasn't much, just a quickie at first. Oh, God, Trace." Tears flowed down Kim's face as she said, "He pulled out, turned me over on my belly, and fucked me from behind." Tracy watched her sister's throat work. "He fucked my ass. It really hurt at first, but it was exciting, too. I'd never done anything like that before. When my body finally relaxed and he could move inside of me, he fingered my clit and I think I actually came." She expelled a shaky breath at the memory. "He almost suffocated when he climaxed, holding his breath so he wouldn't make any noise.

"As he pulled out, I heard you ask Mom where Andrew was. He bounced out of bed, slapped my ass, then dressed and ran back downstairs. I heard you say, 'Oh, there you are,' and he said he'd been in the bathroom.

"Needless to say, I felt like hell. I called out the window and said I wasn't feeling well and would stay in my room. You came up. Remember?"

Tracy vaguely remembered that evening. She had worried about her sister but had quickly put it out of her mind when Andrew slipped his arm around her waist and pulled her close. "Sure. You looked really flushed and we thought you had the flu."

"It was never the same between us from then on. I wanted to tell you what a shit your fiancé was but I couldn't without revealing what had happened."

"You made your dislike pretty obvious and I always wondered what you had against him. I thought you were jealous since you and Josh had split."

"I think I was jealous, too. You had someone, even if he was a shit, and I had no one." Tears still trickled down Kim's cheeks.

"I guess I can understand why you did it. I felt like fucking the world after Andrew and I split, but I couldn't bring myself to risk it."

"Don't let me off the hook, Trace. I did a terrible thing whatever the reason."

"Yeah, you did, and there didn't have to be a reason. It was dumb, but I've done really dumb stuff, too. Guys do that to girls." She tilted her head to one side. "I think it's genetic."

"You should be furious with me."

"Part of me is, but not for the reason you think. Maybe, if you had told me then, I wouldn't have married him."

"Would it really have made a difference?" Kim asked, totally serious.

Tracy smiled ruefully. "Probably not."

"I feel incredibly guilty. During the past weeks we've gotten so much closer and I've been able to push that night out of my mind. When you asked about anal sex, that's all I could remember but I couldn't tell you."

Tracy rounded the table and lifted her sister into her arms. The women hugged for a long while. Tracy said into Kim's ear, "Andrew was such a shit, you know. He tried anal sex with me, too." The two women parted. "He'd already come once that night but for some reason he wanted to do it the back way. I was so frustrated that it didn't take much for him to talk me into it. Talk? He begged and I acquiesced. He lubed me up good and rubbed his cock through his condom, but try as he might, he couldn't get hard enough to penetrate. It was a fiasco, and by that time I wasn't aroused anymore so I was delighted that it didn't work. I guess the humiliation was too much for him and thankfully we never tried it again." Over the next few minutes, Tracy told Kim about the afternoon Tracy had walked in on Andrew and Sharon. "That was the final straw. He was doing it with her in our bed."

"I figured it had to be something like that. Trace," Kim said, closing her eyes, "can you forgive me?"

"It says on our birth certificates that we're both grown-ups now. Maybe we can start again."

As they grabbed for the tissue box, Tracy said, "This is like a scene from some soap opera or chick flick and I hate it. Let's stop right now."

Each woman took a deep breath and they exchanged watery smiles. "Done," Kim said, taking her coffee cup and heading for the living room. "You asked me a question about the things I talk about and the things I've done. Maybe I can give you a better answer now that I can be totally honest with you. What do you want to know?"

"I guess that forum on bondage and stuff really bothered me. I heard all your reasoning, control and all, but . . . I don't know. Have you ever been, you know, tied up?"

"First, bothered you how? Good bothered or bad bothered?"

Tracy felt the color rise in her cheeks. "I don't really know. Both, I guess."

"I've done it and it's really exciting. Elliot and I play like that from time to time."

"I just can't picture Elliot—"

"I know, I couldn't either. Actually neither could he. I had played some light bondage games with an old boyfriend and it really turned me on. He'd tie me to the bed and tease me, and himself, of course. When we finally made love, I was so aroused I came from his first thrust."

Tracy was pleased by her sister's honesty and, if she had to admit it, really curious. In the past it might have been embarrassing, but if she couldn't talk openly with Kim, how could she expect to talk in front of a group?

"Elliot and I had been together for about six months when I brought it up to him."

"How did you do that the first time? I'd be too scared. What would some guy think of me?"

"I was a bit worried, but while we were making love one evening, I stretched my hands over my head and said, 'Hold me tight.' He got the idea, grabbed my wrists, and things got really hot. It was dynamite for both of us and it grew from there. Now we have all kinds of games. Sometimes he's in charge, sometimes I am. Frequently we play gin rummy and loser pays a forfeit. You get the idea."

"Have you ever told that story to a group? It would undoubtedly help others who might want to try something unusual with their partner. Finding ways to branch out must be really difficult."

"You mentioned making that a separate forum and I think it's a great idea, and you're right, that story should help." Kim found a piece of paper in an end table and jotted a note. "I guess that brings up the core question. Have you decided about the weekend?"

"Yeah. I think I'm going to do it. Between us we can make it work."

"Dave's helping, too, isn't he."

Tracy blushed. "He's helping, too." Tracy paused, then said, "I've had such bad experiences with sex that I wonder. Has sex always been good for you?"

"Of course not. Elliot and I communicate so well now that if it's not good for me, I can ask for what I want. Before Elliot, I had lots of lousy evenings."

"With Andrew it was pretty bad most of the time."

"For both of you?"

Tracy considered. "I don't really know whether it was satisfying for him."

"Neither of you said or did anything to make it better?"

"I thought it was my fault."

"So many women do. You know, we need to work that idea into one of the forums. Sex isn't always wonderful. Sometimes it's just ordinary and sometimes it's plain awful. I remember evenings of pure frustration and times when I had no idea what the guy wanted me to do. I thought I was the least-talented lover on the planet."

"Me, too." Hesitantly, Tracy told her sister about Andrew's attempt to get her to perform oral sex on him. "I threw up and ran into the bathroom."

"Good for you." Funny, Tracy thought, that's just what Dave said. "Oral sex can be wonderful, but not every woman enjoys it. I'm sure he made it seem like it was your fault." When Tracy just stared at her hands, Kim continued, "There's no fault. There are no good lovers, only good couples. Sure, some people are better at sensing what their partners want and need, but it's the job of both to send and receive."

"Kim," Tracy said. "There's one thing about the weekend. I'll do it, but I feel like I'm cheating the couples who pay all that money for Miranda—you."

"I've been thinking about that," Kim said. "How about sending everyone who's already registered a letter that explains everything. We'll give them an opportunity to cancel, and if they don't, we'll refund two hundred fifty dollars. Will that make you feel better?"

Tracy couldn't keep the grin from her face. She'd been thinking along the same lines for several days but hadn't wanted to ask Kim to give up all that money. "Are you sure? It will take quite a bite out of the proceeds."

"I would never want anyone attending to feel cheated. We can write the letter together, decide on what to say about your credentials, and when we're both satisfied, ship it out."

Tracy couldn't believe her relief at having the weight lifted from her shoulders.

"Let's call Dave," Kim suggested, motioning Tracy to the extension phone in the kitchen.

Dave was delighted and quickly agreed to contribute fifty of the two hundred fifty dollars. "You don't have to do that," Kim said.

"I know I don't, but I want to. This is a joint effort. I hate to bring this up, but have you ladies considered what you're going to do about April?"

"We're a team now," Kim said, "and we can handle the weekends from here on."

"Absolutely," Tracy said.

After their conversation with Dave, the two women talked for several more hours until they heard the front door open and shut. "Hi, girls," Elliot called. "How's the gab session going? Is it safe for a mere man to come inside?"

As Kim rose to meet her husband, Tracy tried to picture him tying Kim to the bed. As Kim and Elliot walked back in, arm in arm, it was all Tracy could do not to burst out laughing. "Don't you dare, sis," Kim said, reading her mind.

"Gin rummy later?" Tracy said, now unable to control herself.

Elliot turned to his wife and raised an imperious eyebrow. "What have you two been talking about, as if I didn't know? Can I ever look my sister-in-law in the face again?"

Tracy stood and embraced her brother-in-law. "You're the best," she said. "Most important, you make my sister happy." She laughed again. "And you're hot. We've decided." Tracy grabbed the thick envelope of Kim's columns that Kim had given her at their lunch together and headed for the door. "Soon, guys," she said over her shoulder.

As she drove home, she thought about bondage and anal sex. Many of her preconceptions were slipping away, and she liked the feeling. Between Dave and Kim, she was starting to believe that she had been wrong about herself and the whole subject of sex.

Several weeks later her new resolve was put to the test. She and Dave had been out at least once a week since that first weekend. The weather had turned late-October cold, the nights crystal clear, the sky filled with what seemed to be a million stars. Dave arrived at Tracy's house for their usual Wednesday dinner and she had cooked a large steak. After their first few dates, when they had been able to think of nothing but sex, they had begun to get to know each other. Dave had a married older sister who lived in the Midwest, and his stepfather had married his mother when Dave was in his early teens. They had met when he had been hired to run his father's three hotels in the Catskills, and although a bit overbearing, his stepfather seemed to care about him. Now, while the older man ran the two largest ones, Dave owned and managed the Catskill Lake Resort, with some of the profits placed in a trust fund for his mother and sister.

A few weeks earlier Dave had confessed to Tracy that his original interest in her had been the weekends and to avoid an I-told-you-so from his stepfather. Although initially stung to hear him say it out loud, Tracy had let her brief anger go. Now they lay on her bed, naked and entwined. Candles burned and the music was classical, which they had discovered early on that they both enjoyed. As a Chopin Étude played softly, Dave's hands expertly pressed her higher and higher, while she ran her fingernails down his chest and felt him shiver. His cock was fully erect and she wrapped her fingers around it and felt the soft skin with the hardness beneath.

Dave turned so his mouth was against her mound and his cock rested against her breasts. As his lips found her, she was afraid that he wanted her to put her mouth on him. Paralyzed, she stared at his cock as it twitched against her skin. Dave rolled away. "You just shut down. Tell me what's wrong."

"I know you need me to put my mouth on you and I can't."

"If I needed it, I'd ask for it. I don't, but I would like it if you did it."

"I can't."

"I understand and it's not important." He scrambled beside her and held her. "There's nothing you ever *have* to do with me."

"But I want to make you happy."

"You do make me happy. What frightens you so much about oral sex?"

"I told you about Andrew and how I threw up. I'll gag and do something dumb. I just know it."

"And if you do?" When she said nothing, Dave said, "I think you have the wrong idea about oral sex. Despite what Andrew did, you don't have to perform deep throat. I'd like it if you'd just lick me like a lollipop. The touch of your tongue would be heavenly. That's not a demand, just a request."

"I want to. Just don't hold my head. Please."

"Why would I do that?" He stretched out on his back, reached up, and grabbed the headboard. "Let's pretend that my hands are tied and I can't move."

Somehow that made it more possible and she wanted to give Dave as much as he had given her. Tentatively, Tracy knelt between his legs and held his erection. Hot and heavy, she had learned to love the feel of it both in her hands and in her body. Could the taste of him be too bad? She bent over and experimentally touched the tip of her tongue to his shaft. The skin was smooth and there was little taste. He smelled of heat, and sex, an aroma she'd grown to enjoy over the weeks of their lovemaking.

She felt him tremble and touched the tip again. His cock twitched, his knuckles whitened on the headboard. He looked as if he were in pain but his pleasure was obvious. She used the flat of her tongue to lick along the length of him and watched his face. The power she felt at being able to give him such joy was enormous. Experimentally she blew cool air on his wet skin and he shuddered again. Although she didn't think she was ready to take him into her mouth, she realized the amount of pleasure she could give him and felt something deep inside of her let go, releasing her fears and uncertainty.

"I don't think I can take much more," Dave groaned.

"What do you plan to do about it?" Tracy said, now feeling light and playful.

With a loud roar, Dave grabbed her around the waist, lifted her, and set her down straddling his erection. Levering herself up on her knees, she placed the tip of his cock against her opening and slowly lowered her body. When his hips bucked to ram his penis home, she moved away. "You're becoming quite the monster," Dave said with a grin.

The look on his face made her feel all-powerful. "You made me that way, Doctor Frankenstein." She lowered her body until an inch of his shaft was inside her, then started to lever herself upward. Dave grabbed her hips and flipped her over, driving himself into her to the hilt. Aroused by their aggressive play, Tracy came first, with Dave's orgasm only moments after.

Throughout the remainder of the fall, Tracy thought a lot about the power of sex, the ability to give so much pleasure, her ability to tease, then to satisfy. It was a heady sensation. Between her weekly meetings with Kim, reading her columns and letters, and devouring every sex book she could find, Tracy found her eyes opening wider on the world of great sex.

She and Dave occasionally discussed their relationship, and Dave kept expounding on how great sex could be without commitment. As she felt her feelings for him strengthening, Tracy found his declarations a bit troubling. Well, she reasoned, I'll hang on for the ride and hope that he and I end up in the same place.

The week before Christmas, Dave arrived at Tracy's apartment with a large package. "What's in there?" Tracy asked, after a long, satisfying kiss.

"I stopped by Diana's place and she gave me something that, if we open it, will mean that we won't get dinner until late." Grinning, he asked, "How hungry are you?"

Tucking a strand of hair behind one ear, she said, "I can wait." They settled side by side on the sofa and placed the box across both their laps. They pulled off the tape holding the lid and opened the box. Inside was a sheaf of paper, the cover sheet of which proclaimed the contents. "Diana's Beginners' Bondage Kit."

When Tracy's hands began to shake, Dave asked, "Do you want me to put this away? I can look it over another time to see what she's going to be selling at the weekend. You don't have to be involved at all. Nothing's important enough to make you uncomfortable."

Was she uncomfortable? Of course, but was it a negative feeling or something deliciously scary? "It's okay."

"Are you sure?" When Tracy nodded, Dave put the papers aside and continued, "Diana said the pages contain a list of rules for bondage sessions, like safe words and trust, and several of Kim's columns about power games. There's also a short story that Diana wrote about a couple who play and how they do it."

"It sounds like she's covered all the bases."

"Let's see what she packed." Dave rummaged in the box and pulled out a set of velvet and Velcro wrist and ankle restraints. He rubbed the soft black fabric through his hands and Tracy felt her vaginal muscles twitch. She reached into the box and withdrew several long chains with large rings at the ends and a plastic pouch with three small padlocks with keys attached. There was also a length of soft, nylon rope and a black satin blindfold.

Tracy saw Dave stare at her as she placed all the items on the sofa beside her. "Fear, or excitement?" he asked softly.

"I'm not sure. Have you ever done anything like this before?"

"Yes," he said. "An old girlfriend loved to play bondage games. She loved to be tied to the bed and tormented." Dave seemed a bit unsure of himself and Tracy found it wonderfully attractive. "Do you think you'd like to try? I'd love to stretch you out on your bed and fasten your wrists and ankles to the bedframe. I've dreamed about you that way."

"You have?" When he nodded, she said, "It's tempting."

"There are rules. We have to trust each other. Do you trust me completely?"

"Of course."

"Not 'of course' at all. You're paying me a gigantic compliment. The safe word is *mushroom*. If you say it, I'll stop. I promise. And you have to trust me to do that. But there's another part, too. You have to promise to say mushroom if anything makes you uncomfortable, either physically or emotionally. Agreed?"

"Agreed," she said. "Mushroom."

"Good girl." Dave took Tracy's hand, and with the box under his other arm, they made their way into the bedroom. Setting the box on the bed, Dave took Tracy in his arms and kissed her, his hands roaming her sides, then cupping her breasts. He pinched her nipples and pressed her belly against the ridge of hard flesh beneath his zipper. "You can't imagine how this turns me on," he said, pulling her sweatshirt off over her head, then removing her jeans.

Tonight Tracy was wearing a red satin bra and matching panties. "How much do you like these?" Dave asked, indicating her underwear. "Can I destroy them?"

Not totally understanding what Dave meant, but trusting him to have something delicious in mind, she nodded.

"Good. I'll enjoy buying you new ones."

"What should I do?"

"For now, just stand there," he said, taking the velvet restraints from the box. Slowly, he stroked the soft fabric over her arms, her neck, her belly. Then he looped it around her upper thigh and stroked it back and forth over her sensitive skin. Eventually he lay her on the bed and fastened one strip of material around each wrist, then tied the ends to the headboard, spreading her arms wide. "How does it feel?" he asked.

"I'm ashamed to admit it, but it's making me really hungry."

Dave's grin widened as he repeated the process with her ankles. "Mushroom. Say it."

"Mushroom."

"Remember it."

Leaving her stretched out, not quite uncomfortable, Dave lit candles and put on a CD of Liszt's piano concertos, turning the volume low. While he busied himself around the bedroom, Tracy watched him, her fluids running freely, her nipples hard, her body deliciously tense. He took something from the box, then approached. "If it's okay with you, I'm going to cover your eyes," he said. "You'll find that it makes it more intense." She raised her head and he fastened the silk behind her head. "Now you can only imagine what I'm going to do."

Tracy quickly realized he was right. Everything shifted into sharper focus. She was aware of the rustling of his clothing as he moved around the room, the lilac scent of the candles, the sound of the soft piano music. She wondered what he would do to her next, and shivered in anticipation.

She thought briefly about trust and she realized that she trusted Dave totally. She knew that he would never do anything to hurt her in any way. He cared for her and she cared for him. They were so much more than friends and could share everything about themselves. Was that what love was all about? Had she ever felt quite that way about Andrew? Love?

Her thoughts were interrupted by cold. Icy cold. Dave had placed something heavy on her belly and the sensation was driving her crazy. Then the cold slipped beneath her, snaking around her waist. One of the chains from the box. She heard the click of a lock and it was scary, yet exciting. She had no control over what was happening. All she had to do was feel.

His hands were all over her, first on her lips, then her toes. He pulled at her nipples, then licked her wrist. She didn't know from one moment to the next where she would feel him. He bit her index finger, then pulled the crotch of her panties to one side and jammed three fingers into her sopping pussy. When she started to writhe to press his fingers more tightly inside, he pulled away.

"I brought you something besides what was in the box," he said. "Just remember the magic word."

"Mushroom," she said. Then she felt something cold against her inner lips. Slowly, inexorably, it filled her. He had brought a dildo and now it was inside her. She'd played with a small shampoo bottle in the tub when she masturbated, but this was something altogether different. A thick plastic phallus stretched her, the base pressing against her clit. He moved the crotch of her panties over it to hold the dildo in place, then left her.

It was like being fucked, yet not being fucked. She tightened her vaginal muscles to make better contact, then moved her hips, but it was no use. The dildo didn't move. It kept her terribly excited, yet she couldn't push herself over the orgasmic edge. "Terrible, isn't it?" Dave said. "You want, yet you can't have."

"Oh, God, Dave. This is torture."

"It certainly is." He tapped on the base of the dildo, making claws of hunger rake her. How long would he keep this up? She heard clothing rustle, then a metallic snapping sound. "You said you didn't mind if I destroyed your gorgeous, sexy undies." She felt cold metal against her hip, then the snipping. He was cutting the sides of her panties.

God, she is gorgeous, Dave thought, spread out for me. He knew he could do anything, try anything, and he trusted her to tell him if he was getting too far out of line. He'd had some of the same feelings with Caitlin, a long-past girlfriend, but it had never been like this, so overwhelming, so completely consuming. He wanted to take, yet he wanted to give. He cared for this woman. It terrified him.

He pushed those thoughts aside and watched Tracy move, undulating, trying to drag all the feelings from the dildo still tightly lodged in her sweet pussy. His cock was so hard it hurt, but still he watched. The chain around her waist caught the candlelight and winked at him. Her lips pursed, her tongue flicking out to lick them, and her head thrashed from side to side. His eyes roamed the restraints, black velvet against her white skin. God, she was fabulous, so uninhibited, so willing to try new games. She was totally his. It terrified him.

Shaking his head, he pulled the dildo from her body and crawled between her legs. He pressed the tip of his condom-covered cock against her slippery opening and slowly, ever so slowly, pushed it inside. Eventually he was fully lodged inside her, pressing his body against hers to hold her still. "Don't move."

"I want to feel you."

"I don't want you to move. Hold perfectly still."

"I can't."

He pulled out and sat back on his haunches, silent. "All right," Tracy said, "I'll be still."

Again he pushed slowly into her, then slowly pulled out a fraction, then pressed in again. Tiny movements and he knew they were driving her mad. He watched her face around the blindfold as she concentrated on not moving. He loved torturing her this way. In and out, the most minute movements. Then he touched her clit and she exploded, her inner muscles pulsing and squeezing his cock until he could resist no longer. With a loud scream he came, and collapsed on top of her.

"God, that was incredible," Tracy said, her speech punctuated by labored breaths. "Never before." She grinned. "If we keep doing this, I'll be dead before I'm forty." She paused. "Do you have any idea how much I love you?"

I love you? The words terrified him so he ignored them. "It was wonderful," he said, to fill what was now an uncomfortable silence.

Later, over dessert, Tracy said, "I told Kim we'd come over for Christmas. Next Christmas the twins will be almost a year old," she said dreamily. "I can't wait for us to be able to buy them stuff."

"Right." He could feel his stomach clench. Next year? Tomorrow, maybe next month, but next year? An awkward hour later he pulled on his ski jacket and kissed Tracy lightly on the forehead.

"See you Saturday," she said.

"Yeah, sure," he said and hurried out the door.

Later, on the drive home, he thought about the depth of the feelings he had experienced during the evening. Shaking, he wiped his palms on the thighs of his jeans and turned the radio up. He pressed the CD play button and heard classical piano. Annoyed, he pressed the eject button and, driving with one hand, inserted a CD of loud, pounding jazz. "There," he said aloud, "that's better."

He didn't call Tracy that week, and when she called, he let his voice mail screen her out. On Friday he had the people at the front desk call and tell her that something had gone wrong with the Christmas Show and Sale Weekend and he wouldn't be able to see her.

He would be forced to see her during the Creative Loving

Weekend, but he had more than two weeks before the workshop to get himself and his feelings under control, and he would succeed. He knew Tracy wouldn't understand and would probably be really upset, but he couldn't worry about that.

Once the semester was over, Tracy went to Kim's apartment almost every day. Kim was on complete bed rest now but the doctor was totally upbeat. Everything was going along fine. Except for Kim. She was climbing the walls. She had gained almost thirty pounds and her midsection was immense. "This is all bullshit," she lamented, three days after Christmas. "I feel fine, but I'm lying here like some enormous slug, getting waited on by my sister and my husband."

"That's right," Tracy said, "and you're going to lie there and take it. For the babies." They had spent the holiday together and all the presents for the babies were stored at her apartment and in the trunk of her car to avoid jinxing anything.

"Shit. I hate this. I've got to watch my weight constantly, I haven't seen my toes in weeks, and except for the workshop and my column, I've totally forgotten what sex is all about." She groaned. "Remember that kelly green robe Elliot got me for Christmas? I put it on and looked at myself in the mirror in the bathroom. I look like a green pea with feet."

Tracy's laughter was good-natured but her voice was stern. "Behave. Remember you could be in the hospital."

"Thanks," Kim said acerbically. "I'll pay homage to the appropriate gods when I get the energy."

"You're in a pissy mood today."

"I know. Elliot and I tried to make love last night. We figured out a position that worked but neither of us got much out of it. Me, the expert. I didn't climax and I didn't even feel like letting Elliot help me after he did."

"Just stay calm, sis. You've only got a few months to go.

Anyway, remember what the great Miranda would say. There's a lot of good fun to be had that doesn't involve penetration."

"Shut up," she said, her grin taking the heat out of her words. "A few months. It feels like a few years."

Tracy patted her sister's belly. "It will be so worth it. You can live without sex." Could you? She hadn't seen or heard from Dave in two weeks. He hadn't returned any of her phone calls, and when she got through to one of the staff, they all said he was just really busy.

Dave wasn't looking forward to Tracy's weekend. The bookings were great. Only a few of the couples had backed out when they read Kim's letter and those vacancies had been quickly filled from the waiting list. Even at the reduced rate, the weekend would be a resounding success.

Sitting at his desk the Thursday before her arrival, he assured himself that Tracy could handle it. She'd matured into an understanding, open-minded woman, interested in all aspects of sex and creativity. That last evening had been the culmination of many weeks of experimentation. She had become a walking wet dream. So why was he staying away from her? That was an easy one. She was getting too close, and he wanted nothing to do with anything long-term.

He picked up the phone and dialed the front desk. "I don't know whether I told you," he said to Annelise. "Give Tracy McBride Number 214." That was the room with the perfect view of the lake that she had had during the previous Creative Loving Weekend.

"You've told me twice," Annelise said. "It's all taken care of."

"Right. How's the weekend looking?"

He thought he heard a sigh. "We're at about sixty-five percent overall, with the Creative Loving section almost entirely taken. All the meeting rooms in that building are booked for the weekend and six of the cabins are rented."

He knew all of that, but he needed to get his mind back on his work. Tracy was arriving the following afternoon, and he had to be ready—casual, friendly, but distant. That was the best way.

Chapter

9

Elise and Bob Prescott lay on a king-sized bed in their room at the Catskill Lake Resort. They had arrived midafternoon, and since the plane ride and long drive afterward had been tiring, they had stretched out on the bed and dozed off. The drapes were open wide, and the bright white light from the rising full midwinter moon lit their room almost as if it were daytime. "What time is it?" Bob asked, rubbing his eyes. "I can't make out the numbers on the clock radio without my glasses."

"It's almost six," Elise said, gazing at the bedside clock. "We must have fallen asleep. The welcome session is at seven-thirty so I guess we should think about getting up and having some dinner." She yawned, combed her fingers through her short, salt-and-pepper hair, and fell back on her pillow.

Bob had been looking forward to this weekend for several months. Creative Loving. New things, new toys, new something. He loved good sex and lamented its slow disappearance from his life. Adding spice to his sex life, however, had been only part of his reason for convincing Elise to sign up. He'd realized over the past few months that his wife was becoming more and more depressed, obsessed about her weight, and because of that, their sex life was going to pot. While he was horny much of the time, she always seemed to be making love just to please him. Maybe this weekend would enliven her.

Bob, balding, with deep brown eyes and a hint of a double chin, propped himself up on his elbow and gazed down at his wife of almost twenty-six years. How could she not believe that she was sexy? Okay, if he was being honest, he'd have to admit that, at fifty-three she was rather overweight and her breasts drooped, but to him she was still the sexy, exciting woman he had met and married all those years ago. As he gazed at her, he felt himself harden. He play-leered at her. "Actually, I'm thinking about lots of things, and 'up' has something to do with every one."

"Bob, please," Elise said, her tone a bit exasperated, her shoulders tightening.

He knew that he could tease her into a little lovemaking before dinner. Ignoring her body language, he asked, "Please what?" Finding her large sweatshirt-covered breast with his free hand, he rolled her nipple between his thumb and index finger. Since she had slipped out of her bra before napping, he could feel her nipple tighten and his voice became husky. "Please what?"

Elise gazed at him and he felt her body relax. She smiled up at him and her eyes softened. "Just please," she said softly. He settled his lips against hers and felt her mouth open. For long moments their tongues stroked as she held the back of his head. When he could wait no longer, he raised her shirt and found her now-erect nipple. He suckled the way he knew she liked and felt her heavy breathing.

When she arched her body to meet his, he suspected that she was indulging him, but right now he didn't really want to think about it. His cock was hard and he wanted to fuck his wife. He played with her breasts, lightly biting and sucking. She unbuttoned his shirt and laid her hand on his chest, pulling lightly at his chest hair, and he felt his cock stiffen still more. God, he wanted to ram it into her. Quickly, he climbed from the bed and pulled off his clothes, while he watched his wife remove her jeans and panties, leaving her shirt in place. He loved the feel of his wife's naked body against him, but he knew better than to ask her to completely undress. As she stretched out on the bed, she growled, "Do it."

Was she in a hurry because she was excited or did she just want to get it over with? He slid his hand down her belly until he found her coarse black hair, then combed his fingers through it until he found her small clit. He moved his tongue around in his mouth until he could wet his fingers and transfer the moisture to Elise's inner lips. When he pressed the tip of his cock against her vagina, Elise wrapped her legs around his waist and pulled. As he had wanted to since he awakened, he thrust hard into her and watched her brown eyes close and her head arch back, exposing her soft neck.

He pulled back and rammed into her again. Over and over he thrust until, long minutes later, he tightened his buttocks and poured his semen into Elise's waiting body.

His breathing labored, he collapsed on top of her. "God, that was good," he said, panting. "Fast, but good."

"And a really nice way to start the weekend," Elise said softly. "Right in tune with the theme."

"Very nice indeed," Bob said, rolling off the bed and heading for the bathroom. "I'm going to grab a very quick shower and then we can go downstairs."

"Leave the water running," Elise said. "I'll shower after you."

As Bob closed the bathroom door behind him, Elise sighed. She loved giving her husband pleasure and he certainly enjoyed sex with her. As she grabbed a wad of tissues and pressed them against her vagina, she accepted the fact that she really hadn't been aroused. How long had it been since Bob hadn't had to wet his fingers to make her slippery?

Bob didn't seem to realize that she was never aroused these days. Earlier in their marriage, even with a house full of kids and little time or privacy, they still had managed hot sex at least once a week. Over the past few years, however, her excitement had taken longer and longer to build until now it was almost nonexistent. Their lovemaking had become a series of once-a-week quickies, good for Bob and rewarding for Elise since she loved to please her husband. Since Jeremy, the last of their five children, had left for school three months earlier, however, Bob seemed to want to make love all the time. Occasionally it was really annoying.

She accepted the fact that the way their sex life had developed was more her fault than his, since she had never really asked him to slow down. Now it wouldn't make any difference anyway. Actually, she speeded things up just to get it over with. She was a dried-up old woman, and since Jeremy left, she'd gained another ten pounds. She'd gone from chunky to just plain fat, and she seemed to be unable to work up the desire to diet. Food was such a comfort.

Elise lay back on the bed and fantasized as she often did. In her dream she was five eight rather than her five three, and slender, with a figure reminiscent of a *Playboy* centerfold. She had a tiny waist, narrow yet provocative hips, and long, long, long legs. Her breasts were full and high, with none of the droop and flab she saw when she looked at herself. Her entire body was tight, as if she had been working out several hours each day.

She stood in the middle of a totally white room walled with mirrors wearing a diaphanous beige gown that clearly revealed her magnificent body. Everywhere she looked, she could see and admire her perfect figure. Several men stood around her, reaching out long arms to touch her. As the fantasy had developed over the last few months, the men had become more numerous and now there were several dozen, all good-looking, lean, and hard. At first she had felt guilty that Bob was nowhere in the dream, but then she stopped worrying. It was just a fantasy, after all, and she certainly didn't intend to act it out. It wasn't really her anyway.

In her dream she was the most desired woman in the world, worshiped for her sensuality, and with a long, slender finger, she selected four of the men to approach. The remaining men appeared disappointed, but sat on the thick white carpet and watched. Behind her was a white leather upholstered lounge chair and she was gently lifted and laid upon it. The men opened her gown and touched her skin. First they stroked her hands and feet, sliding slender fingers between her toes and scratching her palms. Hands pulled at her fingers as if they were thin cocks to be milked. The varied sensations made her skin tingle and she felt her tissues swell and heat. She looked up and saw that the ceiling was mirrored like the walls and she could watch the men caress her, long dark fingers on her flawless white skin.

The men moved upward on her arms and legs, touching, rubbing, stroking. No inch of her skin was ignored. They turned her over and fondled her buttocks, stroked her back and shoulders, then turned her again onto her back. The hands fondled her belly and then found her breasts, swollen with hardened nipples aching for attention. Fingers pulled and squeezed, kneading her flesh. One man moved behind her head and combed his fingers through her long, moonlight blond hair, spreading it on the chair like a halo.

In the mirrored ceiling she watched the men seated around

the chair open their clothing and pull out their erections, now thick and hard. Hands stroked turgid cocks while eyes watched the men touching her and envied them.

Finally, when she was pulsing and ready, they spread her legs and one honored man touched her sopping flesh. He moved at the perfect pace, sliding his fingertips over her slippery skin, while two others placed their erections into her hands. Slowly, ever so slowly, fingers filled her while others found her clit and rubbed. The man at her head moved so her mouth was filled with him, the tip of his cock wet and salty from his obvious excitement.

Unable to do anything but revel in the worship the men were lavishing on her, she allowed her arousal to build while giving pleasure to the men in her hands and the one in her mouth. When the fourth man thrust his large cock into her body, she ceased being able to concentrate on anything so she just let herself respond.

Molten heat speared from her belly to her breasts, her groin, her entire body. Her pulse pounded as the men pinched her nipples and scraped their nails over her skin. Unable to keep the growing heat from engulfing her, she let it all go and surrendered to the swirling lava. Spasms filled her, and as she crested, the four men came, covering her hands and filling her mouth.

As the fantasy faded, she sat up and straightened her black velour sweatshirt. What was she going to do? How could she tell Bob that she was so down much of the time? Maybe she should talk to Dr. Pfeffer about antidepressants, although she'd read articles in several women's magazines that said that they often reduce the libido still more. What would happen when she couldn't make love to Bob at all anymore?

She didn't even get wet anymore, at least not the way she had before she'd stopped getting her period. Well, she reasoned, maybe her libido was waning but she'd just have to get used to it. She hated the idea of never feeling that exhilaration again, and sex had always been such a good part of her marriage. However, what were her choices?

Maybe this weekend would help. Creative Loving. She hadn't been anxious to attend but she knew how much it meant to Bob and she really couldn't see any reason not to. So, although the price was rather steep, they had signed up. Maybe . . . As she stood up and flipped on the light, her gaze flicked to the mirror over the dresser, and she quickly turned away. No need to look. She knew what she'd see. With a resigned sigh, she headed for the shower.

Twenty-seven-year-old Debbie Stafford and her husband Paul entered the room they had been given and looked around. "It's charming," Debbie said, gazing at the wood-beamed ceiling and the bird prints on the walls. The two double beds were covered with deep green and beige striped spreads and the thick carpet was deep green tweed. Paul put the suitcases on the bureau and unzipped his.

Debbie took a deep calming breath. This weekend could be the beginning of something great, she thought. Paul had insisted that they sign up for Creative Loving and had explained that it would be a wonderful way to enhance their love life. A weekend away from the distractions of the city, of their jobs, of the house, and their friends and family. She had been dreaming about it for weeks.

In her dream Paul was patient, warm, and loving, sensitive to her needs. She had fantasized so often it had become almost real. She smiled inwardly as she relived it. Paul would unpack his things then turn to her . . .

"Debbie, I'm so glad we're finally here." He closed the distance between them and wrapped her in his arms. "It's been so hectic that we've sacrificed so many good things. For this weekend let's forget everyone and everything else and concentrate on our pleasure. Then we'll try to take the feelings home with us."

"Oh, Paul," she sighed, "that would be wonderful." She lay her hands on his chest and allowed him to pull her closer. "So wonderful."

Their mouths met, his soft and warm, teasing, nipping at her lower lip, his tongue darting out to caress her. Slowly she slid her hands around his neck, threading her fingers through his soft, curly hair. The kiss lasted for long minutes as they drank their fill of each other, hands caressing, breath quickening, hearts pounding. When her knees were too weak to hold her, Paul lifted her in his strong arms and lovingly placed her on the bed. As she watched, he slowly removed his clothes.

When she started to unbutton her shirt, he stilled her hands with a slight shake of his head. "Please. Let me undress you," he whispered. He peeled off her shirt and kissed her neck, her shoulders, her collarbone, then licked the inside of her elbow, making her shudder with pleasure. He stroked every inch of her skin with the tips of his fingers, then tickled her with the tip of his tongue and abraded her skin lightly with his short mustache.

Her flesh was alive with him as he pulled off her jeans and socks, then repeated his lovemaking up her legs to the insides of her thighs. When she reached for him, he pressed her arms back onto the bed. "Let me pleasure you," he said, his voice hoarse with his need for her.

She lay still as his teeth nipped at the sensitive skin of her inner thigh and his fingers played with her erect nipples. He leaned over her cotton-covered mound and breathed hot air until she wanted to scream with her need. She felt him pull the crotch aside and play with her sopping flesh. Dragging in a shaking breath, she moaned, "Please. Please. I want you."

"Not yet," he said, his voice strained as he controlled his need, concentrating on her pleasure. He rubbed his naked erection against her thigh and she knew how difficult it must be for him to hold back, but he continued to give to her, touching, stroking, licking, driving her higher and higher until she could almost embrace the climax.

He removed her remaining clothing and knelt over her, his turgid penis reaching for her. Yet still he waited as his mouth found first one nipple then the other. Unable to delay any longer, she wrapped her legs around his waist and pulled him inside of her. It took only a few thrusts for her to come, and as vibrant colors swirled in her head, she rubbed her mound against his pubic bone. Moments later he pounded hard into her and she felt his orgasm overtake him. Later, dropping to the bed beside her, he held her close and whispered nonsense words of love and passion in her ear.

"Not bad," Paul said, opening one of the dresser drawers and yanking Debbie back to reality. "I'll take the top one, you can have the second." He lifted two sets of underwear and a dress shirt and settled the stack inside. When he looked back into the suitcase, he said, "I don't see my tan sweater. You did pack it, didn't you?"

Debbie felt her hands begin to shake and her underarms prickle. "You told me you wanted your blue one and your Rutgers sweatshirt."

"God, you're hopeless. You'd think after eight years of marriage you'd be able to remember which sweater I like. I distinctly recall telling you that I wanted the tan one."

Debbie remembered the conversation, but didn't argue. She never argued with Paul. Maybe she was wrong. Maybe he had asked her to pack his tan sweater. "I'm so sorry, dear. I'm sure you'll look fine. You know how I like you in the blue one." She really did like his blue sweater. It brought out the blue of his eyes and complemented his sandy hair. Although he certainly wasn't a stud, he was nice-looking with an outgoing personality that seemed to attract people. He had a large circle of friends, both male and female. She didn't make friends easily and usually felt lost at the gatherings they attended each weekend, content to watch her husband, always the life of the party.

"Yeah, right," he muttered. "Well, I'll just have to make do. God, you're useless."

As Paul continued to put things in the drawer, Debbie quietly unzipped the top of her suitcase and leaned over to open the second dresser drawer. When Paul didn't move out of her way, she placed her clean underwear and tops back in her suitcase. He'd be finished soon enough, she thought, so she sat on the edge of one of the beds and folded her hands in her lap.

"All right," he said, dropping his now-empty suitcase beside her. "I'm going downstairs to look around. When you're done here"—he waved at the dresser—"I'll probably be in the dining room. The brochure they gave me when I checked in says that dinner's served from five-thirty to seven-thirty. Don't be late."

Debbie watched the door close behind him. She stood, moved his toiletries from the top of the dresser to the shelf in the bathroom, then put her things in the second dresser drawer. Why had he wanted to come to this thing? she wondered. It's not as if we need help in the bedroom. She had always fulfilled all of Paul's needs. As a matter of fact, she did things with him that she really didn't like, but she knew that a man had his needs and it was up to her, his wife, to satisfy them.

Well, it couldn't hurt to attend whatever sessions there were. She might even learn ways to better please her husband. Maybe he'd be more loving if she did.

* * *

Paul galloped down the stairs and checked the map in the brochure. He found the Cayuga Room, the main meeting hall, and the Onondaga, Seneca, Albany, and Putnam Rooms, where the stuff would be for sale. Nothing was open yet. God, he couldn't wait. Gerry had told him that if he played his cards right, this would be a swinging weekend. Lots of sex talk to keep everyone hot, and couples who might be interested in threesomes or foursomes. He wouldn't cheat on his wife, but if they could play with another couple . . .

Gerry had told him what he and Darcy did in the hot tub after the lectures when he'd attended the same weekend here in July. He remembered how his body had hardened when Gerry had told him that, after a forum on bondage and discipline and a cocktail in the bar, Darcy had been more than willing to play kinky games with another couple. He and Gerry had recently started to talk about swapping.

He couldn't imagine what Gerry saw in Debbie, but he was already thinking about spending an evening or more with Darcy. Gerry's wife had always turned him on, with her big tits and luscious mouth. He could picture her lying wide open on their king-sized bed, her wonderful red hair not quite covering her magnificent tits. He smiled as he wondered whether her pussy hair was that same deep russet. In his fantasy she squirmed on the bed begging him to fuck her. He imagined himself pushing a thick plastic dildo into Darcy's wide open pussy, then forcing her to lick her juices from it. Eventually she'd use her magnificent tongue on his dick. God, he felt himself getting hard yet again.

Maybe, just maybe, he could find another couple to play with this weekend. Then Debbie would be more willing to play when they got back home.

* * *

Tish Johnson and Owen Hargrove sat in the large lobby, holding hands and watching several groups of people all trying to check in at the same time. The three harried young people behind the desk were being patient and helpful, assisting guests as they filled out registration forms, directing them to the correct area of the hotel and motioning them toward the dining room, up the short flight of stairs at the side of the lobby.

The theme of the hotel was the lake, and more specifically the wild life that surrounded it. There was a relief map of the Catskill Mountains on one pine-paneled wall with walking trails clearly marked. There were photos, drawings, and paintings of birds and small animals on the walls, and there were small, randomly placed shelves everywhere that held dozens of old-fashioned weather vanes and birdhouses.

Since it was almost six, the lobby was full of people heading for dinner, and Tish wondered how many of them would be attending the Creative Loving Weekend. She had read most of the literature they had been given when they checked in, and she saw that although the lobby and dining room were common areas, all the meeting attendees were housed in a separate "Adults Only" building with its own meeting rooms, hot tub, and pool. Good idea, she thought as she read about all the forums and products for sale. They would also have a separate part of the dining room, set with mostly tables for two. "I can't believe we're really here," Tish said. "I've wanted to come for such a long time."

Owen squeezed her hand. "I know, sugar. I've wanted to as well but it's pretty expensive . . ."

"We're here," Tish said. "No use rehashing it all again." They had been talking about going to the Creative Loving Weekend for more than a year, but until they won five thousand dollars with a joint lottery ticket, the cost had seemed prohibitive. When they cashed in their ticket, however, they agreed that four thousand would go in the bank and they would spend the rest for the weekend. Now, with the reduced rate, they had another two hundred fifty to put away. "I'm a bit embarrassed," she said, feeling her palms sweat. "All these people will know what we're doing at night."

"All these people will be doing the same thing," he said with a wink. "They won't care about us one way or the other."

Tish giggled and looked at the brochure that listed all the forums. "There's a forum here called Storytelling and the Art of Nonverbal Sexual Communication." Perhaps she could get Owen to share some of his deepest fantasies. Then she could act them out with him and he'd realize that they had to spend the rest of their lives together. She'd become the perfect sex partner, doing whatever he wanted.

"Yeah," Owen said, peering over her shoulder. "There's also one called Toys, Games, and Role Playing. I looked at the map and it seems there will be places to buy things, too."

Toys. God, maybe that would be what clinched the deal.

Tish allowed her mind to wander for a moment. He'd have a large dildo, and when she was hot and hungry, he'd fill her with it, then pull back and probe her opening agonizingly slowly until she could barely contain her climax. Then he'd flip a switch and the vibrations would drive her over the edge. As she was coming, he'd pull out the toy and ram his cock into her, throwing his head back and bellowing as he came. "Oh, sweetheart, I get so hot watching you," he'd say, panting. "We have to make this last forever. Marry me. I want you so much. Please, make me the happiest man in the world."

Marriage. White dress. All their relatives. She and Owen had been together for almost three years and it was time. Time for children, or at least for planning on a family. She knew that Owen had come to the weekend just for fun, games, and new sexual ideas, but for her it was a last-ditch attempt to gain what she wanted most: a plain gold ring on the third finger of her left hand. Well, she'd play it cool until some of the forums helped her learn everything about Owen's desires. Then she'd satisfy them all and he'd realize that he wanted her permanently. "The place is really lovely," Tish said, biding her time. "How about we walk around and check the place out. That will let the crowd thin out a bit before we have dinner."

"A wonderful idea and just what I was thinking." Owen stood and, holding Tish's hand, walked toward the large main staircase.

As they walked down a long, carpeted hallway, Owen looked at Tish. This weekend would either make or break their relationship, he thought. They had moved in together more than two and a half years earlier, but neither had wanted to mess anything up with marriage. Who cared, they'd said often, whether they had some expensive party, with some guy in a church saying meaningless words over them?

Recently, however, Tish had been hinting that it was time to make their relationship official. After all, she'd said several times, she was almost thirty and her clock was ticking. Tish had honed in on the workshop on sexual communication. Maybe if they could really talk about what life would be like if they married, he could settle his stomach and make the commitment. He wrapped his arm around Tish's shoulders and hugged her close against his side. She was such a tiny thing that she fit quite comfortably, her head against his chest. He leaned over and kissed the top of her head through her short, kinky hair.

He loved her so much but he just wasn't ready for a commitment. His friends teased him, on both sides. His best friend Levon, who had gotten married the year before, told him marriage was the best. Hot food, a warm bed, and all the free pussy a man could want. Levon had a mouth like that. Owen had asked him why he would buy the cow when the milk was free. Ball and chain. He loved her, though, and wanted to spend his life with her. Didn't he?

Maybe . . .

Chapter

10

"Good evening, everyone, and welcome," Tracy said, swallowing her nervousness and locking her shaking knees. "You all know by now that I'm not my sister Kim. As the letter you got several weeks ago told you, she's at home awaiting the birth of twins." She couldn't resist a grin. "In less than two months, I'm going to be an aunt twice over." There was a ripple of applause. "Thanks to all of you who have expressed concern, and I can assure you that she's doing great." Every test had proven that. "However, she's on complete bed rest at her doctor's orders, so here I am." She tugged at the bottom of her vest and squared her shoulders.

"What sexes are the babies?" someone in the audience yelled.

"She didn't want to know so I haven't got a clue. Knowing Kim and Elliot, I'm sure that, in about fifteen years, they will either be advising the boys about condoms or building a ten-foot-high fence around the girls with Elliot guarding the gate with a shotgun." There was another burst of laughter, a good sign that she was connecting with the audience. So far, so good.

She turned serious, nervous about the next section of her

introduction. "I don't purport to be the expert that Kim is, but I'm hoping to be able to give you some of what she, and her alter ego Miranda, have given to these weekends in the past. I'm delighted that so many of you agreed to attend." She paused and looked around. "Of course, the lower rate helped, didn't it?" She raised an eyebrow and was gratified to hear slightly embarrassed laughter. She might be able to pull this off after all.

She took a deep breath, perched on the edge of the front table as she had watched her sister do so many times, and continued. "So, let's get started."

As she launched into the welcome speech she and Kim had discussed, she saw Dave walk in and stand at the back of the room. She hesitated momentarily, then mentally shook herself, locked eyes with him briefly, and as he left, continued.

"Isn't she just wonderful?" Debbie said, as they left the Onondaga Room after the kick-off speech. She was about five-three with a nice figure, soft green eyes, and long, fine hair that she kept in a ponytail most of the time. She'd wanted to cut it for years, but Paul insisted that he liked it long so she merely had the ends trimmed a few times a year. She looked over at her husband, so tall and handsome, with his curly, dark blond hair, charming, open smile, and well-trimmed mustache. He really did look good in his blue sweater. It accentuated the deep blue of his eyes.

Debbie had wanted to attend a forum on communication right after Tracy's introductory remarks. She'd been reading *Ask Miranda* for several years, and if Tracy was as honest, genuine, and informative as Kim, she knew all the forums would be fascinating. Paul, however, had nixed that idea right away. "I don't need any self-proclaimed expert telling me how to talk to my wife about sex. We communicate just fine."

"Of course we do," Debbie said with a resigned sigh.

"What does she know about it anyway? She said she's been married and divorced. That's not a good advertisement for great sex. I'd bet she couldn't even keep her husband satisfied. What does she have to teach us?"

Puzzled, Debbie asked, "So why are we here? It cost the earth even with the discount. Is anything bothering you? Is there something I'm not doing?"

Paul started to speak, then he stopped and his voice softened. "Nothing's bothering me," he said, "and I'm not really worried about anything, least of all whether we have great sex. I know it's good. Most of what she said was nonsense, geared for folks who don't have it as good as we do."

"Okay, so then why did we come here? God knows there are lots of other things we could do with that money."

Paul seemed evasive. "Don't you worry about that. We're here to have fun." He leered, then reached over and squeezed her breast. "Lots of fun and games."

"I wish we could attend the rest of tonight's forums. After all, we paid for everything."

With a long-suffering sigh, Paul said, "You're hopeless, believing that that woman has the key to anything. Most of what she spouts is nonsense."

"I don't think it's nonsense." Debbie had listened very carefully and had agreed with everything Tracy had said. Tracy. She was so comfortable with her that she already thought of Kim's sister by her first name. Tracy had been right about quite a few things. "She talked about good sex and how we're all entitled to it." *Am I?*

"Of course we're all entitled to it, but we're lucky. We already have it."

Not both of us. "She said we're each in charge of our own orgasm."

"Don't be silly. Remember that she also said that orgasms aren't everything. Getting there is half of the fun." Paul leered at his wife again.

Debbie looked up at her husband, now climbing the stairs to their room a step ahead of her. Was getting there fun? She couldn't remember when it had been. Their foreplay was just perfunctory. If Paul was erect, he kissed her, rubbed her, used a lubricated condom so she wouldn't get pregnant, and went at it. Wasn't she entitled to more than that?

Paul dipped his card key in the lock of Room 207 and walked inside, Debbie following. He didn't turn on the light and Debbie almost crashed into his back. He turned and embraced her. "You know," he said, his voice husky, "all that talk about sex has made me horny." He grasped her hand and placed it on his hardness. "See what just thinking about sex does to me?"

Debbie felt his fully hard erection and tried not to sigh. *Here we go.* He placed his mouth softly on hers then, as she opened her mouth, pushed his tongue inside. *He's still a pretty good kisser,* she thought as he changed the angle of his mouth. She lifted the front of his sweatshirt, found the thick hair on his chest, and tangled her fingers in it the way she knew he liked. Even after five years of marriage, she still enjoyed his kisses and the feel of him. It was too bad that what inevitably followed was so unpleasant.

"Oh, Deb, you make me so hot." She felt his hands slide down until they cupped her buttocks, and he pressed so her pubic bone rubbed up and down his erection. Then his hands were inside her slacks, kneading her ass cheeks.

Slow down, she begged, but she didn't voice her need. *Let me show him,* she decided. Tracy had mentioned a few things about how to show your partner what you wanted, then invited everyone to stay for the next forum. Maybe she could show Paul.

She pulled back slightly and tried to let him know that she wanted more kissing. Her breasts felt full and her nipples hard. Touch me there, she thought as she tried to pull his hands from beneath her panties. She rubbed her breasts against his shirt, trying to make him understand. She cupped his face and gently kissed his lips but he turned his face away. Kissing was over.

Instead he pulled her cheeks apart and wiggled his fingers until they were in contact with the sensitive skin around her anus. God, she thought, knowing immediately what he intended. She hated this part. "Oh Deb," he groaned, "you make me crazy."

Oh, Paul, please. Take some time. I might even enjoy what you're doing if you gave me a chance, but you never do. Quickly he pulled off her slacks and panties and removed his jeans and shorts. She heard the ripping of foil, then he turned her back to him and stroked his lubricated, condom-covered penis against her rear hole. "I don't think I'm ready," she whispered, finally able to verbalize something.

When she tried to pull away, he wrapped one arm around her waist and inserted a now-slippery finger into her rear. "You know I'll take care of you so don't worry about anything," Paul said. Pressing, he slowly filled her with his finger. "See? You know you love this."

"I don't," she whispered, but she knew he wasn't listening. Now his erection pressed against her, and with a grunt, he entered. "God, you're so tight. I love this." He'd done this often enough that Debbie wasn't in much discomfort. As he pushed and withdrew, he idly rubbed her clit and slowly she found herself getting aroused. Maybe this time . . .

Suddenly she felt him tense and, with a series of grunts, come. Almost immediately he pulled out, then collapsed on the bed. "Deb, I've never come that fast. That was fabulous."

Debbie pulled off her remaining clothing, stretched out on

the bed beside him, and put his hand on her breast. "Umm," he purred. "You know just what I like." He kneaded her flesh, but as she closed her eyes and enjoyed the sensations he was creating, his movements slowed and soon she could hear his light snores.

Tracy is right. It's my body and I'm responsible for its pleasure, she thought. She climbed from the bed and went into the bathroom. She should brush her teeth and wash her face, she thought, but instead she raised the cover on the toilet and sat down. She didn't really have to pee but she pulled off a length of toilet paper anyway, and rubbed it gently over her heated, swollen flesh. I'm responsible. She dropped the tissue and used her fingers to explore. She found herself very wet so she lubricated her fingers and found a place where it felt good to touch. I'm responsible.

She touched, rubbed, and stroked. Her clit was erect and very sensitive. She couldn't touch it too hard or rub it too fast, but she quickly learned what made it feel particularly good. Over and over she stroked until she felt the bubble of orgasm grow. She knew that if she continued, she'd climax. I'm responsible. She found the small ball of pleasure and nurtured it, helped it expand, then held her breath as it suddenly overwhelmed her. She held her lips tightly closed and allowed only a tiny sound to escape her throat.

"Hey, Deb, where are you?" Paul called sleepily. "You know I don't like it when you're not next to me."

Debbie took a deep breath and forced her voice to sound normal. "Just a minute." She leaned over and ran the water in the sink to cover her need for a moment to calm down and catch her breath. After about two minutes, she stood, brushed her teeth, and walked back into the bedroom.

"I missed you," Paul whined. "You know I hate to sleep without you."

Debbie slowly climbed into bed and, with Paul's chest against her back, fell asleep.

Dozing, Paul was thinking about the couple he'd met while Debbie had gone back to the room for a few minutes before the introductory meeting. Jerome and Betts were about their age, and although they weren't married, they had been living together for more than three years. Jerome was well over six feet, with an athletic body and a completely shaved head, a full brown mustache with a tiny tuft of hair below his lower lip, and small oval black-framed glasses. Betts was sensational, about the same height as Debbie with very black hair, white skin, and wonderfully large tits that jiggled when she walked. Paul had spent quite a bit of time wondering whether she wore a bra. They'd gotten to talking as Paul stood in front of the sign that advertised Matt's Adult Toy Box, irritated that the store wasn't open yet. After they'd made quick introductions and chatted for a few moments, Betts had asked softly, "Are you a toy collector? One of the reasons we come here is for Matt's displays. He's always got the latest stuff."

"You've been here before?" Paul asked.

"Sure," Betts said. "This is our third time. We're from a tiny town in rural Wisconsin, not a hotbed of sexual activity so this is a great way to expand our horizons, so to speak."

"I'm from New York City but I wouldn't go into a toy store there. Too many perverts."

"Are you interested in anything in particular?" Betts asked with a wink.

Paul wondered how much to say, but then threw caution to the wind. After all, he had less than forty-eight hours to make a connection. "I'm interested in paddles and stuff like that. I think my wife would really enjoy that sort of thing."

Betts giggled. "That's amazing. Jerome, honey, it looks like we've found a kindred spirit." She dragged Paul to a small seating area and, sitting diagonally from him, placed a hand on his knee. "Have you ever completely dominated her sexually? Demanded that she do your bidding?"

"Well," Paul admitted, trying to sound sophisticated, "not yet, but I know it's something she'd like."

Betts was wearing a V-necked sweater and now leaned forward and Paul got a fabulous view of the swell of her large, full breasts and the valley between. She rubbed her hand up and down his thigh. "I'm sure she would, since it's so exciting. Maybe we could show you and your wife a few things." The doors of the Onondaga Room opened and several couples rushed inside.

"Jerome," she said, "get us a seat, will you?" Jerome hustled off from behind her chair. "Maybe the four of us can meet at breakfast tomorrow morning and, well, see what happens. About seven-thirty in the dining room?"

"That's great. I know Debbie will get in the spirit."

He'd wanted to sit near the couple during the first session, but when Debbie arrived and they entered the room, the only seats left were in the back, and Jerome and Betts had stayed for the later forums. Just like his wife to be late and keep him from introducing them that evening. Well, they'd meet over breakfast.

Elise and Bob had stayed for the forum on communication and the one on kissing and foreplay. Now they made their way into the hallway. Bob slipped his arm around his wife's waist. "Tracy said there's a woman who sells lingerie, a confectionary, and a bookstore. Wanna see what's there?"

Elise thought about the lingerie store and cringed. The bakery was much more her speed, but when Bob led her to Diana's Lingerie Shop, she meekly followed. They entered the Seneca Room and Bob made a beeline to the corsets and bras. He was really so sweet and she hated that her depression was disappointing him so much. She wanted their sex life to be explosive, but it never would be again and she'd have to get used to it.

She watched as he fingered a soft camisole, his short fingers playing with the satin. As he stared at price tags, he pushed his wire-rimmed reading glasses up toward the bridge of his nose in a gesture so familiar that it made Elise ache with tenderness. She loved him, from his balding head to his crooked toes. If only she could be what he wanted.

Elise looked around and saw the display of satin shorts for men and decided to buy something slightly outrageous for her husband. Maybe that would scratch his itch for tonight, she thought.

"Those are really cute," a woman's voice said from behind her as Elise picked up a pair of satin boxers, "but how about something for you?"

"I don't think I'm the type for lingerie like this," Elise said as she slowly turned. One look at the person who had spoken and Elise gasped. The woman must have weighed at least two hundred pounds and wore a lacy, bright red slip with a black peignoir over it. She was only about five feet one, but her spike heels made her taller than Elise's five-three. Her hair was deep brown with slight reddish highlights and her makeup was evening-heavy but not really overdone, a stark contrast to Elise's makeup-free face.

"I'm Diana. I didn't think I was either several years ago," she grinned, "but I decided that I might like the feel of this stuff so I said to hell with all the propaganda and bought a few things. It feels just as good as I thought it would and my husband just adores the way I look."

"Do *you* like the way you look?" As the words slipped out of her mouth, Elise tried to pull them back. What a presumptuous question!

"At first I thought I looked like a well-dressed piano, but one look at Tommy, he's my husband, and I realized that he really thought I was sexy and it made me feel better about myself. It took a while and lots of Tommy's kind of reinforcement—if you know what I mean—but I found that I enjoyed wearing sexy things like this." She grasped Elise's arm lightly, leaned forward, and whispered conspiratorially, "I think you might, too."

To cover her discomfort, Elise asked, "Is your love of this kind of thing the reason for the store?"

"I get everything I want wholesale so what could be better?" The woman smiled. "I also try to be a poster girl for lingerie like this in plus sizes." She twirled slowly on her toes so the peignoir swung wide. "You'd be amazed what something really hot and sexy can do for a woman's ego."

Surprisingly comfortable with this unusual woman, Elise couldn't conceal her slight grin. "You're quite a saleswoman."

"I try. Can I show you something?"

Elise couldn't bare the humiliation of seeing herself in an outfit that would just be an advertisement of an overweight, dried-up old woman. "Thanks for the pep talk," she said, not wanting to offend the woman, "but I think I'll just take these." As she paid for the black satin boxers, she saw Bob poking around in the back of the room so she waited beside the door until he had finished his explorations.

"You bought something," he said, as he saw the small paper bag in her hand.

"It's a surprise. For later."

Bob's grin nearly split his face. He probably saw me with the shorts in my hand, she reasoned. I think they'll look and feel great. She looked him over. He had just celebrated his fifty-second birthday but he looked just as attractive as he had when they first met. Sure, his hair was graying and getting thin on the top and his face was deeply lined, but it was the same face she had fallen in love with. He now needed reading glasses, which he wore folded against his chest suspended by a thick cord around his neck, and he wore his jeans a bit lower so his belly hung over a bit, but he really hadn't changed much at all. She placed a quick kiss on his mouth.

"Mmm, that was sweet," he said. "How about another sweet before we go back to the room and you can show me what you bought?"

They wandered into Sweets to the Sweet and were in turn amused and shocked by the pastries and candies. Penis- and vagina-shaped chocolates and several that looked like double D breasts with rosy erect nipples, candy hearts with all kinds of rude phrases on them, cakes and cupcakes with icing designs depicting everything from kissing to orgies. There were even spun sugar paddles and whips.

They bought an outrageous pastry covered with chocolate and powdered sugar, slightly embarrassed that the small cake was shaped like a vagina. They settled at a tiny white wrought iron table, and as Bob dipped his fork into the center of the confection, he winked and she smiled and winked back. This is like the old days, she thought, before five kids, pendulous breasts, and stretch marks.

Later, back in their room, Elise handed Bob the small pink paper bag. He opened it, and as he removed the black satin boxers, she abruptly realized that he was disappointed. He smiled quickly and thanked her, but she could see that he had thought she had bought something for herself. Sorry to disappoint you, she thought, but I just couldn't.

Quickly Bob changed into the boxers and said, "These feel really great. Here, touch." He took her hand and rubbed it over his hard penis. "See what they do to me?"

"I certainly do," Elise said. She reached behind her, turned off the lights, and stretched out on the bed. Their lovemaking was quick and hard, and Elise smiled as she cuddled against her husband afterward.

His voice thick and sleepy, Bob whispered, "I know you'd feel just as good in something sexy and satin as I did. Tomorrow we'll get you something. I insist. And maybe a toy too. I saw something you just might enjoy."

Elise lay still in Bob's arms. Tomorrow she'd head him in another direction. Maybe toys would distract him from lingerie.

After the introductory sessions of Creative Loving, Tish and Owen also wandered into the lingerie display. "Oh, hon," Tish said, "these are all so gorgeous."

Owen looked at her. Although she was only five feet tall, Tish had a lush figure and deep café au lait skin that would look really hot in something red or, even better, white. The contrast against her skin would be so sexy. She held up a soft pale pink teddy with satin laces up the front and Owen found himself getting hard picturing her full breasts spilling out over the top. "Get that one," he said, licking his lips and leering at her. "I can't wait to see you in it."

Tish looked at the price tag and blanched. "It's very expensive. Are you sure?"

"We saved two hundred and fifty dollars on this weekend," Owen said. "Let's splurge."

"We should really put that money away for the future."

Shut up about the future, he wanted to rail at her. "Let's not worry about anything but this weekend," he said instead. "We're only going to do this once and everything else is already paid for, so we can splurge a bit."

"If you insist," Tish said with a shy smile. "I really like this one."

Owen took it from her and handed it and his credit card to

the large, amazingly dressed woman manning the small cash register. As they left, Tish said, "That woman's quite something. She must weigh about two hundred but she really doesn't look half bad in that outfit she's wearing."

"Frankly, I like looking at women in sexy lingerie." He winked and leered at her. "Or wearing nothing at all."

That teddy might just do the trick, Tish realized. Owen had been willing to spend almost a hundred dollars on it so it must have turned him on. Clutching the small pink paper bag, Tish watched Owen as he walked slightly in front of her. He is so gorgeous, she thought, deep ebony skin, so tall, with broad shoulders and really great buns. She loved to walk behind him and watch the massive muscles in his behind move beneath his tight black jeans. She couldn't help smiling. He was big all over. One of his hands could envelope both of hers, his arms were so strong as they held her, and his cock was enormous. She recalled that the first time they made love she'd been dubious. Would her body ever be able to adapt to his size? Her grin widened as she remembered how well they had fit together, and still did.

She wanted him permanently. She was almost thirty and her clock was ticking. Maybe, if their sex life was even better, he would be willing. She'd make it better and that teddy would be only the beginning. She'd make him want her so much that he'd agree to marry her just to keep her with him. They'd attend every session and she'd learn exactly what turned him on, and what kept him high. She'd do anything.

As soon as they were back in their room, Tish disappeared into the bathroom. She could hear the sound of voices through the door so she realized that Owen must have plugged the TV in. Movies. That was an idea. Owen had always wanted to rent an XXX-rated film but Tish had always vetoed the idea. Maybe they'd wander into the book and video display and pick out something that didn't look too awful. It seemed moderately disgusting to watch some couple, obviously acting, pretending to enjoy some form of kinky sex. This weekend, however, would be devoted to whatever Owen wanted.

Tish pulled off her clothes and put the teddy on. She had brought along a pair of black high-heeled shoes with long black stockings. They might not match the pink of the teddy but Owen wouldn't really care. As she attached the teddy's garters to her hose, she realized that the garment had a detachable crotch. Quickly she found the tiny hooks and removed the small bit of fabric. She refreshed her makeup and then hesitated at the closed door. With a grin, she lifted her breasts so they almost fell out of the lacy, underwired cups of the bra section, her areolas clearly visible.

As she stepped into the bedroom, she discovered Owen naked with all the lights in the room off and the bed open. He had obviously found an XXX-rated channel and was peering at a movie. "I couldn't resist," he said, his back to her, "but I can turn it off if you want."

"That's all right," Tish said, her voice a bit hoarse, staring at Owen. His eyes were riveted to the TV screen. Okay. If he wanted to watch XXX-rated films, she would put up with it.

Her gaze moved to the scene on the screen. It was a silly costume drama in which a woman wearing a powdered wig was stretched out on a period chaise longue in a gaudy room filled with gold-framed paintings and old-style furniture. Her pink puffy skirt was up around her waist and her large breasts spilled from the neckline of her dress. A naked man crouched between her legs, obviously eating her out and enjoying it tremendously. His hands were on her breasts, his fingers pulling at her large nipples. The woman thrashed and moaned, her hands tangled in the man's hair, holding his mouth tightly against her pussy.

Tish knew that it was all for the camera but it certainly looked like she was enjoying it. "Owen," she said softly.

He turned and looked at her for the first time. "Holy shit," he whispered, slowly standing. "That's absolutely fantastic. You look so hot."

Tish couldn't control her wide grin—the expression on Owen's face was worth anything she could do. Gracefully she settled on the edge of the bed. With the grunts and moans from the TV in the background, Owen pressed Tish back onto the bed, his hands finding her full breasts and playing with her nipples through the fabric. As he leaned over her, she realized that they were in a similar position to the couple in the film. Colored lights from the TV played on the walls and Tish found her eyes straying to the scene on the screen.

Owen's hands were all over her, sliding up and down the satin over her ribs, over her belly and her lace-covered breasts. Deftly, he scooped her breasts from the cups and his mouth settled on one nipple. Tish stared at the screen. The man's head was buried between the woman's legs, and she could hear slurping sounds.

Tish had never cared about oral sex one way or another but she knew Owen enjoyed it. She slipped off her shoes and pulled her feet close to her buttocks, her knees in the air. With a touch, she guided Owen's face between her legs. "Oh, sugar," he groaned when he discovered that her pussy was uncovered. His mouth found her hot, swollen flesh and his tongue flicked her clit. Somehow the noises from the TV excited her and she found her back arching and her fingers tangled in Owen's hair. "Don't stop," the woman on the TV said.

Tish thought about the forum on nonverbal communication she and Owen had attended just a few hours ago. "You have to communicate what you want," Tracy had said. "He wasn't born knowing. Use words, and if you can't, purr, moan, scream,

or use your hands. Tell him what feels really great, then hope-
fully, by omission, he'll know when you're quiet that something could be better." She remembered her homework
assignment, to say, "That's good," at least once during lovemaking. She must get Owen to express himself, too, so, as embarrassing as it might be, she'd do it.

What did she want? If he didn't press his mouth against her
so hard, it might feel sexier. She placed her hands against the
sides of his face and pushed him away just slightly. His touch
lightened and his tongue flicked over her clit. "Like this?" he
said, his hot breath erotically tickling her wet skin. His tongue
flicked again.

Tish felt stabs of pleasure between her legs. "Oh, hon,
yes," she whispered. "Just like that. It's so good."

His tongue kept working, lightly caressing, then stabbing
between her inner lips. His mouth felt so good that it quickly
became difficult to control her hips. Then his index finger was
pressed against her sopping opening. Slowly it slid only about
an inch inside, then withdrew. In and out it teased as she
writhed on the bed. Never had she been so excited. She
wanted him to fill her, yet she loved what he was doing, too.
For long minutes he continued, driving her nearly mad with
need.

Then his cock was against her, slipping in only that same
inch. He pulled out and asked, "Like that?"

"More," she said.

In and out, in and out, never quite filling her, yet never
quite leaving. Each time he drove inside, she thought he
would finally end the torture, yet again he'd pull back. She
opened her eyes and saw that he was doing exactly what the
man in the movie was doing. God, she thought, you can learn
a lot from a movie.

As she watched the couple on the screen, they finally stood
up and exchanged places so he was stretched out on the chaise

and she was crouched between his legs. His cock was massive, thick and hard, and the woman extended her tongue and licked the length of it. Then she surrounded it with her hand, pumping as she ran her tongue over the head.

Owen had often suggested that she perform oral sex on him but she had usually demurred. She didn't really know how and she had always been sure that she'd do a poor job. Now, as she surreptitiously watched the woman on TV, she thought she might be able to begin at least. Hadn't the purpose of this weekend been to expand their sex lives?

She moved and guided Owen until he was lying on his back on the bed. With a last quick look at the TV, Tish crawled between his legs. She stuck out her tongue and licked the length of Owen's erect cock. Wow, she thought, it's just as big as the guy's in the movie. She wrapped her fingers around the shaft and flicked her tongue over the head as she'd seen the TV lady do. "God, sugar," Owen moaned, his hands cupping her head, "I love what you're doing. My God."

She sucked on the tip of his cock, tightened her grip, and moved her hand slightly toward the head. When Owen said, "Don't do that," Tish jumped back.

"Sugar," he explained, "one more move like that and I'll come in your mouth." He flipped her over on her back, and with the fabric of the teddy sliding over their skin, he plunged his cock into her.

Her last coherent thought was that he must have liked what she was doing. Then she felt the beginnings of her orgasm, but before she could hold on to it, Owen came with his usual bellow. Disappointed, she relaxed as he collapsed on top of her, his softening cock slipping from her body.

"Damn, Tish," Owen said, a few moments later. "That was so good it just got away from me. I didn't give you time." He reached between her legs and idly fingered her clit. "Let me help."

"You don't have to," she said.

"I know." His fingers danced over her soaked skin then he thrust into her with his thumb. "I want this for you."

"It's really okay," she said, her voice catching in her throat.

He grabbed her hand. "Do it for me, sugar, like the woman on TV. I want to watch both of you."

He had watched her masturbate before, so she moved so she could watch the scene. The period movie must have ended and now a naked woman was lying across a bed covered with red satin sheets, her hand working furiously between her legs. Slowly the camera panned close, and while Tish watched the woman's hand, she rubbed her pussy.

The erotic combination of doing and watching was doubling Tish's excitement. The woman's hand moved faster, then so did Tish's. She was lost in a sensual world of hands, fingers, and slippery flesh.

Owen shifted so his face was between her legs and he could watch both her ministrations and those of the woman on TV. His breath was hot on the insides of her thighs. Tish wanted to come. She felt her orgasm boil inside her.

"Yes, do that," Owen whispered as he watched. "Oh, yes, sugar. It's so good."

It was good. Very good, and although she knew that the woman on TV wasn't actually close to coming, Tish was. All of a sudden she felt Owen slide three fingers into her, filling her completely. She closed her eyes, touched the side of her clit, and pressed. Climax crashed over her, and not wanting to be distracted by his movements, she held Owen's hand still as wave after wave of pleasure engulfed her. After what felt like hours but was probably only a few moments, her entire body relaxed.

"I felt it," Owen said, his voice filled with wonder. "I felt the muscles inside you hold me, grip me."

"Was it okay?" Tish said, her voice barely audible.

"Okay? It was magic. I've never felt anything like that." Propped on his elbow, he leaned over and kissed her gently. "That was the most beautiful thing I've ever experienced. Next time we make love, I want to feel you come with my cock quiet inside you. God, sugar, that was dynamite." Using the remote, he turned off the TV. As she started to get up to undress, he asked, "Would you wear that all night? I'd love to find you in it in the morning."

She cuddled against him and they fell into dreamless sleep.

Dave slipped into the Onondaga Room and stood in the back, listening to Tracy end the final forum of the evening. She looked so capable, so professional, but he knew what an animal she could be in bed, naked, thrashing around in the throes of orgasm. God, once she finally opened up, she had become the hottest woman he'd ever been with. Why the hell did she have to spoil it?

She'd said things that told him that she was already picking out dishes and linens, setting up bridal registries, picking out a church for the wedding. He watched her guide the discussion, letting everyone have a chance to express their views. God, he thought, his body tightening, she certainly is quite something.

As the couples filed out of the meeting room, several stopped to chat with Tracy. One asked her to give their regards to Kim. "This is our third winter here," the woman—Tracy thought she'd said her name was Kaylee—said, "and we're disappointed that Kim's not here." Tracy remembered the unusual spelling from the list of attendees.

"Not that you aren't wonderful," the man, whose name was Harry, said, "but we like your sister so much. She saved our marriage, you know."

"Of course, she doesn't know," the woman said, "but two years ago we were on the verge of a breakup. We came as sort of a last resort, hoping sex would cure us."

Kim had always said that good sex doesn't cure a bad marriage, Tracy thought, but if these two thought it did . . .

"Sex didn't cure us, of course," Kaylee said, "but the communication skills we learned did. After almost ten years, we finally learned how to talk to each other and here we are."

"I know how busy you will be for the rest of the weekend so I'll ask you now. Will you tell your sister that Harry and Kaylee send our love and to please let us know when the babies arrive?" He pulled out his business card. "This has my e-mail address. Please ask her to drop me a note."

"Of course. I'll take care of it personally." Tracy put the card in her purse.

"Thanks so much," Kaylee said. "I hope the birth goes easily." As she launched into a monologue about her pregnancies, her husband tugged at her arm. "Darling," he said, "there are others waiting to talk to Tracy." As the two walked away, Tracy could hear her continuing to talk about giving birth. Three other couples also asked to be remembered to Kim and Tracy started a list of e-mail addresses so she could announce the birth of the twins.

When the room was finally empty, she straightened several stacks of handouts. She'd seen Dave walk back into the room toward the end of the session but she'd ignored him, not knowing exactly what to say. "Hi," Dave said from behind her.

"Hi," she said. "I think the evening went pretty well." Nothing too personal.

"I'm sure you were a smash." There was a long pause. "Tracy, I'm really sorry about the way it all worked out."

"Whatever," she said, trying to keep the bitterness from her voice.

"It got to be too much. I felt overwhelmed."

"That's fine. It just might have been nice to call and let me know what was going on. At first I was worried that something might have happened to you. Then I called and your minions kept telling me that you weren't available. Finally I got the message."

"I'm really sorry."

"So am I but I'll get over it." She swallowed the lump in her throat. Softly she said, "I thought we had more."

"Tracy," Dave said, almost relenting.

She shook him off. "Don't confuse the issue. If you don't want to see me anymore, that's the way it will be. Just don't expect me to welcome you with open arms one moment and then watch you walk away the next. I'm not that strong." Not strong at all.

Tracy watched him heave a giant sigh through moist eyes. "I'm sorry."

"I know, Dave. Listen, I've got a lot of things to do so if you'll excuse me." She stepped away. She wasn't going to lead with her chin so she needed to get away. She left him standing beside the long table.

When Tracy returned to her room later that night, she called Kim. "The evening went amazingly well, sis," she said. "I was amazed. All the people seem to have bought into the story that I'm as qualified as you are to run this thing."

"You are, Trace," Kim said. "You don't realize how much you've learned and the ways you've changed."

"Whatever is different, I owe it all to you."

"Not just to me," Kim said. "Dave had a lot to do with it, too. How is he?"

"He's just fine, working hard. Actually I've hardly seen him." She hadn't given Kim any of the details of their estrangement. All her sister knew was that they hadn't seen much of each other in the past two weeks and Kim had assumed that it was just the stress of the weekend that had affected Tracy's mood.

"Give him my love," Kim said with a huge yawn.

"Get some sleep and I'll call you tomorrow."

"Call anytime if you need me for anything," Kim said, "or just to catch me up on how it's going. All I do is eat and sleep anyway so don't worry about waking me."

"You need your rest—for all three of you."

She could hear rustling, then Elliot's voice. "She's climbing the walls here, Tracy, waiting for news about the weekend, so call anytime, night or day."

"Will do, Elliot. Keep her quiet as best you can and I'll call her tomorrow."

Chapter

11

Bob and Elise awoke almost simultaneously the following morning, as they often did, and she turned so that her back was cuddled against his chest, her rear comfortably cradled in his groin. Bob's arm snaked around her chest and his hand found its natural place over her T-shirt-covered breast. "I enjoyed making love to you last evening," he said, his breath warm and sleepy on her neck. "You're one hot, sexy woman."

"You're one hot guy yourself," Elise said, loving Bob more for trying to help her feel sexy. And the sex had been good the previous evening.

"I loved the feel of those satin boxers you bought, too. Today we've got to get you something outrageous. You can't understand how delicious wearing something satiny against your skin can be until you try it."

With a slight shake of her head, Elise said, "If it's all the same to you, I'd just as soon not get anything."

Elise could feel Bob's body stiffen just a bit. "Sweet, one of the things last night's forum taught me was that I can ask for what I want, and I really want you to get something at that lingerie store." She could feel his deep breath. "I know you have bad feelings about your body and I'm aware of your depression. I think this weekend could be the beginning of a change, and I think Diana's stuff might be just the way."

Elise turned so Bob's hand slipped from her body. "I know you mean well, darling, but I just can't. Don't you understand anything?" She felt control slipping and her eyes filled. She didn't know why lingerie had become a symbol of everything she'd had to give up about her sex life, but she did know that every time she thought about the issue, it made her stomach hurt. "That part of my life is over. I'm old, fat"—she swallowed hard—"and dried up. It's done."

"That's ridiculous. You're fifty-three, not ninety-three. Okay, you're overweight, but I don't care." He turned her face so she had to look at him. "Don't you understand? When I look at you, I don't see what you see. I see a loving, wonderful woman who turns me on. Can't that be enough?"

Tears flowing freely, Elise said, "It's not enough for me. I'm finished." After a long pause, her voice barely above a whisper, she continued, "Maybe you should take a lover."

Bob's words nearly exploded from his mouth. "You've got to be kidding! I don't want anyone but you." He took a deep breath. "Did you see that woman who sells the lingerie? She's twice your size and she obviously enjoys the way she looks. She's wearing a wedding ring so I assume her husband does, too."

"She's who she is, and I'm me. Let it rest." She looked at her husband. "Why is this underwear thing so important anyway? Can't we just go on the way we've been?"

"I love you. Is it that you've stopped caring about me?"

Elise's heart was pounding. She and Bob hadn't spoken this openly in many years. "Of course not. I love you very much and I thought our sex life was okay for you."

Bob cupped her face and stared into her eyes. "For me. That's the key. I'm not stupid. I know you've been faking it most of the time and that's not enough for me anymore. I love you so much and I want us to be sexy with each other." Elise heard Bob's voice harden. "I've been focusing on this weekend, hoping it would change things, but you're so darn stubborn . . ." Without another word, he climbed out of bed and silently stalked into the bathroom.

Elise couldn't remember the last time they had had a fight, even a little one like this. Was it so little? she wondered. Was she just being stubborn? Maybe she was, but it hurt so much. This lingerie thing had become some kind of sticking point and she could no longer think about it rationally. Perhaps she should talk to Diana later today. She seemed like an intuitive and understanding woman and just might be able to help. She swung her legs around and sat on the edge of the bed, listening to the shower. Bob had sounded more upset than she could ever remember. Wasn't he worth some effort on her part?

Paul and Debbie walked into the Creative Loving area of the dining room just before seven-thirty. Paul had awakened just after six, so excited by their meeting with Jerome and Betts that he couldn't get back to sleep. He had rushed his wife just a bit but he hadn't wanted to mention the importance of their breakfast date. They would like her, he just knew it. If they didn't, maybe they would be willing to have a threesome.

"You've seemed in such a rush this morning," Debbie said, as Paul peered at the occupants of the many tables. "The first session isn't until nine. What's the hurry?"

"I met a couple last evening and I wanted to introduce you to them," he said.

"That's really nice," Debbie said. "When did you meet them? I thought we spent all of yesterday together."

"You were late for the opening forum and I ran into them outside while I was waiting for you."

She had been late because Paul had sent her back to the room after dinner to get his cell phone although they'd been admonished in the brochure that phones and pagers weren't welcome. She shook it off. "What are these people like?"

Paul finally spotted Betts seated in the corner. She'd put two tables together and the larger surface was set for four. "Over there," Paul said, pointing. This morning, Betts was dressed in a demure-looking black jersey top that, while not as openly revealing as the one she had worn the previous evening, to Paul it was just as hot. His cock stiffened at the sight of her massive breasts, tightly hugged by the stretchy fabric. As they approached the table, Jerome returned from the buffet with plates for himself and Betts.

"Thank you, darling," she said to Jerome, as Paul and Debbie approached. She patted the seat next to her and Jerome sat down.

"Betts, Jerome, I'd like you to meet my wife, Debbie."

"I've been anxious to meet you," Betts said. "Paul told us how lovely you were, and he wasn't exaggerating. We combined two tables. I hope I wasn't presuming. Join us?"

"Yes, thank you," Debbie said softly, as Paul slipped into the chair beside Betts and she took the one beside Jerome.

Debbie looked at the couple, so different from the type of people Paul usually associated with. Betts was attractive in an overblown sort of way, with a bit too much makeup and hair so black that it had to come from a bottle. Jerome was a large man with mile-wide shoulders, a totally bald head, a full mustache, and a little bit of beard below his lower lip. They exchanged pleasantries and she learned that the couple was from somewhere in Wisconsin. In a way she was glad they didn't live closer since she didn't think she cared much for them. While Betts seemed open and quite talkative, Jerome was just her opposite, almost totally silent.

While Paul talked with Betts, to make conversation Debbie asked, "Jerome, what do you do for a living?"

"I work at Home Depot and I do some home construction on the side."

"Oh, that's interesting," Debbie said, keeping her voice bright. "Paul's an accountant." When he seemed unwilling to say anything else, she asked, "Does your wife work?"

"No, and Betts isn't my wife, although we've lived together for almost three years."

Not Paul's type at all, Debbie thought. He always ranted about people who were unwilling to make a lifetime commitment. "Oh." She turned to her husband. "Want to get some breakfast?"

"In a minute," he said, waving her off.

Jerome caught Betts's eye and she nodded. "Can I get you some breakfast?" he asked Debbie. "Tell me what you'd like."

"Thank you, Jerome," Debbie said, "but I'll wait for Paul."

"As you wish." He lapsed into his now-familiar silence.

Several agonizing minutes later, during which Debbie caught a few words of Paul and Betts's conversation about the Sexual Control and Power Games forum that evening, Paul rose and headed for the buffet. As she stood to follow, she thought she caught a slight look of pity on Betts's face, but it was gone before she was sure.

As Debbie helped herself to eggs, Paul walked up behind her. "We're going to get together with Betts and Jerome tonight for drinks after the evening forum."

"Okay," she said hesitantly, "but Jerome's really difficult to talk to. You and Betts seemed to hit it off, though. Maybe I'll just go back to the room."

"I want you there. I mentioned that you might want to go to bed early and suggested that just the three of us get together but Betts wouldn't hear of it."

Debbie nodded and used a pair of tongs to put several slices of bacon onto her plate.

"That's really not good for you," Paul said. "Bacon's poison for the body."

Debbie couldn't put the bacon back and she hated to waste it, but she knew now that she wouldn't eat it.

Paul got back to the table before his wife, and Debbie noticed a quick, animated discussion between Paul and Betts, which ceased when she got within earshot. She slid into her seat and Betts faced her and said, "I thought we would attend the forum on role playing early this afternoon, then Jerome has things to do, as, I gather, does Paul. I have an appointment for a massage at three-thirty and I thought I'd make one for you, too."

She'd never had a massage in her life and it couldn't be cheap at a place like this. "Thanks, but no thanks. I'll curl up in our room with a book."

"Don't be silly," Paul said. "You'll just be in my way and I think you should take Betts up on her offer. It will give you girls time to get to know each other."

Girls. She almost rolled her eyes. How she hated that term. "Really. I think I'd be just as happy reading. If I'm in your way, I can move to the lobby."

"Listen, Debbie," Paul said, his voice taking on that tone she hated, making it sound as if she were being a recalcitrant child, "you're just being difficult. I think you should take advantage of Betts's knowledge of this stuff. We've got all that money left over from the discount so why not take advantage of it."

"I'd like it if you would," Betts said gently. Was there a tiny conspiratorial note in her voice? What the heck was going on?

"Fine. Okay." Debbie was amazed at the way Betts's sudden smile changed her face. She's really pretty, Debbie thought, and there was a lot of warmth, too.

"I'm glad you'll be joining me," Betts said. "I think we'll have a lot to talk about."

"I'm glad that's settled," Paul said, patting Debbie's hand as if she were finally behaving. Mystified, Debbie was going to play along and see what this was all about.

"Great," Betts said, addressing the group. "The four of us can have lunch together and then we can all go to the forum. I know we can all have some fun with that." She seemed to be addressing Paul specifically.

"Sounds like a plan to me," Paul said, looking at his watch. "It's almost eight, and as I said, I have a lot of work with me. Debbie's got her book so we'll see you later."

As they left the dining room, Debbie said, "Which of the morning forums are we going to?"

"Please," he said, with an exasperated look on his face. "Oral sex, anal sex, we know all about that, and I've got more than enough work to last me until lunch."

"Right," she said softly. "Maybe I'll go to one or both by myself if you don't mind."

"I do mind. It's a ridiculous waste of your time. Wouldn't you rather be reading that slushy romance novel you brought with you?"

With a resigned sigh, she said, "Of course."

Tish awoke later than usual, just a bit sore from their sex of the previous evening. Owen was in the bathroom so Tish had some time to think about her plan. Their sex had been wonderful and Owen certainly seemed satisfied. She was going to use the day's forums to learn still more ways to please him.

She heard Owen turn on the shower and decided to continue her campaign. Sliding out of bed naked, she walked quietly into the steamy bathroom and slipped into the shower behind the man who soon would be her official fiancé. She'd never been a very adventurous lover, but now she was determined to do it all. As water sluiced down their bodies, she rubbed her water-slick breasts against Owen's back.

"Good morning, again," he said with an audible gasp. "I love what you're doing."

"I hope so." She picked up a bar of soap and lathered her skin, then again rubbed against Owen's back. Her lathered hands smoothed over his furry chest. "I've got to get you all clean."

Owen turned and rubbed his body against Tish's. "Clean isn't what I have in mind right now. Actually, I've got lots of dirty thoughts." With a chuckle, he soaped his hands and massaged her breasts.

"Like what?" Tish asked, eager to learn more about what turned Owen on. "Tell me everything."

Owen took Tish's hand and put it on his growing cock. "He's hungry for you."

Sensing there was something more, she asked, "How would he like me to satisfy his hunger?"

Water pouring over them, Owen fondled her breasts. "Do you really want to know?" When Tish nodded, he continued, "Kneel down."

"Do you want to be in my mouth?" she asked, doing as he asked.

Her breasts were at the height of his dick, and he took them and pressed them around his rampant erection. "Like this," he said, his voice now hoarse, his breathing ragged. He grabbed the soap and spread a thick coating of lather on both his cock and her breasts. Then with trembling hands, he held her flesh tightly and thrust his slippery cock in the valley. "God, I love your tits. I've imagined you this way," he said, each word wrung out of him.

Tish reached around and grasped his buttocks, feeling the play of his well-developed muscles beneath his wet skin. "Do it," she said, enjoying the feel of his dick. She took a chance with her language and said, "Fuck my tits."

As if in response to her words, he came, semen spurting from the tip of his erection, muscles trembling. Bingo! She'd aroused and satisfied him again. Not wanting him to fall, she eased him down until he was sitting on the floor of the tub. Turning off the water, she wrapped him in a towel and rubbed his skin.

"My God, Tish. Where did you learn to do that? It was amazing."

"You taught me just now," she said, folding a towel sarong-style around her chest. "You can teach me a lot."

"I may never move again," Owen said.

Giggling, Tish said, "You better move pretty soon, stud, because I'm not bringing you breakfast."

His expression becoming serious, Owen said, "You didn't come."

"I got enough pleasure from watching you to last me a long time," she said flirtatiously. "Or at least until later."

Tracy stood at the buffet table, scooping scrambled eggs with cheese and peppers onto her plate. "Good morning, Tracy," Dave said from behind her. It infuriated her the way his voice affected her. Her knees wobbled, her breasts tingled, and her pussy swelled and moistened. Forget it. He's not really interested, or maybe he's too interested, and whatever the problem is, it's his, not mine. "Good morning," she said, adding a single sausage to her plate.

"Are you ready for this morning's forums?"

"Of course. Well," she said, deciding on honesty rather than curt, single-word replies, "as ready as I'll ever be."

"How's your sister?"

She accepted that he was making an effort to be pleasant, so she said, "She's doing fine, but totally pissed at having to stay in bed. I hope she survives until the babies are born without committing suicide."

"She's due the end of February?"

"Actually the doctor's told her that she'll probably be early but they're trying to prevent labor for as long as they can, which is why she's climbing the walls lying flat on her back." She laughed at her silly phrasing. "Anyway, she's already more than thirty-three weeks and so far, so good." As she'd been talking, Dave had poured her a cup of coffee and added milk and sugar just the way she liked it.

He carried it to a table in the corner. "Any one-on-ones before the first forum?"

A frown coloring her voice, she said, "No, and I expected it. Until everyone gets to know me, I don't expect many."

"Be patient. When they know you as well as I do, they'll come flocking."

Her eyebrows shot up. "Thanks for the compliment."

There was a long, and somehow intimate, silence. Then Dave stood. "I've got work to do. I'll see you as the day goes on."

"Right," she said, both disappointed and relieved. Keep it professional and you'll survive this weekend.

Dave walked toward his office, unable to get Tracy out of his thoughts. She was wonderful, sexy, and in most ways perfect for him. Why was he being so thick about it? Why couldn't Tracy have left well enough alone? They'd known each other for only a few months. It was certainly too soon to get serious. Wasn't it? Couldn't there be a compromise? Couldn't they continue as they had been?

Chapter

12

E lise and Bob had taken a break in their room after lunch and were lying on the bed side by side. They had attended a morning forum on using erotic stories for sexual communication. Bob took Elise's hand and said, "Once upon a time there was a man in love with an overweight woman."

"Stop it," Elise snapped, a bit annoyed at Bob's one-track mind. "I'm sure that's not what Tracy meant by storytelling. You're supposed to be whispering sensual things in my ear, not telling stupid tales with even stupider morals."

She could hear Bob's long, exasperated breath. "Elise, listen. Our relationship is the most important thing in the world to me. I love you, more, it seems, than you love yourself. I don't know how to get it through your head that your attitude about yourself is what's ruining it all, not my feelings about the way you look."

"Ruining it all?" she gasped. Tears gathered at the back of Elise's throat, threatening to choke her. She'd done more crying this weekend than . . . And she'd foolishly thought this would be the beginning of the next phase in their lives, whatever that might be. She cleared her throat. "I believe you mean what you say, but it only takes one look in the mirror to make me forget it."

"What do you see when you look in the mirror?" Bob asked softly.

Elise took in a shaky breath. "I see an elephant. I see drooping breasts and a fat stomach. I see what used to be salt and pepper and now is salt and salt and salt and pepper. I'm old and dried up." She knew that she was ranting now, but she couldn't seem to help herself. "Sex stinks. I'm never excited anymore. You've noticed that I'm never wet anymore, haven't you?" When he hesitated, she shouted, "Haven't you?"

"Yes, I've noticed that you're not as lubricated as you used to be, but it doesn't prevent us from making love, does it?"

Her body shook from the tears she was still trying to suppress. "That's not the point. I'm old and it's all gone."

"There's something else going on here and I don't know what to do anymore. Maybe Tracy can help. She's supposed to be the expert."

"Kim's the expert," Elise said, then hesitated. Anything had to be a step up. "I don't know, Bob. I just feel so awful."

"I feel just as bad. I'm not only losing sex, I'm losing you. I don't intend to do that without a fight."

After a long argument Elise agreed to talk to Tracy. She had no confidence that Tracy could tell either of them anything they didn't already know, but she'd do it, if only to make Bob happy.

They found Tracy sipping coffee in a quiet corner of the Creative Loving section of the dining room. She was dressed in the same mint green and white striped shirt and jeans she had been wearing that morning. Charming as always, Tracy invited them to join her.

"You probably don't know exactly who we are. I'm Bob Prescott and this is my wife Elise. We've been married for almost twenty-six years and we need some advice." Bob quickly outlined the argument they had had earlier. "Something's terribly wrong and I don't know exactly what it is or how to fix it."

"If you'd just give up on this lingerie fetish you've got . . ." Elise snapped.

"It's not a fetish and it's not the crux of the issue. Wearing sexy undies has just become a symbol of so much more and you and I both know it." Bob put his arm around his wife. "I love this woman very much but I feel her slipping away. It's not that sex is the most important thing in my life, but I don't want that part of our relationship to end. She's obsessed with her weight and her age and she thinks sex is over. I know enough to realize that it's not over unless she thinks it is. I don't want to fight, but I don't want to give up everything we had. I don't know what to do. I'm afraid our marriage is in real trouble."

"And you, Elise?" Tracy asked.

Elise felt as small as her voice sounded when she said, "I'm terrified."

Tracy was amazed at the honesty and understanding Bob had shown about his relationship with Elise, and she could understand Elise's problems, too. She immediately realized that this was her first real test. Could she actually help a couple with a serious problem? Kim had dealt with body image problems often in her columns and Tracy had learned a lot from them, and from all the books she had read on sexuality. All she could do now was synthesize all that information and try to make Elise take a serious look at herself. "Bob," she said, "maybe Elise and I should chat alone for a few minutes."

"Sure," Bob said, and left the table.

When she was alone with Elise, Tracy began. "Elise, is Bob pretty much right about what he said about your feelings?"

"I guess," Elise said softly.

"Have you met Diana? She's really the poster child for a great body image."

Elise's smile was small and wistful. "We met last evening and she's just wonderful. I wish I could be like her but I can't. Bob wants me to get a piece of sexy lingerie. He thinks that if I just wear something sexy, I'll feel sexy. I wish it were true, but the image of me in a skimpy lace outfit just accentuates the problem. Sex isn't exciting for me anymore, partly because I keep seeing myself as Bob must see me."

"Isn't it a bit presumptuous for you to decide how your husband sees you? He says he finds you sexy and attractive. Is he lying?"

Tracy watched emotions flash across Elise's face. "No. Yes. I don't know."

"Do you make love occasionally?"

"Yes. As he said, sex is, or at least was, an important part of our relationship. Now with the kids gone, the situation's just gotten worse."

"Worse how?"

"We've got an empty house so he wants to make love all the time."

"Is that so horrible?"

"I'm just not what I used to be. I don't get excited anymore."

"Did you ever?"

"Sure. When we were first married, it was great. While the kids were growing up, we used to tell them we had private things to do, lock the bedroom door, and make love. But as they grew, so did I. Now, with the changes and all, I just know that sex is all over."

Tracy searched for the perfect words, then decided to say what she thought without censorship. "Your weight is important to your good health, of course, but in the bedroom it's only important in the way you see yourself and the way it affects you and Bob. You can change your weight, or not, but what's more important here is that you can change the baggage that goes along with it."

"Baggage?"

"I'm fat so I'm not attractive or sexy. I'm fat so Bob doesn't want me. I'm sure he doesn't say that, or even feel it."

"He says he doesn't, but I know what I look like. How can he want me?"

"He says he does, doesn't he?"

"Yes, but sex doesn't work anymore." Her answer came slowly. "I'm never excited."

"Does Bob get erect?"

"Sure." Elise shook her head slowly. "All the time."

"Every time you make love, it's another glaring example of how bad it is for you. Right?"

Elise's face softened. "You do understand."

"I assume you're going through menopause?"

"Went through. I stopped getting my period about three years ago."

As much as Tracy knew medically about menopause, it shouldn't cause a complete loss of libido. "Is that when you stopped getting excited by your husband?"

Elise's shoulders drooped. "I guess so."

"You know that there's no reason not to have a great sex life until you're in your eighties, or beyond." Tracy suddenly had an idea. "How do you know you're not excited?"

Elise hesitated. "I'm just not. I don't get wet and I don't feel aroused." Tears began to flow down her cheeks. "Sometimes I'm so dried up that Bob uses spit to lubricate his penis. It's humiliating."

"Let's tackle that problem first. Menopause can cause your

body not to produce as much fluid as you have in the past. That doesn't mean you're not excited, it's just physiological. Have you and your doctor discussed hormone replacement?"

"We did about a year ago, but with all the new studies we decided against it."

"Okay. How about just dealing with the lubrication problem? Many women find that using something like K-Y Jelly solves that problem rather easily."

"Really? Feeling slippery was the way I always knew I was ready for intercourse. I don't think I'd like some phony stuff."

"Would you rather lose your husband? You've got to begin to feel better about yourself before you two will be able to rebuild all the good stuff you used to have. Perhaps something as simple as a vaginal lubricant can be a start."

"That isn't going to solve the real problem. I'm still fat."

Tracy looked at Elise, who was probably at least sixty pounds overweight. "I'm not going to kid you, you're overweight. I assume you've tried dieting and exercise."

"I can't do it. I've tried and I just can't. Diets don't work and exercise is so boring."

"Sex is great exercise. I read somewhere that really good sex can be worth about three hundred calories. At thirty-five hundred calories to the pound, all you have to do is make love about a dozen times a week and you'll lose several pounds a month."

Elise's smile was teary, but genuine. "Right. Thanks for that anyway."

"I'm not a weight loss specialist and you'll lose or not as you see fit. The problem is all the stuff that you carry around along with the extra pounds. You're fat and that makes you worthless and sexless, ugly and unattractive." Elise nodded. "Well, it's up to you to sever the connection between the weight and all the rest of that junk. I can't solve your problems in one ten-minute chat, but maybe counseling would help, both with a weight loss specialist and with a psychologist. However, let me give you two pieces of advice."

God, Tracy thought. Let me be able to make a difference, even just a small one.

"First, go into Matt's and buy some lubricant. Don't think about it or judge why you need it, just do it. Give it to Bob and explain that sometimes you're just not as wet as you feel you want to be. If it bothers you to talk to Bob about it, go into the bathroom and smear some on before you make love. Either way, enjoy the cold, slippery feel of it and see what happens."

"What if it doesn't work?" She looked so terrified that Tracy reached out and held her hand. "What if I'm just not into sex anymore?"

Tracy thought about all her fears before she first made love with Dave. "The fear of finding out that you were right all along is the most threatening thing in the world. It seems that you're better off not knowing whether it's real or not. I know. I was there quite recently, but I finally decided that, for me, not knowing was even more torturous."

"Were your fears groundless?"

Tracy's smile was wide and genuine. "They certainly were, and when I realized that, it was like a great weight had been lifted from my shoulders."

"I can give the lubricant a try. What kind should I get?"

"Talk to Matt or just pick something. Then, when you discover that it works, you can buy several kinds and do a consumer test."

Elise giggled, the first relaxation Tracy had seen. "That's a creative idea. You said you had two suggestions."

Tracy nodded. "Talk to Diana. I've never been more than my current ten pounds overweight, and it's never played a big part in my sex life. You and she should be able to talk about that with much more understanding than you and I can. She can probably give you some positive thoughts, and thinking positive thoughts is the best start I can suggest."

Elise nodded. "I'll try," she said, her voice quavering.

As Elise walked away, Tracy crossed her fingers. Please . . .

Matt's Adult Toy Box was doing a brisk business when Elise walked in. Maybe Tracy was right about lubrication. Feeling slippery between her legs had always been a sign of arousal for her. Bob had often commented that she flowed like a fountain. "You'd make a great porn star," he'd said once, many years earlier. Feeling really embarrassed, she selected a plastic bottle of something called Wet Stuff, paid for it, and quickly put the bag in her purse.

As she pushed her card key in the door of their room, she thought about Bob and his bravery. He'd been willing to take risks, to discuss their problem. Maybe he deserved the same willingness from her. She closed the door behind her and saw her husband lying on the bed, his arms folded behind his head. "I talked to Tracy," she said.

Bob turned to gaze at her. "Was she able to help sort stuff out? You know that if she's suggested anything that I can do, I want to help."

Elise huffed out a small breath. "I know that and she suggested something I hadn't thought of." She took the bag from her pocketbook and handed the bottle to Bob. "I don't feel sexy when I'm not wet. Tracy said it might just be due to my changes so I bought this."

Bob grinned and waggled his eyebrows. "Is that an invitation?"

Elise thought about it. Was it? She was certainly curious. "I guess it is." She climbed onto the bed as Bob put the bottle on the bedside table.

"You know," Bob said, "I've been doing a lot of thinking since I left you and Tracy. I think I've been taking you and our lovemaking for granted and I'm sorry about that. While you were talking to Tracy, I took some of her advice and did a bit of shopping." He rolled off the bed and opened a drawer in the dresser. When her stomach clenched, he quickly said, "No, nothing from Diana's. I merely got a few things I thought you'd like."

He opened a paper bag and pulled out several pillar candles, placed them around the room, and lit them. "I know you don't like making love with the lights on, but I was hoping that this might be an exception." He flipped off the room lights and closed the drapes to shut out the midday winter sun.

"The scent is wonderful," Elise said, inhaling. "What is it?"

"I haven't the faintest idea. The label said Sensuous Mist." He quickly stepped into the bathroom and returned with something behind his back. With a flourish, he whipped out a bud vase with a single pink plastic rose inside. "They didn't have any real ones so I hope this will do."

Elise couldn't contain her grin. Pink roses had always been her favorite. She remembered that early in their marriage Bob used to bring her flowers almost every week. "It's lovely, and so thoughtful of you."

"I want the rest of this weekend to be just for us. I want us to remember how it was, and decide to do whatever we need to to make it that way again." He turned on the bedside radio and Elise heard a familiar seventies song. "I also found a station that plays music of the seventies and eighties." He listened a moment, then said, "Remember this one? That silly apartment you had for a while?" He held out his hand. "Remember dancing?"

Elise melted into his arms and they held each other, moving their feet slowly to the music. As she closed her eyes, she was transported back to their dating days. "I don't remember dancing longer than one song," she said, her head on Bob's shoulder. "We never lasted longer than that."

"No, we didn't, but I want to take my time now." Bob's hands caressed her, gliding down her back then beneath her sweatshirt. "I love the feel of your skin," he said. "Over the years I've forgotten to slow down and appreciate how good you feel."

Elise pulled Bob's shirt from his jeans, and her hands snaked up his back. "I don't know which feels better," she said, "my hands on you or your hands on me."

For several minutes they stood, hands massaging, caressing. Then Elise's head fell back and Bob's lips were on hers. The kiss was deep, long, and caused tendrils of heat to unwind in her belly. The flame was small, but it was more than she'd felt in quite a while.

"I love you, Elise," Bob said. "I want you as much as I ever did, but I want you to understand something. If we never made love again, I'd still love you and want to be with you. Always."

"I love you, Bob." Then his mouth was on her neck, and her ears and eyes. Soon they were on the bed, Bob naked, Elise in just her sweatshirt. Hands were everywhere, touching, fondling. Then Bob reached for the bottle on the bedside table. He squirted some of the liquid in his palm, then pressed it against Elise's mound. "Yipes," she squealed, "that's cold."

"Is that bad?" he asked.

She considered. "Not really. It was just a surprise." His hands knew all her hot spots and soon his fingers were buried inside her.

"Tell me," he said, and she remembered Tracy's advice the previous evening. "That feels good," she said, as he thrust in and out. "Slowly. Fill me slowly." The slippery feel of the lubricant and his fingers filling her heated her blood and she wondered at the change in her reactions. She took his hand. "Touch me here," she said, placing his hand on her clit. "Slowly."

For several moments, with the room filled with the scent of candles and the sounds of soft music, he touched her. The fact that she was actually aroused surprised and delighted her. She didn't think she'd climax but this wonderful feeling was certainly a beginning. "Be inside me," she whispered.

Bob poured more of the cold, slippery liquid in his palm and rubbed it on his cock. Then, with an ease she hadn't experienced in a long time, he slipped inside, then moved. It was wonderful. She felt him thrust more urgently, and said, "It's all right. Let it happen."

"You're not ready," Bob said.

"Do it," she said, and not needing any more encouragement, he climaxed.

Later, she said, "That was wonderful. Thank you."

"Don't thank me," Bob said. "I'm the one who came. Was it okay for you?"

"It was wonderful. For the first time in a long time I feel like a sexual person. If we can keep this going, orgasms will happen. I'm sure of it."

"Did the slippery stuff help?"

"I'm surprised at how much. Tracy explained that the dryness was probably due to my changes and not my lack of arousal. You know, I never realized how much that wet feeling was connected to feeling excited. Does that make any sense?"

"Sure. I guess it's kind of like my erections. If I'm not hard, then I don't feel like I could possibly be excited."

Elise cuddled closer to her husband. Maybe she'd have a talk with Diana. She'd crossed one gigantic hurdle; maybe she could cross another.

* * *

Tish looked up from the magazine she had been reading as the hotel room door opened. She and Owen had skipped the Sex and the Internet forum so that Owen could take care of a mysterious errand. When he walked in, he had a large box under his arm and a wide grin on his face. "I couldn't resist," he said. "That role-playing forum really turned me on and I got to thinking about a game I'd like to play. When Tracy said that Diana had scenarios all packaged, I had to see whether she had the one I've always dreamed about."

"Did she have something?" Tish had never known Owen to be so free with his wishes, and she was ready for anything if it would get her closer to her goal. Her only reservation was that the teddy they had bought the previous evening had cost quite a bit, and she hoped that he hadn't spent too much more of their lottery money.

In answer, Owen placed the box on the bed beside her. "Actually she didn't have exactly what I wanted, but with Matt's help and things from Diana's store, we built it." As Tish started to open the box, Owen held the top shut and said, "Why don't you take the box into the bathroom and change? I think it will all be self-explanatory and I can't wait to see how you look."

Tish took the package and closed the bathroom door behind her. She set the box on the toilet lid and lifted the top. Inside was a black leather miniskirt and a silver spandex tube top. Beneath was a black garter belt, a scandalous French-cut black bra with openings for her nipples, black stockings, and a pair of black platform shoes with four-inch high heels. In one corner was a small plastic bag containing bright red lipstick, black mascara and a black eyeliner pencil. God, she thought, slowly starting to fume, this stuff must have cost a fortune.

She pulled each item from the box and laid it out on the

sink. This is an outfit for a hooker, she thought with a shudder. Is this what he wants? A cheap slut? Stop that, she told herself. It's just a game, just role playing, and you said you'd do anything. Why does this feel so distasteful?

Owen knew that before they met she'd worked in a bar while she was in secretarial school. Was that the woman he wanted to see? Did he realize that she'd hated every minute of it, parading around in a skimpy outfit, being nice to drunks who might be good tippers? Although she'd been offered money, she'd never, ever sold herself. She had a great body and she enjoyed using it to please Owen, but this outfit he'd bought hit a little too close to home. "Don't be like that," she said aloud. "Owen's only doing what you suggested, freeing all his sexual energy."

She undressed, then as she put the clothing on, she became aware that there were no panties. Finally fully dressed, she looked at herself in the full length mirror on the bathroom door. Cheap slut didn't go half far enough. She carefully redid her eye makeup and added the blood red lipstick. Now she looked like a vampire hooker when all she wanted to be was Owen's wife.

She slipped the shoes on, then, with as much courage as she could muster, she walked back into the bedroom. Owen had closed the drapes against the late afternoon sun and tuned the radio to a rap and rock station. Rolling her hips and trying desperately to get into character, Tish said, "Hello, stud. Were you waiting for me?"

"Oh, my God," he breathed, as he took it all in. "Holy shit." The look on his face was priceless. His mouth hung open and his eyes darkened. He cleared his throat and said, "What's your name?"

She'd play it out just this once. "Candy," Tish said, "and I'm yours for the evening if you want me." Silly question. She could judge his answer by the huge tent in the front of his pants.

"Oh, I want you all right," he breathed. "First I want to see you strut your stuff."

Tish took a deep breath and walked around the room, swinging her hips, her stomach pulled in tight and her bosom sticking out as far as she could push it beneath the tight elasticized top. She almost fell off the ladder-high heels but she managed to do a pretty good imitation of a street corner hooker.

"My God, Tish, I mean Candy." He grabbed her wrist and pulled her down on the bed beside him, his hands quickly under the spandex scooping her breasts from the tiny bra. He buried his face in her cleavage then, his mouth on her nipples, pulled his pants off. Still almost fully clothed, he turned her back to him, bent her over the bed, and entered her vagina from behind in one hard thrust.

She wasn't really wet, but as he moved, she felt her juices flow. He pulled back, then slapped her ass cheek hard. "Slut," he yelled. "Whore." He slapped her again. "See what flaunting your body gets you?" He jammed his cock into her one last time and roared as he came.

It had all happened so quickly that Tish had barely had time to react. As she climbed onto the bed, she rubbed her burning buttocks. The words he'd used echoed in her head. Was he acting or did he think she was some kind of cheap prostitute? She'd thought she was willing to be anything but this struck awfully close to home, to the battles she'd fought years earlier. And he'd never hit her before, even in play.

Owen stroked her burning cheek. "I'm sorry about that, sugar. I got carried away. You told me about your days in the bar and I've fantasized about it ever since. You looked . . . well, I can't describe it."

"Is that what you think I did back then?"

"Of course not," he said. "It's just been a fantasy of mine. And you made it all come true."

"I like making your dreams come true." He hadn't been that quick on the trigger since the early days of their relationship.

"Yeah," he said, a satisfied grin in his voice, "I know. It's never been that fast for me but you drove me crazy." He was silent for a while, then said, "Tish. I know I've been reluctant to get married, but maybe we should. This weekend was so great. I love sex with you."

Tish's heartbeat sped as she propped herself on one elbow. It had been worth all the bad feelings and the slap on her ass. Her plan had worked exactly the way she had planned it. "Do you really mean that?"

He wrapped his arms around her and pulled her close. "I mean it. After all, we've been together for so long, what would really change? We'd be official but we'd still be the same people. We could play out fantasies like this every night."

Not like that, she thought. Never like this again. She lightened her voice. "That's wonderful, and yes, I would love to marry you and have your babies."

"Babies? Sugar, let's not jump the gun here."

She felt Owen's body tense. She wanted children but she'd let it go for the moment. After all, she'd gotten her marriage proposal. "Well, not right away, of course, but that's what marriage is all about, isn't it?"

"Sugar . . ."

"Listen, we just got engaged so let's forget the difficult stuff, get dressed, and have a drink to celebrate."

"Get dressed? We are dressed."

"You need pants, and I need real clothes."

"Of course. These," he said, tugging on her leather skirt, "are only for me to see."

As she changed back into the clothes she had been wearing earlier, Tish wondered why she was so sad. She had what she wanted, didn't she? He'd asked and she'd accepted. The rest would work itself out. Wouldn't it?

They shared a drink in the bar and talked, although the subject of marriage didn't come up again. Eventually they made their way into the dining room and had dinner. Tracy entered as they were finishing dessert and Tish waved her over. "I just wanted to thank you," Tish said, as Tracy pulled a chair over and sat beside them.

"I'm delighted you've gotten something out of the weekend so far."

Tish took Owen's hand. "He asked me to marry him," she said, "and I said yes."

"That's wonderful," Tracy said, leaning over and giving Tish a kiss on the cheek and shaking Owen's hand. "Congratulations."

"We really have you to thank," Owen said. "I never realized that sex could be this good. Tish has really gone out of her way to show me how great the rest of our lives can be together."

"That's wonderful."

"Owen," Tish said, "I'm really chilly. Could you go back to the room and get my sweater? It's on the bed."

"Sure, sugar," Owen said as he left the table. "I'll just be a minute."

"Tracy," Tish said as she watched Owen's retreating back, "I need to talk to you."

Tracy studied Tish's face. For a woman who just got engaged, she looked troubled. "Okay. I gather you don't want Owen to be part of our discussion so maybe we better talk fast."

"I was so happy when Owen agreed to marry me, but now I don't know whether this is really what I want." She quickly described her plan to get Owen to pop the question and his response. "I have two problems. First, I think he asked me to marry him because I played the prostitute in his fantasies. I'm not that person and our sex won't be play acting every night."

"It can be if that's what you both want."

"That's just it. I want a comfortable life. Sure, hot sex has its place and we'll explode from time to time, but I don't want him to think that he's marrying a hooker with all the tricks."

"So tell him just as you told me." Tracy hesitated and looked carefully at Tish. "There's something else."

Tracy watched the other woman take a deep breath. "I don't think he wants children and I do. I'm not sure I'm doing the right thing."

Tracy leaned on her elbows. Please let me be able to help. She heard Kim's words. When in doubt, try to find out what they want and how they feel. The key is that people can change behavior, not feelings. "Tell me exactly where you see yourself and Owen five years from now."

Tish's eyes became dreamy. "We live in a little house and we've got a few kids. I really want kids."

"If you knew he was never going to want children, what would you want?"

There was a long pause. "I don't know."

Tracy took Tish's hand. "That's what you have to figure out. You can't make him want kids."

"I want kids, but I love him so much, too."

"Now it's a matter of what's most important to you, him or children. It's a pretty simple question from the outside and very difficult for you."

"What if I really can't decide?"

"Then you might want to set a deadline for the two of you. Talk to him, without nagging or issuing ultimatums. Discuss your concerns and suggest that you both take, say, three months to figure out what you really want."

"He doesn't know what he wants."

"You're dreaming. He knows exactly what he wants. He wants what you two have now, with or without the label of marriage. You need to decide whether that's okay with you.

"I understand where you're coming from as well. Your clock is ticking and Mother Nature has ways of ensuring the continuation of the species. They tweak your hormones and society tweaks them further. It's not the same with men. Children change everything for a man. Suddenly he has dependents. Money becomes a big issue and he feels that all his freedom is down the tubes. Some men never get past that, and that's fine for them. You need to make up your mind."

"Three months?"

"If you wouldn't stay with him if there were never to be children, then you have to move on. Just remember this isn't blackmail. It's not 'Make a baby with me or I'm out of here.' He has to do the same job as you do of figuring out what he wants. If, to him, not having kids is more important than his feelings for you, then he needs to split, too."

Tracy saw Owen returning with Tish's sweater and stood. "He's back. Think about it. It's your decision."

"Here's your sweater," Owen said, sitting back down.

"I've got a few things to do before the evening session," Tracy said, "so I'll be running along. Again, congratulations. I wish you all the best."

"Thanks," they both said.

I hope I said the right things, Tracy thought. I guess I can only do the best I can do.

As she walked away, Tracy considered her conversation. Did Dave have feelings similar to Owen's? Was that the reason he'd dropped her? While Owen was willing to commit to Tish at least to the extent of living together, he was really reluctant to take the next step. Was that Dave's problem too, taking the next step?

Maybe it was time to have a serious conversation with him, even at the risk of finding out that he had other reasons for not wanting to see her. When she spoke about sexual communication, she talked at length about taking risks. Now she had to believe her own rhetoric and take risks herself.

Chapter

13

During the early afternoon role-playing forum, Paul had insisted that he and Debbie sit with Betts and Jerome. Debbie found herself a bit uncomfortable sitting beside Jerome. He was so big, so imposing, yet so quiet that he made her feel just a bit creepy. Paul sat on her other side and she held his hand throughout the forum. When someone mentioned a scenario that involved multiple partners, Paul's grip tightened. He also reacted to a question about dominance. Interesting.

Debbie wasn't blind and she knew that there was something going on between Paul and Betts. Did he want to have an affair with her or some kind of kinky threesome? If he wanted to play around, why was he making such an effort to get Debbie and Betts to like each other? Although she hadn't particularly taken to the woman, Debbie would just play along and see what happened.

As the forum ended, Betts gathered the other three around her. "Okay, guys, go play. Debbie and I are going to the spa. We'll see you when we're done." As she walked away, she turned back, winked, and said, "Don't wait up." Debbie followed.

It was a long walk through several hallways to the spa, and when they arrived, the area was almost deserted. "I usually find that late Saturday afternoon is a pretty quiet time at places like this."

Curious to find out more about this woman who had so obviously caught Paul's attention, she asked, "Do you visit spas often?"

"Jerome and I spend quite a few weekends at places like this and I do love to unwind before Saturday evening activities."

Debbie couldn't help but wonder how the couple managed the expense of many weekends at places like this. Jerome worked at Home Depot. "Do you work, Betts?"

"No." Her smile softened her face. "You're wondering about the cost. I inherited quite a bit of money from my parents and a maiden aunt so neither of us ever have to work."

"Oh. Jerome said he works at Home Depot."

"I let him do that because it makes him crazy to stay home all day. He's rebuilt most of our house and really needs something to do."

I let him? Interesting choice of words. A woman dressed in a soft pink uniform approached the two women and extended her hand to Betts. "Welcome back, Ms. Galgani." The well-coiffed and made up woman turned to Debbie. "You must be Ms. Stafford. We're ready for both of you."

"Both of us?" Debbie said. "I don't have an appointment."

"I'm sorry, Deb. I stopped in earlier and took the liberty of making an appointment for a massage for you right after mine."

"Thanks, but no thanks," Debbie said. Betts had called her Deb. She'd always liked the shorter version of her name but Paul always insisted on calling her Debbie.

Betts motioned Debbie to the far side of the waiting room. "Listen, Debbie. There's a lot going on here and we need to talk. I thought we could do it while feeling totally pampered. Indulge me."

She was eager to hear what was going on but nevertheless she didn't want to spend the money on a massage. "I've never had a massage and I think I'll pass. I'll sit in the room while you have yours and we can talk."

"I told your husband that I had made the appointment and he called in his credit card number. Indulge us both." When she turned on the charm, as she was doing now, Betts was difficult to resist. "Please."

Reluctantly, Debbie nodded. "Great," Betts said. They changed in a small locker room.

"What does one wear to get a massage?" Debbie asked.

"You can wear your underwear if being nude beneath a towel makes you uncomfortable. I just strip to the buff and wrap." She grabbed a large fluffy bath sheet and unself-consciously removed her clothes. She looked as if she worked out, with a flat stomach, great thighs, tight buns, and large breasts with deep brown nipples.

Debbie knew that her body was a mess compared to Betts's but what the hell. She might just as well get into the spirit of whatever was going on. And something was definitely going in. She quickly removed her clothes and wrapped herself in a towel.

"You have a lovely figure," Betts said, sounding sincere, "and you shouldn't be nervous about being nude."

Unable to think of an appropriate reply, Debbie remained quiet. Together they entered the massage room and Betts stretched out facedown on a narrow padded table. Debbie had wondered how she'd react to some man having his hands on her, but she didn't have to worry. The massage therapist who walked in was a woman of about forty. She had graying hair, a sharp profile, and a rather ordinary figure. She wore a pink uniform, sneakers, and socks. "Hi, folks," she said, her voice bright. "I'm Carol. I gather you're here together and the appointments are for thirty minutes each." She wound an oven timer and Debbie watched her set it for half an hour. "This way no one feels gypped."

Betts turned her head toward Debbie as Carol arranged the towel so it covered only her buttocks. Carol poured oil in her palm from a small bottle that sat in a warmer and rubbed her hands together to warm them. "Carol," Betts said, "Debbie and I need to have a very private conversation. I assume you'll do your work and be deaf as a post."

"Of course, Ms. Galgani. Nothing said in this room ever goes out the door. Especially during the Creative Loving Weekends."

"What's so special about these weekends for you?" Debbie asked.

"No details, of course, but frequently couples come in for his-and-hers massages. They've become open to all kinds of sensual pleasures after all. I pay no attention to what goes on after I leave the room." Her giggle made her sound like a teenager. "Let's just say my tables get a workout from more than massages."

Debbie formed a picture in her mind, then chuckled. Carol put her hands over her ears. "Say whatever you like, ladies," Carol said, then covered her mouth. "I'm now not only deaf, but dumb as well."

Betts was silent for several minutes as Carol worked on her feet and legs. Finally, with a long exhalation, she said, "Tell me about your relationship with Paul."

Okay, that was that. Betts might be a great organizer and have Paul snowed with some scheme, but her marriage was none of the woman's business. "It's a marriage. Why don't you tell me about your relationship with Jerome?"

"I'm sorry. You're right. I'm asking a very personal question without reason or explanation. Let me tell you about Jerome and me and about what plans Paul has, and then you can run away or we can continue. Okay?"

When Debbie nodded, Betts continued. "Jerome is my bottom." Debbie was totally confused and Betts must have noticed. "Sorry. Let me put this all in English. Jerome and I have a slightly unusual relationship. I guess the best way to explain it is to say that he's my slave. He does what I want, when I want, both in sex and in everyday life."

Debbie just stared, her mind reeling. She knew that such things existed, of course, but she never expected to meet real people who enjoyed that kind of thing. And Betts and Jerome seemed pretty normal. As she thought, pieces clicked into place: Jerome's deference; I let him work; the secret glances; questions asked; permission granted. It all made sense now.

Betts had let her think for a few moments, and then continued, "Hear me out, then you can leave if you like." Carol might have said she was deaf, but she was obviously listening to every word. Betts went on, "We met just over three years ago at a party thrown by a mutual friend who knew our desires rather well and was sure we'd hit it off, in all ways.

"Jerome was, at that time, a very successful architect but instead of building things with his hands and imagination, he watched his designs gutted by cost-cutting and linear-thinking executives who parceled everything out to the lowest bidder. Just before we met, there had been an accident on a building he designed. He wasn't responsible, of course, but it troubled him deeply. He wanted out, and after we talked, he realized that he wanted nothing more than to be told what to do. He'd have no decisions to make with no consequences to anything he did.

"I was, and still am, a spoiled rich kid. I've got more money than I can spend in several lifetimes and I was totally tired of dealing with a world full of men interested in my body or my wallet. I wanted a man who would be all mine, for my pleasure only.

"Jerome and I hit it off almost immediately. We share a lot of the same interests."

Debbie was both amazed and curious. "For example?"

"Despite his incredibly busy schedule, he had found the time to become a life master at bridge. I have to say I play a great game myself. We both love old black-and-white films, particularly old science fiction. We idolize Bela Legosi and Vincent Price, for example. He loves Shakespeare but hadn't had the time to go to performances as I had."

Debbie's mind was boggled. This was so different from her preconceptions of both people.

"You look surprised and I don't wonder. It's very complicated."

"Jerome's so quiet. How did you ever find all this out originally?"

"He's not as quiet as he seems. He's just forbidden to speak more than one or two sentences unless I give him permission."

"Excuse me?"

"Everything he does, from morning to night, is under my control. I tell him when to eat, and what, when and where to sleep, what to wear." Carol poured more oil on her hands and moved from Betts's legs to her back and shoulders. "It's been like that from the first."

"How did this all begin?"

"After we spent that first evening talking, I invited him back to my place. We had briefly discussed the lifestyle I was looking for, and when we got to my door, we kissed." A wisp of a smile crossed her face. "What a kiss that was. It was as if we put our entire soul into it, all the needs, all the desires.

When we came up for air, I realized that we had an opportunity to have everything each of us ever wanted. I told him that, if he entered my home, he would belong to me. He could walk out anytime, no questions asked, but if he stayed, I would control his life. He still can walk out, by the way."

"But he didn't leave."

Betts beamed. "Nope. We made love almost the entire night. I taught him exactly what I enjoy and he taught me a few things, too. Now he pleases me whenever and wherever I want, in whatever way I want. I know how to please him, but I frequently withhold pleasure because he loves my control over him." Carol motioned for Betts to turn over. "Listen," Betts said to her, "this towel is annoying me. Do you have any problem with nudity during a massage?"

"None at all," Carol said, and Betts let the towel slip to the floor. Carol began again with her legs.

"Go on," Debbie said. "I'm a bit embarrassed to admit it, but I'm fascinated by all this."

"Jerome quit his job the following morning and the rest is history. I don't know whether it would work for anyone else, but frankly I don't care. It's worked for Jerome and me for almost three years and I'm not about to change it."

"I'm pretty open-minded," Debbie said, "but I don't quite understand what this has to do with Paul and me."

"There's a little more you need to know about us before I can answer that question. Jerome and I also have an open marriage, although we're not exactly married. I lend him out from time to time and I take an occasional lover, too."

Debbie gasped, "You lend him out?"

"He's the most magnificent lover any woman could imagine. It's almost as though he reads minds. I taught him everything I know about pleasing me and he's taken it several steps further."

"Oh," was all Debbie could say, but she felt herself getting aroused. Her vaginal tissues swelled and moistened from the thought of the perfect lover making love to her.

"I can see you're not turned off by our way of doing things. Anyway, last evening your husband and I got to talking. He told me that he's looking for another couple to swap with, and when I explained how I live, he was really hot to play with me."

"He wants to swap. You and Paul, me and Jerome." Although Debbie had suspected as much, hearing it said aloud caused the air to whoosh from her lungs.

"I've put together what I believe is a pretty accurate picture of your marriage and I wanted a chance to talk to you about all this before tonight." Carol was working on Betts's abdominals, and watching her hands on Betts's white skin was making Debbie even more aroused. Not a good thing.

"How did this all start? You and Paul, I mean."

"Paul met us in front of the toy store, lamenting that it wasn't open. We started talking and he confessed that his sex life was really boring and he was looking for something to spice it up."

"He said that?"

"I told him about Jerome and me and he said that he might want to get together for a double date, so to speak."

Debbie's body stiffened. "He assumed I'd agree?"

"He described you as a little mousy thing who could use some love lessons and said that you'd agree if he told you to. His words, by the way." Betts gazed at her, then said, "I can see that you had no inkling of any of this."

"None," Debbie managed to say.

At that moment the timer went off and Betts sat up on the massage table. "Your turn."

While Carol went to a small sink in the corner and washed

her hands, Betts wrapped herself in her towel, climbed off the massage table, and settled in the plastic chair that Debbie had vacated. Debbie was so shocked by what Betts had said that she climbed onto the table and stretched out facedown without conscious thought. Carol returned, arranged the towel over her behind, and went to work on her legs. God, it did feel good.

"Now tell me about your marriage," Betts said.

"We've been married for almost six years. Paul runs an accounting firm, and I work for his company."

"No children?"

"No. Paul doesn't want any."

"Of course not. That way there's no one he has to share you with."

Debbie had never thought of it quite that way. "We're happy. We have lots of friends and that's about it."

"Are you happy?"

"Of course. I love our life together."

"Listen, Debbie, I'm not going to play shrink here, but I've met a lot of men in my life and I think I know your husband's type. I might be way off base here, but indulge me for a moment. Like Tracy said in that first session, don't answer, just think about the answers."

Carol's fingers were digging into the backs of Debbie's thighs and it was loosening her up a great deal. And all the talk about sex . . . "Okay."

"Do you really like your friends? Seriously."

If she were being honest, she'd have to admit that she liked a few of the couples, but for the most part, the group was shallow and boring. Betts continued, "Does he please you in bed?"

Of course he does. "No knee-jerk reactions now," Betts said. "Does he please you in bed? When was that last time you came?"

When was the last time she had climaxed? She couldn't remember.

"Does the idea of being with Jerome while I'm with Paul excite you?"

Did it? She'd never been with anyone but Paul, and Betts painted Jerome as some kind of sex guru. She would certainly love some really great sex. She thought about her life. She had been settling for Paul's idea of sex for a long time. She'd been settling for Paul's idea of everything for a long time. How had it evolved to this stage? Paul wasn't a monster, but he wanted things his way. He had a right to have things his way, didn't he? He was the man, the primary breadwinner.

Her mother had always told her that it was the wife's job to satisfy her husband by doing whatever he wanted. Did the fact that her father had run off when she was two years old have any bearing on her mother's teaching? There were so many ramifications of what Debbie had just learned.

She thought back to when she and Paul met. They had hit it off quickly and dated for almost a year. In the beginning they had been equals, made decisions together. As time passed, however, it had just gotten easier to agree with him on everything, to please him in every way. That way she didn't have to think, didn't have to argue.

Debbie felt Carol move to her back, clever fingers finding tight muscles and relaxing her body, giving her mind freedom to wander into areas of thought she'd never considered before.

"Debbie?" Betts said.

"Sorry, Betts, you're giving me a lot to think about."

"If you want to talk about it, great, but there's a more immediate issue that you need to consider. Paul wants the four of us to get together tonight in the hot tub, to play."

"I don't think so," Debbie said.

"Don't dismiss the benefits out of hand. I don't offer Jerome to just anyone, and maybe my being with Paul for one night isn't as much of an issue as you might think. Maybe I'm wrong. Be as honest as you can. How does all this talk make you feel?"

"I'm not sure what to think."

"I can understand that. Remember that Jerome and I are from the Midwest and we'll probably never see each other again. Maybe you need to talk about some of this. If not, I'll butt out and we can all go our separate ways. I won't do anything with Paul without your wholehearted consent."

"Please don't butt out," Debbie said, as Carol indicated that she should turn over. "It's just really difficult to talk about any of this. There are so many things going around in my head that it's impossible to sort them all out." She settled on her back, her towel covering her from underarms to thighs, and Carol began with her arms and shoulders.

"For right now, your marriage isn't the question. Tell me how you feel about being with Jerome."

Debbie was surprised to realize that, while an hour ago Jerome made her uncomfortable, now the thought of being with him made her knees quake. She swallowed hard and looked at Betts. "The idea turns me on."

Debbie was surprised to see a smile on Betts's face. "I thought so. God," she said, "I'm so good at this, I should get a TV show."

Debbie backpedaled. "I don't know how I feel about you with Paul. It's just . . ."

"It's just that you want your pleasure. If you had choices, what do you really want? Hours of oral sex? Orgasms whenever and for however long you want?"

A shudder ran through Debbie's body. Orgasms. Yes, that was what she wanted. She felt her juices flow and her nipples tighten against the roughness of the towel. That was what she wanted. Once she had that, everything else would follow. She moved restlessly on the table.

"Carol," Betts said, "when's your next appointment?"

"Not for half an hour," she said, lifting her hands from Debbie's body.

"Good," Betts said, signing the receipt for the massages, "why don't you take a break?"

Then, as Debbie lay on her back, she heard the door close behind Carol. She suspected what Betts had in mind and she couldn't let it happen. Could she? "Hungry?" Betts said softly, her mouth next to Debbie's ear.

She couldn't deny it. "Yes," she whispered.

"I can fix that if you'll let me, but if I make you uncomfortable, just say so and we'll shower and dress."

"I'm not into women," Debbie said.

"I know, and I'm not either as a rule, although I've been with a few, but that's not what this is all about. It's about orgasms." Her hands began on Debbie's thighs, kneading her flesh. "Tell me to stop at any time and I will."

The atmosphere was so erotic that even though Debbie would never have dreamed of being with a woman an hour ago, it all seemed possible now. Orgasms. Debbie relaxed as Betts's hands worked on her muscles. Her thumbs were on the insides of her thighs, pushing closer and closer to her pussy beneath the towel. "Can I get rid of this?" Betts asked.

Surrendering to her feelings while telling her brain to shut up, Debbie nodded and Betts pulled the cloth from her body. "Close your eyes," Betts said. "Imagine whatever gives you pleasure." Then her fingers were on Debbie's nipples, pulling, squeezing, arousing. Heat flowed through her like liquid fire, settling between her thighs. Betts was silent, in no way reminding her that the hands giving her pleasure were a woman's.

Hands. Betts's were everywhere. She knew all the places that not only felt wonderful but pushed her closer to the crest. Fingers now played with her vaginal lips, pulling, then pinching slightly. Fingertips caressed, finding crevices and creases soaked with her juices.

Empty. She needed to be filled. She pictured a huge erect cock. Jerome's? Why had that thought jumped into her mind. He was such a big man that Debbie wondered whether he was built like that all over. Then fingers were sliding into her, one then two then three, stretching her wider than she had ever remembered. It was almost too much. Almost. Her body throbbed, her pulse pounding in her ears, her breathing hot and rasping.

Close. She was so close. She needed. She craved the carnal stimulation of those hands. Then the wonderful fingers found her clit, and with a few well-placed strokes, she felt orgasm overwhelm her. Her body spasmed, her back arched, and she couldn't keep the long, loud moan from echoing through the small room. "Oh, God," she cried later, when her body had calmed and Betts was back sitting in her chair.

"How long has it been?" Betts asked softly.

"Forever."

"I'm glad I could give that to you," she said, winking, "but you're really not my type. This is my week for blondes."

Their laughter was cleansing and made everything all right. "Quite a learning experience," Debbie said.

"I'll bet. Now we have to decide what to do about later."

They talked for a long time.

Instead of going back to her room, where she suspected Paul would grill her on her afternoon with Betts, Debbie found a quiet corner of the lobby and settled into a wood-framed chair. She realized quite quickly that she wasn't bothered by the sex with Betts. She had no problems with her heterosexuality. She was very bothered, however, by her new insight into her relationship with her husband. How had she let it go on so long?

She thought about the fact that she acceded to all of his

wishes and in doing so had become smaller and smaller. She had no will of her own anymore. How had she not seen it? It had become a pattern and she had allowed it. She and Paul had become—what did they call it?—codependent. She felt smaller and smaller, and by helping her to be small, Paul felt big. It seemed so obvious now.

Had she always been like this? She thought about high school. She'd been a member of the student senate and had been urged by some of her friends to run for class president. She hadn't been interested in the extra work but she might have won. She had value. She'd worked for a few years before she and Paul had met, and she'd been given steady raises and a promotion to assistant office manager. She'd had value then, too. Even now she had some power at work, although her job at Paul's firm was a very minor one. Why was it so different at home?

If her marriage had become some kind of codependency, some dance of inferiority and put down, whose fault was that? Not Paul's alone. Didn't she have to accept some responsibility? After all, she had allowed it to spiral this far downward.

What did Paul think of her? Did he really believe that she was a total dunce, a clumsy dolt who couldn't do anything right? She could ask him, of course, but she quickly realized that she wasn't willing to confront him yet.

As she sat, she saw Tracy walk through the lobby and glanced at her watch. It was almost five o'clock and she realized that the last forum of the afternoon must be over. She should really go back to the room, but then what? When Tracy nodded a greeting, Debbie motioned her over. "Have you got a minute to talk?" she asked.

"Sure," Tracy said, and dropped into a chair diagonally across a small side table. "What can I do for you?"

Debbie took a few minutes to describe her marriage and her doubts about her husband's attitude. She omitted the part about the swapping and just filled Tracy in on their relationship. In telling it, it sounded so ugly. Was it? Tracy only interrupted once to ask whether Paul had ever gotten physically violent. Debbie assured her that Paul had never struck her. "But he is emotionally abusive," Tracy said.

Debbie started at the use of those words, then forced herself to admit, "Yes, I guess he is. I don't know how much of this is really my fault, though."

Tracy took a deep breath. "Let's dispose of one thing right off. Determining who's at fault is a pointless exercise. Suppose you come to the conclusion that it's your fault, or his. Does that change anything? How you got to where you are is of little consequence, except to learn how not to do it again. The question really is where do you go from here." She leaned forward and took Debbie's hands in hers. "I know very little about the kind of marriage you describe, and I think some of your description is colored by your feelings. Without talking with your husband, I have no clue what the real story is. Actually, neither do you. I can tell you a bit about my marriage, and I think it might help."

Tracy seemed completely comfortable telling Debbie about her husband Andrew and his extracurricular activities. She described her feelings when she saw Andrew with Sharon. "I was lucky, I guess. He really gave me no choice but to leave, so I never wondered whether I should shoulder some of the blame. To me, at that moment, it didn't matter. I ran, and licked my wounds."

Debbie thought about Tracy's situation for a while. While her husband had played around behind Tracy's back, Debbie was sure that Paul would never do that. Not behind her back, but in front of her face? As she thought about it, she realized that Paul had been dropping not-so-subtle hints about something like that for several weeks. Then he'd been talking about his friends Gerry and Darcy, how sexy Gerry was.

She took a deep breath. Although the long-term problem of her marriage was important, she had a concern that was more immediate. Did she have to go along with what he wanted for the evening? Did she want to? "Can you answer a question for me?"

"Sure."

"Isn't it a wife's job to make her husband happy, to satisfy him?"

"It is, but it's also a husband's job to satisfy his wife." When Debbie looked surprised, Tracy continued, "Why is it the job of one partner more than another?"

Why indeed? "I don't know. I'm afraid I don't know much of anything right now." What should she do about later?

"Do you have to know something 'right now'? Let me make a suggestion. Take a few weeks and just observe. Look at your interactions with Paul through eyes colored by your new understandings. The most important thing you have to do right now is figure out what you want, and until you know what you have, you can't know that."

"What about dealing with Paul's—unusual desires?"

"I don't know exactly what you're talking about, but if it gives both of you pleasure, go for it. If not, say so."

"I know he wants to."

"His desires aren't any more—or less—important than yours. If you care about each other, you should each want what's good for the other." Tracy's smile was warm. "Easy to say, difficult to do."

Debbie nodded and for the first time in more than an hour she didn't feel frantic to figure things out. She didn't have to do anything yet. "Observe. That's a great idea. Thanks, Tracy. I think I'll do just that." The two women talked for a few more moments and then Tracy left to return to her room. Debbie thought about what she had said, then stood and walked up the stairs to see Paul.

Observe. That's what Tracy had advised and it was sound advice. She had no idea what her marriage had become, much less whose fault it was. Tracy was right again. Fault didn't matter. Where was she going? Where were they going? Did she love Paul? Thinking about it in the abstract, she realized that she hadn't a clue. Observe.

She dipped her card key and opened the room door. "Where the heck have you been? I was getting really worried," Paul said.

"I'm sorry. I got a bit sidetracked."

"If you're going to get sidetracked, let me know, will you?"

"Sure. I'm really sorry." That phrase echoed in her mind. How many times a day did she say it? *I'm really sorry.*

"That's fine. Why don't you change for dinner and then we'll go to the evening session?"

"I'm not sure I want to go," Debbie said, interested in Paul's reaction. She really did want to see what he had planned for the evening, but she just wanted to watch their interaction.

"Don't be silly. Of course you do. We planned on it." He walked over and patted her on the fanny. "Now hustle into something decent to wear and let's get going."

Debbie looked down at her long-sleeved shirt, jeans, and leather vest. "This isn't decent?"

"We have a date with Betts and Jerome after the forum. You certainly don't want to go looking like that."

She remembered what she had been wearing, or not wearing, earlier with Betts but said nothing. Observe. As she changed her clothes, she thought about their interchange. Everything Paul had said had put her down, either overtly or subtly. She wasn't dressed poorly, and if she didn't want to go to the forum, it was her right to say no. How often did he say, *Don't be silly?* She wasn't silly. Or hopeless. Or difficult. She wasn't any of those versions of *Don't be silly* that he used. Speech habits or subtle attempts to make her feel smaller?

Observe. She would do just that, and make decisions based on what she wanted.

Chapter

14

Elise was feeling wonderful when she walked into Diana's Lingerie Shop shortly after dinner Saturday evening. That afternoon she and Bob had had mind-blowing sex, the kind they'd had when they were first married. Maybe she hadn't climaxed but something inside her believed that it would happen eventually. She wasn't a dried-up old woman after all. All the good things that were said about sex after fifty must be true. It could be wonderful, and she and Bob had just proved that. Now she wanted to do something really nice for him, and Diana was just the person to help her. She'd shooed Bob off to their room, saying that she had an errand to run. He probably suspected what she was doing, but she wanted to do this alone.

"I want to buy something Bob would like to see me in," she said, as Diana approached. That evening Diana was wearing a sheer midnight blue peignoir over a white teddy. Dark blue hose and silver high-heeled sandals completed her outfit.

"You don't want something like this, do you?" Diana said, motioning to her own outfit.

Sweat began to trickle down the middle of Elise's back and

all her resolve trickled away with it. "No." She huffed out a breath. "I can't."

"Of course you can't," Diana said with an indulgent smile. "You're not ready for this kind of outfit." She hugged Elise's shoulders. "Honey, you have to learn to walk before you can run." She led Elise between a few tables to a rack of night-gowns in larger sizes. She checked a few colored tags, then pulled a hanger from the brass bar and draped a black satin gown over her arm. "Something like this is walking."

The gown was demure, the satin cut high over the breasts and falling, full to the floor beneath a slightly empire waist. "This looks fabulous over it," she said, adding a long open lace jacket to the gown. "How about going in the next room and trying the two on?"

Elise stared at the garments and pictured rolls of flab flopping over the top. She couldn't look at herself that way. As her head shook, Diana said, "Just try. You don't have to buy them but you need to do this, if not for yourself, for your husband." She draped the two pieces over Elise's arm, all but pushed her into the hall, and aimed her at the try-on room next door with a slight shove.

The adjacent room was another small meeting room but Diana had set up screens for changing and several full-length mirrors. Diana's selections still over her arm, Elise stood and looked at herself, dressed in a black sweatshirt over black sweatpants, sneakers, and socks. Although the clothes were baggy and totally concealed her body, every extra pound was visible to her, all fifty of them. She held the nightgown in front of her, grimaced, and wondered what size it was. She found two tags. One stated the outrageous price; the other, which should have given the size, was solid green. Just green, no numbers. She frowned, then checked the labels inside but found that the one with the size had been neatly removed. That was odd.

With a sigh, she stepped behind one of the screens and pulled off her shoes, socks, and outer clothing, then reluctantly removed her oversized bra. After a minute's hesitation, she slipped the gown over her head. She adjusted the garment, lifting her large breasts into the cups in the front and looked down past the spaghetti straps. Well, she told herself, it doesn't look too bad from here. Barefoot, she walked into the room filled with mirrors.

She looked, then looked away, then looked again. She wasn't a fashion model, even for larger sizes, but it wasn't as bad as she had thought it would be. She turned left and right, watching the gown's skirt swirl. She reached down and felt the hem. There was a slightly weighted band around the bottom that helped it flow when she moved. She held up her arms and looked at the flab drooping beneath. She had always hated her arms and all of their jiggly fat. She closed her eyes but the image remained.

Okay, she told herself, give it all a chance. She stepped behind the screen and slipped the jacket on. As she looked in the mirror again, she saw that the jacket was long sleeved, made of black lace roses. There was a small frog fastening at the waist and she pushed the black satin toggle through the loop.

The jacket hid her arms and, together with the heart-shaped top of the gown, outlined her ample cleavage. She usually let her short gray-streaked hair fall forward around her face, but now she finger-combed it back and fluffed it out. Determined, she grabbed the small makeup case from her pocketbook and put some lipstick on. She had often wondered why she carried it, since she wore lipstick so seldom, but now she was pleased with the way she looked.

"Not bad," she said out loud. She checked the tags on the jacket and found two, one with a price and one plain yellow. No size there either. She smiled. Diana's a clever lady. She quickly put her street clothes back on and carried the two pieces back into Diana's sales room.

"I don't think I have to ask how you liked them," Diana said, as she saw Elise approach. "You look well satisfied."

"I am. There aren't sizes on either of them," she said. "They're color coded, aren't they?"

"Of course. When I started shopping for myself, I found I was appalled at having to buy clothes with big numbers. They call them half-size or stuck a W on the end, but to me those numbers always screamed FAT LADY. So when I started to carry lingerie in larger sizes, I decided to remove the numbers and just use colors."

"So what size did I just buy?"

Diana just grinned. "Not a chance. I'll never tell and you shouldn't ask. Just decide whether you like yourself and, more importantly, whether your husband likes you. The look on his face when he sees you will tell you everything."

Nodding, Elise handed Diana her credit card.

Since they weren't going to the evening forum, Elise knew Bob would be in their room. With her package under her arm, she made her way up to the third floor and slid her card key into the lock. As she entered, Bob turned. "Hi, sweet." She watched his eyes flick to her pink-wrapped bundle, but he remained silent. Wordless and unsure, Elise crossed to the bathroom and closed the door behind her. Before what little courage she had deserted her, she yanked off her clothes and put the gown and jacket on. She freshened her lipstick and ran a comb through her hair before slowly opening the door.

Bob turned from the TV and just stared. Finally, when Elise thought she would shatter into a thousand pieces, she heard Bob's hoarse voice. "You look wonderful. Just wonderful."

Letting out the long breath she had been holding since she'd walked out of the bathroom, she said, "Really?"

She could see Bob's Adam's apple bounce as he swallowed. "Oh, yes, really."

Elise watched his eyes as they ranged over her body as though she were naked and stacked. "It's not—"

"It's everything." He opened his arms and she slowly walked into them.

Tish thought about her future with Owen for a long time. During dinner he commented on how quiet she was being, but she just said that she was thinking about the weekend. Instead of going to the Power and Control forum, they spent the evening watching movies, including an X-rated one Owen had rented. Although her churning mind didn't leave her enough peace to watch much of the film, she had to admit that this one at least had a story. After the movie ended, Owen was so hot that they made hard, quick love. Spent, they lay together, then Tish rolled to one side and lay beside Owen, holding his hand. "I think we have to talk."

"Phew," Owen said, "that sounds ominous."

Tish stared at the ceiling. "I've been doing a lot of thinking and I'm not sure that we should get married."

Owen popped up onto one elbow. "You're not sure?" There was an edge to his voice. "You've been trying to get me to ask you for months. I asked and now you're not sure?"

"No, I'm not. Let me try to explain. I love you. That's not in doubt."

Owen let out a breath. "You had me worried for a moment there."

"I have to say a few things so let me get this out. First, I haven't been honest with you this weekend. I set out to get you to ask me to marry you. I've done everything I could to show you that I could be everything you could want."

"You did," Owen said, looking a bit baffled.

"The woman you made love to earlier wasn't me and might

not ever be me again. I don't ever want to be slapped again, even in sex play. And I won't be made to feel like a hooker. I never was and I don't like the idea that you think of me that way."

"I understand. I guess I did get pretty carried away."

"It's not just that, I'm afraid. I have a pretty firm idea about where I want to be in five years." She didn't mention that her thoughts had crystalized after her conversation with Tracy. He might not want to hear that she had discussed the problem with a stranger. "The more I consider, the more I realize that having children is very important to me. I also realize that to you marriage isn't much of a change from the way things are now. I'd have a different last name but nothing much would be different. That's not how I see things."

Owen remained silent so Tish continued. "I want to feel like a forever unit, moving toward my personal goal of being a mother. You've said often that you don't want to even consider children. That's fine for you, but not for me."

"I'm not sure I know what you're trying to tell me."

"You're very important to me. I love you as much as any woman could love any man. I want us to be forever. But if that means that I have to give up my dreams of a house full of kids, then I'm not sure I want to be with you." Saying the words out loud made them sound so real that they terrified Tish, yet she realized that she meant them.

Owen looked totally shocked. "Are you saying we're through?"

God, that sounded so harsh. "No, I don't think so. Here's what I'd like to do. I want us to take three months and decide what we really want. No talk of anything during that time. We'll just try to decide what each of us really wants. I need to find out whether, if at the end of those three months you say no kids"—she swallowed hard—"whether I need to leave and try to find someone who wants what I want."

"You say you love me, yet you'd leave me and date other men?"

"I need to make a life, Owen."

"This sounds like blackmail. Kids or I'm out the door."

That's exactly what Tracy had said. "It's not blackmail. I'm trying to be as honest as I can. I've finally admitted to myself that you have a right to your feelings about having children. I'm not about to make you a reluctant father."

"What happens during those three months?"

"I guess from the outside nothing much changes. On the inside we both think and make some hard choices. I need to find out whether having children is important enough to give you up. You need to figure out how much of your reluctance to create a family is knee jerk and how much is deeply important to you."

"Three months?"

"We can make it more or less time, if you really think that would matter."

With a sigh, Owen said, "Okay, three months."

At seven-fifteen Tracy sat on the edge of her bed. The Power and Control forum was the most difficult one for her to lead. Yes, Dave and she had played once, and she'd read books about power games, but she was unsure of her own attitudes about control activities.

As she had done three times before that day, she dialed Kim's number. "So how's it gone since I last talked to you, Trace?" her sister asked.

"Actually I'm really nervous about lots of things."

"I know this forum is giving you trouble, but we both know you'll be fine. What else?"

"I had to give some serious advice to a few women today and I just hope I got it right."

"I know you told them what you felt based on what we discussed and your own good sense. What's the problem?"

"What if I encouraged someone to do something and it ruins their marriage? That scares me to death."

"It scares me sometimes, too," Kim admitted, "but when people ask for advice, most of the time they already know what they should do or what they feel and are merely asking for validation."

"I know," Tracy said with a sigh. She and Kim had discussed this problem over and over in the weeks before the weekend.

"Tell me what you said."

In a few sentences she outlined the problems she'd discussed with Tish, Elise, and Debbie. "What the hell do I know about the problems of overweight women? Sure, I have a few extra pounds, but Elise has at least fifty. I suggested that Elise talk to Diana."

"Great idea. She's so sane about the body image thing. What about the woman with the domineering husband?"

"I didn't know what to say, so I suggested that she merely observe their relationship. She has no idea who's responsible for the pit they've dug for themselves so what could I tell her?"

"Sounds like you did good. And the one who wants to get married and have kids?"

"I told her that she has to decide what she wants out of her boyfriend. I used your trick and asked, 'If you thought he was never going to want children, what would you do?' She didn't really know. She thought that when he asked her, it would all fall into place. Now she's realized that, although he has proposed, he doesn't seem to want the same future that she has in mind. I think they both have some serious thinking to do and I told Tish that. I suggested that she give both of them a specific amount of time to decide what they want, then fish or cut bait."

"Seems to me that you handled everything just fine, Trace."

"It sounds like that to me, too, but it still terrifies me."

"I know. Me, too. How's Dave?"

"I've barely seen him. Actually he's been avoiding me," she said, resigned to having to admit her failure to her sister.

"Want to tell me what's up?"

Throughout the weekend Tracy had been thinking about Dave and what must be going through his mind. "Dave dropped me like a hot potato about three weeks ago."

"What?" Kim gasped. "I thought you two had a real thing going."

"We did. I think I'm in love with him, and in the heat of passion I may have said the words. Sis, I think I blew it. As I talked to Tish about Owen, I started to understand where Dave's head must be right about now. He's always been involved in short-term relationships, anywhere from several weeks to several months. All superficial. I think that we got too tight too fast. I think it scared him to death."

"And you?"

"I thought it was for real."

"What are you going to do about it?"

"Do? There's not much I can do. You and I have talked about this topic lots of times. The person who's less involved has all the power. I can't pull Dave closer and he can, and has, pushed me away."

"You can't pull him closer but you can lure him closer. You've become the sexpert so do something about it."

"I can't. It's just not like me. I'm not a siren and I'm not a lurer."

"Trace, you are whatever you want to be in this life. Remember that you only go around once. If there's something out there that you want, go after it. You might not get another chance."

"What if he doesn't want to be lured?"

"Then what have you lost?"

"My pride?"

"Pride is cold comfort," Kim said.

"He doesn't love me."

"Of course not, and you don't love him. Not yet."

Tracy's voice was almost inaudible when she said, "I don't?"

"Listen, Trace, love isn't something that can happen in an instant, all those romance novels to the contrary not withstanding. Love is only real when you've had time to learn who the other person really is. I'm no expert on the proper definition of love but I think I've learned this much.

"To be sure of love, you have to be pretty sure that, barring something truly unforeseen, whatever happens in the future your feelings won't change. There will be bad times and you have to know yourself and your potential partner well enough to know how he will react when those come. You need to have been together when he has a terrible case of the flu or a serious reversal at work."

"I guess," Tracy said softly.

"You can be in lust easily and that's a great reason to fuck your brains out. Making life choices requires more than that."

"So you're saying I'm in lust, not in love."

"I guess I am, and you're probably sending vibes that Dave doesn't like so he ran for the hills. Trace, I put myself out there as some kind of expert on relationships, and I'm not really. Every relationship is different just as the two people who make up the relationship are different. Why don't you let Dave know that you want to get to know him, in and out of bed, and maybe in six months or a year you both will know more about things."

"Kim, I'm glad you're my sister."

Tracy could hear the catch in Kim's voice. "And I'm glad you're mine."

Tracy took several minutes that she didn't have to consider

her sister's words. It was so easy to give advice to perfect strangers but so difficult to step outside yourself and see your own problems for what they were and figure out what to do. Kim was right about everything. Love, lust, it all needed time to grow.

Dave was certainly worth fighting for. She checked her watch then called the front desk and plotted with Meg for several minutes.

The Power and Control forum began more easily than Tracy had imagined. Only about half of the weekend attendees were in the room so she suggested that everyone move closer. She noticed Debbie and a soft-looking man with curly hair who must have been her husband sitting beside an extraordinary-looking couple she'd noticed earlier, a gigantic man with a totally bald head and a black-haired woman with mammoth cleavage in a revealing deep green latex stretch suit.

As Kim had, Tracy began with a description of power games, safe words, and the responsibilities of the two participants. She listed the benefits to both partners of the kind of communication that can go on in such situations. Then she asked whether anyone in the audience had played such games and a few tentative hands were raised.

"Tracy," a man in the middle of the room said. He was of average height, with a pointed chin and slightly projecting ears. "My wife Suzanne and I have been to a few of these weekends with your sister and each time I've volunteered both myself and my wife to help folks understand control." He motioned to his wife, a striking redhead with a bright smile and intelligent eyes, who stood up and said, "Frank is my husband, my lover, and my master." She was wearing a sweater in soft maize and a short black skirt with dark stockings and low-heeled shoes. She was also wearing a leather band around her throat and narrow leather wristlets. "I'm his willing and loving slave and it's the only way I can imagine living. It wouldn't work for most people, but for us, it's fabulous."

There was a gasp from the audience. "I can't thank you enough," Tracy said as the buzz quieted, "for letting us all share your experiences. I know we all have questions but you say you've done this before so why don't you just tell us about it."

Suzanne smiled openly. "Frank and I met about nine years ago. We're both attorneys in the Midwest. I'd rather not reveal exactly where for obvious reasons."

"Actually," Frank said, "most of the members of our firm know about our lifestyle but I'm not sure how our clients would view it."

"That's why we come here," Suzanne said. "The freedom to just be ourselves out in the open is great."

"You think clients would give you trouble?" Tracy asked.

"Why take the chance?" Frank said. He turned to Suzanne and said, "Tell them about our first date."

Suzanne grinned. "We were working on a case together, and after a long evening in the law library, we went out to eat. We ended up at my place and, well, one thing led to another. While we made love, Frank grabbed my wrists and stretched my arms over my head. As he held me, he forced me to take all the things he could give to my body. It was, and still is, a fabulous luxury."

Tracy remembered the evening Dave had done that and how excited she'd become.

"I went nuts," Suzanne continued, "and, well, the sex had never been better for either of us."

"The rest," Frank said, "is history. Although she's my slave and will pleasure me at any moment and in any way I like, I often order her to take from me."

A man at the side of the room asked, "How does it all work? You two don't seem, ah . . ."

"Kinky?" Frank's chuckle was almost indulgent. "We're not. In public we're just like anyone else, except when I choose to give Suzanne an order. In that case, she'll obey without question."

"Like what?"

"If you're prone to be embarrassed, look the other way." He unzipped his fly and pulled out his flaccid penis. He pointed to the floor and snapped his fingers. Without hesitation, Suzanne knelt, took his cock in her hand, and opened her mouth. "Never mind," he said.

There was a hum through the audience while Frank zipped his pants and Suzanne stood up. With a grin he said, "You can look now." Tracy grinned as well, aware that no one had looked away.

A woman at one side of the room spoke up. "That's degrading."

Tracy held her hand up to still the budding arguments. "Degrading is in the eye of the beholder. If both parties enjoy an activity and freely agree to it, it's none of anyone else's business. Frank and Suzanne have found a lifestyle that works for them. Who are we to criticize?" When the buzzing continued, Tracy added, "If any of you want to leave, please do so. This isn't for everyone, maybe not for any but a small minority of couples, but it's not up to anyone to judge." When no one rose to leave, she said, "Okay then, let's ask questions and not make pronouncements."

The woman who had made the previous comment said, "I'm really sorry. I think that was a knee-jerk reaction to something that makes me very uncomfortable."

"It made me uncomfortable at first, too," Suzanne said. "It took a long time for me to accept that this was what I wanted and that it didn't make me a bad person. I work at least twelve hours a day. I'm a criminal defense attorney, and although many of my clients are good, upstanding people in bad situations, many of the people I take *pro bono* are the scum of the earth. When I get home, I want to let everything go. No decisions, no thinking really. Frank makes all the rules and all the decisions."

"Like what?" a man asked.

"Like what to have for dinner, what movie we're going to see."

Frank laughed out loud. "By what to have for dinner, Suzanne means what reservations to make."

There was a gleam in Suzanne's eye when she said, "Of course, master."

"I decide on sex. How, when, where. She merely does what she's told. There are clothing rules in the house as well. She never wears underwear anywhere, even now." He turned her around until her back was to the audience, grabbed her short skirt, and quickly flipped it up to reveal her naked buttocks. "I decide what she'll wear each day to work. No panty hose ever."

"What if she doesn't want to wear what you pick?" a woman asked.

"That's too bad," Frank said, then winked. "However, I have exceptional taste. We shop together and I decide what she may buy."

A man in the back called out, "That's the part of this I like." There was a burst of laughter.

Tracy decided to ask a question of her own. "Part of this forum is about pain as pleasure. Do you two do anything along those lines?"

"Occasionally," Suzanne said. "He likes to slap me across the butt and thighs sometimes."

"That's okay with you?" Tracy continued.

"I love giving him pleasure, and at first that was the reason I liked it when he spanked me. We talked and decided that my doing it for him wasn't quite enough. I finally admitted to myself that I got really hot when he demonstrated his dominance like that."

"My name's Mona," a woman said as she stood up. "My husband Josh loves to spank me when I've been a bad girl." She beamed at the thirtyish man in the seat beside her. "I'm bad a lot."

"You really like it?" someone asked.

"I love it. When my ass gets hot, it spreads to my . . . other parts. It's really exciting. Actually I'm getting hungry just talking about it."

Paul leaned close and whispered into Debbie's ear. "This whole discussion is making me really hot. Did Betts tell you about Jerome?"

"Yes," Debbie said, aroused as well.

"Good. Now be quiet. I want to listen."

The woman named Mona sat down and a woman in her forties, with graying hair and a slight double chin, stood up. "If you've never laid a man across your lap and spanked his bottom while he holds his cock in his hand, you haven't lived." The man beside her yanked at her hand and pulled her back to her seat while the audience tittered.

Tracy stood up and held her hands up for silence. "Let me say one very important thing. We're talking about consensual activities and it's important that you all understand exactly what a consenting adult is. First, a consenting adult understands that no means no and stop means stop. Now. No questions or exceptions. Certainly, after one person vetoes an activity, you can discuss what might work better, but everything stops. No whining or begging, unless it's an accepted part of the game." There was another titter in the audience.

"There's another side to being a consenting adult, however. A consenting adult understands that he or she has, not just the right, but the responsibility to say no if things get even a little uncomfortable. Unless you've decided that it gives you a great deal of pleasure to do something only to make your partner happy, don't do it. A relationship is an equal partnership, each giving and taking in equal measure."

Debbie thought about her marriage. It hadn't been an equal partnership for many years. She gave and Paul took. After her conversation with Tracy she'd decided not to worry about whose fault it was, and merely concentrate on what was happening and she didn't like what she saw.

The forum continued for another half hour. Debbie was amazed at how many people freely admitted to doing unusual things in the bedroom. Throughout, Paul's grip on her hand tightened until she had to shake her hand free. "This is why you came this weekend, isn't it?" Debbie said, when the forum ended.

"I knew you'd be as intrigued as I am by this and by couples like Betts and Jerome. I hoped that you'd realize that lots of people enjoy all kinds of unusual stuff."

Consenting. "I don't know whether I would."

"Don't be difficult. Just keep an open mind and let's talk to Betts and Jerome. They've made it work." He stood and walked toward the rear door just behind the other couple.

"So they have," Debbie said.

They sat over drinks in the Saratoga Bar, with Betts and Paul doing all of the talking. Debbie was deep in thought and slowly she found herself getting angry. He'd engineered this whole thing just as he'd been engineering their lives for years. And she'd gone along with everything. Wimp? Difficult? Silly? She had been for a long time. Tracy had suggested that she just observe and she had. She didn't need weeks to have her eyes opened. She saw it all clearly already.

As Paul and Betts talked, Jerome leaned over and, as
though reading her mind, whispered, "You can be whatever
you want."

"I can, can't I?" she said softly. I don't have to know what I
want from here on, I can just take this one evening and do
something just because. An experiment of sorts.

"How about adjourning to the hot tub?" Betts suggested.
"Bathing suits optional."

"Sounds good to us," Paul said.

Us, Debbie thought. "It sounds like fun to me, too."

"If no one wants bathing suits, we can go right there. They
have towels."

"Good idea," Paul said. "We don't need bathing suits."

"My underwear will suffice," Debbie said, to hear Paul's reaction.

"Be real, Debbie. We don't need clothes. These are our
friends."

Friends. Right. Well, after all, Betts had seen all there was
to see of her, and more, and Jerome . . .

The pool and hot tub area was deserted as they were sure it
would be. Hot and steamy, the sizable room smelled of chlorine and their voices echoed off the tile walls. The pool was
large, and when Debbie leaned down to touch the water, she
found it cool. The spa was rectangular and meant to hold
about ten. As Betts pushed the button, the water bubbled and
swirled. Unselfconsciously Betts and Jerome pulled off their
clothes.

Where Betts's body was small and tight, Jerome's was hard
and muscular, showing that he must work out for hours a day.
Biceps as large around as Betts's thighs, flat abs that positively
rippled, thighs with muscle definition that a bodybuilder
would envy. He looked like a commercial for a new brand of
workout equipment. Debbie couldn't help but gaze at his
now-flaccid cock. Even nonerect it was enormous, probably

five or six inches long. Trying to look away, Debbie found herself imagining how it would feel.

As Jerome dropped his jeans on a poolside chair, he pulled out several small packets and dropped them beside the tub. They had brought plastic cups of wine and they put them on the pool's edge as well. Debbie watched Paul's eyes as he gazed first at Betts's voluptuous naked body, then at Jerome. She wondered what he was thinking. Was he looking forward to getting his hands on Betts or concerned about Jerome's hands on her? Tit for tat, she thought, then giggled at her choice of words.

"What are you laughing at?" Paul asked as he removed his jeans.

"Nothing," she said, pulling her sweater off over her head.

"You know I hate it when you do that. There should be no secrets between us."

"Of course not," she said, an enigmatic smile on her face.

When they were all nude, Debbie climbed into the hot churning water and settled between Betts and Jerome. Paul sat close beside Betts. Debbie could see from the movements of his shoulders that he was stroking Betts's thigh.

Betts and Paul talked about insignificant things for several minutes while Debbie rested her head on the lip of the tub. Suddenly she felt a hand on her leg. Since Paul was still beside Betts, she knew it was Jerome. She caught Betts's eye, and when she nodded slightly, Debbie relaxed. She was going to let whatever happened happen.

She closed her eyes and concentrated on Jerome's hand, kneading her flesh. She had wanted to touch his magnificent body ever since he'd taken off his clothes. "You work out," she said, her voice just strong enough to be heard over the sound of the bubbles.

"I do some exercises. Why do you ask?"

"You don't look like the type who fishes for compliments," Debbie said, sounding slightly flirtatious.

"Okay," he admitted. "You like what you see." It wasn't a question, but a statement of established fact.

As she said, "Oh, yes," she felt his hand take hers and place it on his quads. Eyes still closed, she dug her fingers into his thigh muscle, unable to do more than just dent the skin. With his other hand, he stroked her arm.

Her hand roamed his body, unable to find a soft place anywhere. Anywhere, including the hard shaft of flesh that projected from his groin. Did Paul know what she was doing? Did he care? Did she? When her hands circled his turgid cock, Jerome whispered, "Not yet. Betts has taught me well. I'd get a great deal of joy out of pleasuring you."

Debbie lifted her head and looked across the hot tub. Obviously Betts and Paul were doing more than just talking. Shoulders were moving and Paul's eyes were heavy lidded. Betts caught her eye and a small smile teased the corners of her mouth. She knew exactly what was going on, on both sides of the hot tub. He's yours if you want him, she mouthed.

Debbie did want him. As she had that afternoon, she wanted sexual satisfaction. Earlier it had been a woman who had given it to her, and it had been physically complete, but the fact that it had been with a woman diminished it somehow. Here was a man, however, eager to give to her.

When his fingers found her nipples beneath the warm water and squeezed one between his thumb and index finger, she allowed her head to fall back. What had Suzanne said? Just taking can be incredibly luxurious. Not caring about what went on between her husband and Betts, Debbie gave herself to the pleasures that Jerome's talented mouth and fingers could bring her. He lifted one breast almost out of the water and sucked the erect nipple into his mouth.

Then he kissed her lips, his tongue slowly sliding deep into her mouth until, with a deep exhale, she pressed her entire naked, wet body against his. It was a kiss like the ones best described by the authors of romance novels, totally engulfing, fully involving. His hand cupped the back of her head as his mouth moved and took. And gave. She found that she was more aroused than she had been in a very long time. Her vaginal flesh was swollen, hot and so wet, with none of the sensations having anything to do with the hot water.

Jerome turned her toward the tile wall, spreading her legs on the seat until a jet of water pulsed against her pussy. He propped her back against his chest and held her while the throbbing water created rhythmic spasms throughout her body. "Yes, little one," Jerome purred in her ear, "feel it. Let it take you."

She was amazed to realize that as Jerome murmured in her ear, his hands on her breasts, she had experienced a minor orgasm, one that brought her down just a little. She had read that many women were multiorgasmic, but she'd never suspected that she might be. Tonight she knew that she could, and would, come again.

She felt herself being turned again and lifted until she was sitting on the edge of the tub, with Jerome's mouth between her thighs. His tongue lashed her swollen clit, then softly licked the length of her slit. "Like this?"

Unable to say anything, she grabbed on to Jerome's shoulders and held on while his mouth sucked and his tongue flashed. This time her orgasm crashed over her and she screamed yet Jerome's mouth continued to explore. Now his fingers were inside her, finding secret places that again drove her upward. Again? Oh, yes, again.

Finally she collapsed on the tiles and Jerome picked her up as though she weighed no more than a piece of fluff. He lay her on a lounge chair, unrolled a condom over his immense erection, and positioned himself over her. Without using hands, his erection found her, and stretching her not uncomfortably, he slowly pushed inside. "You take me well," he said. "You're so wet you make it easy. Is it good for you? I wouldn't want to hurt you."

Incapable of speech, Debbie opened her eyes and locked her gaze with his. Then she wrapped her legs around his waist and hung on as he suddenly began to piston into her. "Oh yes," he said. "It's so good." He fucked her for a long time until he finally thrust one last time and groaned loudly as he came. Although she was not able to come again, she reveled in Jerome's orgasm. She wasn't hopeless.

She dozed for a short while, then heard Paul calling her. "It's time to go," he said, his voice tight and his lips pressed together in a thin line. As she pulled her sweater and jeans over her wet body, she realized that Betts and Jerome were in the hot tub, obviously making love. As soon as they were decent, Paul said, "Get the rest of the stuff."

Grinning, Debbie picked up her underwear and socks and headed for the door, leaving Paul to gather the remainder of his clothing and follow. As he caught up, he grabbed her upper arm with his free hand and propelled her up the stairs.

They strode to their room in silence, then, when Paul had slammed the door behind him, he said, "What the hell did you think you were doing?"

Debbie was about to say "I'm sorry" then realized that she was angry. Coldly furious at what had been going on for so many years. She took in a large breath, then let it out slowly. "I guess I was doing pretty much what you were doing."

"It's not the same. I was just having a little fun. You were being fucked."

Her smile was self-satisfied. "Actually I did a bit of fucking myself," she said, putting her underwear on the dresser. "I need a shower to get the chlorine and other stuff off me before I go to bed," she said, heading for the bathroom.

"Stop being difficult and talk to me," Paul said, slamming his clothing onto the dresser beside his wife's.

Difficult? She turned and said, with forced sweetness, "I'm not being difficult. What should we talk about?"

"What was that performance down there?"

"It was lovemaking. Jerome is a very talented lover. Is Betts?"

"That's none of your business," Paul sputtered.

"Okay," Debbie said, turning back toward the bathroom. As she closed the door behind her, she realized that she felt wonderful. She was sexually satisfied for the second time in one day and Paul hadn't had anything to do with either one. She didn't need him. Did she want him? Did she love him? She hadn't the faintest idea, but for now, she couldn't have cared less.

Observe. Boy, she'd observed all right. As for Paul, she didn't like what she saw.

When she finally emerged from the bathroom, considerably less angry than she had been, Paul was sitting on the edge of the bed wearing only a pair of dry underpants. "Are you going to explain yourself?" he said, his voice tight.

"No," Debbie said, unwinding the towel from around her torso and slipping into bed nude. God, she thought, even the sheets feel sensual against my skin.

"Listen, Debbie," Paul said. "We need to talk about what happened tonight."

"Okay." She turned onto her back and looked at him. "Talk."

"I've asked you several times. What the hell was that performance with Jerome?"

"It was just what it seemed to be. He fucked my brains out and I liked it."

"You're hopeless. You obviously don't understand a simple question."

Debbie sat up and let the bedclothes slip to her waist. Her breasts were still a bit swollen from Jerome's pinches and a bit abraded from his rough cheek. "Listen and hear what I'm saying. I don't know what you intended to have happen this weekend, but a lot has. I've discovered a few things. First and foremost, I'm not hopeless or difficult or silly and I won't have you constantly saying that I am. I won't listen to you put me down over and over either."

"Oh, please," Paul said. "I don't know where this nonsense is coming from but I won't have it. I don't like any of it."

Being brutally honest, Debbie said, "Actually, I don't either."

"What the hell does that mean?"

With another sigh, she said, "What happened earlier this evening was an aberration. I have no intention of ever doing anything like that again."

She watched Paul's body relax. "That's a lot better."

"My decision has nothing to do with you, Paul. I just don't want to go outside my marriage again." Without letting her husband interrupt, she continued, "But that's my decision based on what I want for a change."

"You mean what I want doesn't matter?"

"It matters a lot, but so do I."

"So nothing like that will ever happen again."

"No, it won't."

"I'm glad that's settled. Now life can get back to normal."

"If by normal, you mean the way it was last week, not a chance." She hoped she had the courage of her convictions. But she wouldn't go back. No way.

Paul's voice rose. "I want everything to go back to the way it was before this cursed weekend."

"*You* want?" She tightened her stomach muscles and said, "What about what I want?"

"You want the same thing I want. Don't you?"

Holding on to her courage, Debbie continued, "I don't think so. If you want to try to make this farce of a marriage work, there will have to be a few changes. Strangely enough, while I was in the shower, I realized that I really loved you when we were first married. We were good together, equals in this marriage. As you climbed the corporate ladder," she spat, making the phrase sound like a curse, "you changed. Maybe you need to make yourself feel bigger by making me feel smaller. I don't know why and I don't much care. Just know this. It won't work anymore. I'm done."

"What the hell's come over you, Debbie? You're acting like a stranger." There was a whine in Paul's voice.

"Not a stranger. I've simply taken a few hours to observe what I've become and I don't like what I see. Someone said earlier that fault is unimportant so let's not talk about where and how this started. You began to put me down and I began to believe it. I don't believe it anymore.

"We have a few choices. I won't be treated the way I've been treated, and if we can't change the dynamic here, we can separate. That seems the easiest."

With fear in his eyes, Paul said, "You said choices."

"I don't want to throw it all away just yet," she said, "but lots of things will have to change if we're going to stay a couple. Maybe we'll need some counseling to make that happen." The more she thought, the more she doubted that it could ever work. "I don't know whether we can."

"I think you're being silly about this."

Her body stiffened. "That's the first thing that will have to change. You won't call me names ever again."

"I didn't . . ." As she nodded, she watched Paul shrivel. "I guess I did."

They talked for several hours and finally went to sleep at about four in the morning, neither knowing for sure where their marriage was headed. Although they didn't agree, at least some of the time, Debbie thought, they were communicating as equals.

Chapter
15

Tracy thought the Power and Control forum had gone well. After Frank and Suzanne's initial announcement and the discussion that followed, several more couples discussed their sexual activities openly and the questioning was lively. It didn't matter to Tracy whether they'd convinced anyone to try a little slap on the rear or a bit of bondage, she felt good that the couples in the room had come to accept that alternatives existed and that there were perfectly normal people enjoying them.

Now she faced her own dilemma: how to talk to Dave about their relationship, or lack thereof. She didn't know whether there was any future between them, although she wanted one badly, but she had to give it a shot. She put on her ski jacket and got a key from the front desk, then made her way to the cabin in which she and Dave first kissed. Sentimental? Sure, but she needed every trick in her book to at least make Dave listen and lower the barriers he had erected between them.

She had talked to Meg at the front desk when she got off the phone with Kim earlier that evening and was grateful that the cabin she wanted was empty. She had also enlisted the receptionist's help in getting Dave there on the pretext of additional heating problems. She entered the small cabin, turned up the thermostat, and lit the logs already laid in the fireplace. This was a little hokey, but she needed all the help she could get if she was going to repair the damage she'd already done.

She looked around the room, deciding where to sit. It was silly, of course, to worry about making the first impression but it concerned her. A chair? Too isolated. The sofa? Too intimate. As she stood in the middle of the living room, she heard the door open behind her and Dave's voice. "I suspected something like this."

"I'm sorry if you feel duped, but we need to talk and I was afraid you'd continue to avoid me if I didn't do something."

Dave didn't move any farther into the room and his expression was guarded. "I don't think this will get us anywhere. When I didn't call you, it was to avoid a scene just like this. I don't want to 'discuss things' as women are so prone to do. It was fun, and that's that."

"You're right. It was fun and that's the problem. Would you just hear me out? You don't have to say anything or do anything. You can stand there by the door and, when I'm done, walk out if you like. I just want to apologize."

Dave looked surprised. "Apologize?"

"I've spent this weekend pretending to be some kind of expert in relationships, and it took Kim and a conversation with one of the attendees to get things straight in my mind. I'm ashamed to admit that, in my own personal life, I'm not an expert."

"Go on," Dave said, standing just inside the doorway but also slipping his heavy jacket from his shoulders and dropping it on a chair.

"This is difficult for me to admit, but I got carried away." When Dave took a breath to speak, Tracy held her hand up, palm out. "Let me do this. Please." Dave let out the breath he had taken in and nodded. "You're a really wonderful man and you taught me a lot, about sex and, more importantly, about myself." She had formulated her speech but now everything she'd planned to say got stuck in her head so she merely spoke her mind, and heart. "I know you know most of what I want to say, but I need to get this all out.

"Andrew's extracurricular activities hurt me in more ways than I had realized." She huffed out a breath. "Even now it's difficult for me to say that he was a total rat and that I made a huge mistake marrying him. Even Kim knew but couldn't tell me."

"It wasn't your fault," Dave said.

"I know that in my brain, but it's still difficult for me to get my heart to understand. You are the first man I've been intimate with since then and you've affected me in so many ways. You taught me that men aren't all skunks like Andrew."

"But—"

"You told me that you went out with me at first so I would run the weekend, but I'm egotistical enough to think that it grew into more than that. We really did have fun together, even after we stopped jumping into bed every time we were alone with a horizontal surface handy."

"If I remember correctly," Dave said with a small smile, "we frequently didn't even need a horizontal surface."

So far so good, Tracy thought. "You taught me that I wasn't frigid, and at first, the great sex was a toy, something exciting and really good for my ego. I really needed that.

"Then, unfortunately, I began to build my little cottage with the picket fence around it, and put you and me in it." She watched Dave's expression harden but she continued. "I saw forevers where I shouldn't have."

When she hesitated, Dave said, "Go on."

"I made mental plans. It was a nice dream, but it wasn't reality and I understand that now. I'm afraid some of my plans leaked out, if only in my attitude. I've thought a lot about being in love, and that's what I was, and I guess still am. In love. Candlelight, music, intimate dinners, and great sex. That's being *in* love but it's not love."

"Interesting distinction," Dave said.

"It's all semantics, but it's the best way I can express it. I've spent quite a bit of time trying to sort it all out. I talked with a woman who had just received a marriage proposal from her boyfriend and wasn't sure it had been for the right reasons. Then I talked to Kim and she gave me some insights about loving, and I realized that it really is too soon for me to decide that I love you." While she had been speaking, she had been standing in the center of the room. Now she moved to one end of the long sofa and sat down. "I don't want to presume that I know how you feel. Maybe you've stopped talking to me for reasons that have nothing to do with what I'm trying to say, but in case I'm right, I wanted to tell you all this."

Silently, Dave crossed the room and sat at the opposite end of the sofa. "You did scare the hell out of me," he said.

"I was afraid of that. Dave, you're wonderful and I'm crazy about you. I think that given some time to be together I could love you, but right now I'm confusing being"—she smiled ruefully—"in lust, with deeper feelings. Maybe in time there could be something, and maybe not." She took a deep breath and plunged. "I'd like to give it a chance. No promises, no predictions, just dating when we both want to and sex when we both want to. Time to be together but lots of space, too."

"I don't know whether I can spend time with you wondering whether you're measuring me for a tuxedo and a white picket fence."

"I can't be with you on those terms either," Tracy admitted. "I think it would make my stomach hurt all the time. However, I'm not ready to throw this all away either. What can we do to make this all more comfortable for both of us"—she paused—"if that's what you want?"

Dave sighed. "I can't talk about things the way you do, Tracy. Sometimes I don't really know what I feel until some time has passed and I've digested things. When I left you that last evening, all I knew was that I had to run away. I felt like someone was trying to put me in a box and I couldn't let them, let you, do that."

"Do you think we can find a way to make this work, if only in the short run?" She smiled and raised one brown eyebrow. "I'd hate to miss out on all that good sex."

Dave's face softened. "It was wonderful, wasn't it?"

"It was, and I'd like to find some way to change the word *was* into the word *is*."

Dave didn't move closer, but he reached out and took Tracy's hand. "Can we go back to where we were?"

"I'd like to think so. No strings, no promises. Just the occasional date and the occasional roll in the hay."

Slowly, Dave smiled. "Can we make those rolls in the hay more than occasional?" He pulled on Tracy's hand and she tumbled across the sofa until her head landed in Dave's lap.

"That's what I was hoping for." She grabbed the front of his flannel shirt and pulled his face down to hers. With a wink, she said, "Fuck my brains out, stud."

The following morning Dave and Tracy made their way back to the main house holding hands. As Tracy showered, changed her clothes, and prepared for the closing ceremony, she thought of their night together.

Things with Dave had gone wonderfully. The sex had been explosive and Dave seemed comfortable and relaxed when they parted. She thought they were back to where they had been several weeks earlier. She thought the weekend had gone well, too, but she wasn't really sure. Maybe there are unsatisfied couples, she thought, then she heard Kim say, "You can't win them all. You can only hope to win more than you lose and give some couples fun in the process."

As she approached the Onondaga Room, she was stopped several times by couples raving about what a wonderful weekend it had been. More than a few couples had made discoveries of new activities and all were effusive in their thanks. She wondered, however, about the couples with whom she had had personal dealings. How had she fared one-on-one?

As she entered the large room, she noticed Elise Prescott and her husband sitting off to one side, holding hands and talking quietly. When Elise looked up, she caught Tracy's eye and nodded. Pleased, Tracy nodded back. She clicked off one probable success on her fingers. Tish Johnson and Owen, her fiancé, sat toward the back, their bodies leaning slightly away from each other. Uh-oh, Tracy thought. Things didn't go well for them. She hoped it would all work out for the best, whatever that turned out to be. Then she spotted Debbie Stafford sitting alone in the middle of the room. I wonder whether her husband is merely late, or isn't coming at all. One out of three. Not good.

At nine-thirty she stepped to the front of the room and voices stilled. She saw Dave walk in and stand at the back of the room. They caught each other's eyes and grinned. Two out of four.

"Welcome to the final session of the weekend. This is where I ask whether there have been any successes or failures and you grin or frown and remain silent. I'd really love to hear from some of you. What did you like best? What didn't you like? What helped or harmed your relationship? Give me as much feedback as you want. So, any feedback?"

There were a few hands, a few of whom she'd already talked to and Tracy called on several people. Each told her that the weekend had been fun and that they'd learned at least one new thing to add to their repertoire. She saw Elise Prescott's hand and nodded to her. Elise stood up and said, "I was really hung up on my weight and age. I now understand that neither have to stand in the way of great sex. What got in the way was my attitude, but thankfully, with Tracy's wise advice and the help of my wonderful husband"—she squeezed Bob's shoulder—"and Diana, things are so much better now."

"Yeah, they are," Bob chimed in, eliciting a laugh from the audience.

When there were no more hands, Tracy sat back down on the table and said, "I learned a few things myself this weekend. First, sex is easy, love takes time." She paused, then said, "Okay, sex is easy, good sex requires good communication, and great sex requires the willingness to experiment. Lust is right now, love takes patience." She looked at Dave and watched his grin widen.

"I have one last homework assignment for you all. I have here a pile of self-addressed stamped envelopes." She patted the stack on the front table. "I'd love it if you'd write, either when you get home or, even better, a month or two out, just to let me know how it went and what's happened since. You'll find the Creative Loving e-mail address in the brochure you got when you signed in and on many of the handouts you've gotten as well. I've also posted it on the white board outside so, for those of you who prefer to write electronically, do it that way. But please, write. There will be another weekend starting the seventeenth of April, and I think Kim will be able to host part of it, babies in tow. Many of you have given me your e-mail or snail mail addresses and I'll send out announcements when the twins arrive. I would also love to see some of you then, or at another weekend in the future."

She smiled at the audience and, as she summed everything up, realized that Debbie's husband hadn't appeared. "You folks have been great and I thank you for all your help, patience, and feedback. I'm sure you realize that I was very apprehensive Friday afternoon and now you're all like family. I wish you all a safe trip home. No fooling around while you're driving, mind you, but great sex when you get home and for the rest of your lives."

As Kim had done at the previous weekend, Tracy rose, extended her arms, and said, "Go forth and fuck like bunnies."

As the laughter died, couples rose and filed out. Many shook her hand. Several took envelopes, and others wrote down the e-mail address from the board or checked to see that they already had it. Many handed her their address so they could be informed about the babies.

After everyone was gone, Tracy phoned Kim, filled her in on the closing session, and told her an abbreviated version of her evening with Dave. Both Kim and Elliot were generous in their praise and smug in their acceptance of her unqualified success. Warning them not to get carried away until they got more feedback, she hung up.

After cleaning up several odds and ends, collecting unused materials, and tidying up after herself, she packed and gave her card key to Annelise at the front desk. She had lunch with Dave, the first relaxed time they'd spent together since their last date, then she drove home.

Eight weeks later, she and Kim sat on the sofa in Kim's living room, each holding a five-week-old, gurgling baby boy. Boyce, the son Kim was holding, was wearing a pair of tiny red overalls and Matt, Tracy's charge, was dressed in blue. Although the strict dress code Kim used did make things easier, Tracy was now well able to tell the identical twins apart. Elliot freely admitted, however, that he still had trouble.

"They're angelic," Tracy said. "So sweet."

"God," Kim said, turning her eyes heavenward, "thank you for a few minutes of peace and quiet."

"Have you gotten any sleep?" Tracy asked. Nursing twins was taking up all her sister's time.

"Not a whole hell of a lot. When I'm not nursing, I'm changing diapers or giving baths. Elliot's been a rock in the middle of the night so all I really have to do is roll over and offer a baby a nipple."

"He's the best," Tracy said. "You certainly found a keeper."

"I sure did. I gather from the smile on your face, Dave's a keeper, too. How was the vacation?"

Although they had spoken on the phone, this was the first time the sisters had been together since Tracy and Dave returned from a week in Saint Martin. "Dave and I are fabulous. We're exploring and learning so much."

"In or out of bed?"

Tracy giggled. "Both. We're in no hurry but I can't deny that I have high hopes." Reflexively Tracy grabbed a small cloth and wiped milky dribble from Matt's chin. "He's the best thing in my life, outside of you all, of course. He's stopping by to pick me up and see the babies, if that's all right."

"Of course. He's the second best man in my life." She looked down. "Oops, the fourth best." She paused, then said, "Trace, I've done a lot of thinking. I'm seriously considering writing a book based on the workshops. I think there are lots of people who can't attend the weekends but could benefit from everything we've learned."

"That's a great idea. Any idea how you'll go about it?"

"*We'll* go about it, and yes. I've already contacted a woman who attended a weekend last year. She's a literary agent and gave me lots of great advice."

"Hold it," Tracy said, stopping the flow of her sister's words. "What do you mean we?"

"I want you to coauthor it with me. Would you?"

Tracy wasn't sure she could add anything to Miranda's columns and Kim's experience. "I don't know what I have to offer, sis."

Kim handed Tracy several sheets of paper. "These came while you were away. I know we've gotten lots of thank-you notes, but maybe these can convince you that you've got a lot to offer."

The first sheet was a handwritten letter on crisp white stationery.

Dear Tracy,
    My name is Debbie Stafford and my husband Paul and I attended your weekend this past January. I got your note about Boyce and Matt and my best to everyone.
    Paul and I are separated now and are getting counseling. We tried to change things ourselves but it didn't work and frankly I don't think this will either. He can't get used to my being a real person and I can't go back to the way things were.
    You opened my eyes, Tracy, and I can't thank you enough. It won't be easy after so many years of being so small but I'm learning. I've gotten a new job and I've already been given more responsibility. It's nice to feel valuable and happy again.
                                                                Debbie Stafford

Tracy looked at her sister. "That letter makes me sad."

"It shouldn't," Kim said. "When someone tells me that they are separating, I don't automatically say, 'I'm sorry.' Maybe it's the best thing for one or both of the parties. She's giving it every chance and is a better person for everything you told her."

"I know but . . ."

"You told her to merely observe, and if she didn't like what she saw, that's not your responsibility." Kim sipped her water. "Read the next."

Tracy looked at the next sheet, a copy of an e-mail letter.

Dear Tracy,

I don't know whether you'll remember me. I'm Elise Prescott and you helped me so much with my weight and all. I had to tell you what's happened since that weekend.

Sadly I haven't lost any weight and I doubt that I ever will. What's more important is that my size doesn't bother me so much anymore, at least not in bed. I've been doing a lot of talking to Diana. Bob used to be in the garment business and we think the three of us can create our own line of plus-sized lingerie. For now, however, I'm doing lingerie parties for women of all sizes. I actually wear some of Diana's fashions during the evening. Oh, not her type of outfits, but mine.

Well, I just wanted you to know how much Bob and I owe to you and your wonderful weekend. Please also wish Kim all the best with the twins. Having had five children ourselves, we know what a job and what a joy they will be. Hug them all for both of us,

Elise

Tracy looked at her sister. "When I saw her at the final session, I thought Elise had worked through some stuff, mostly with Diana's help."

"Stop minimizing your effect on her. You did good, Trace."

Tracy read through several more letters, one more positive than the last. Finally she reached the last piece of e-mail.

Dear Tracy,

My name is Tish and we talked the evening Owen asked me to marry him. Remember? Well, it's been two months and we've done a lot of talking—even though I tried not to beat it all to death. He's finally opened up about his fear of responsibility and all that. We've decided to get married in September but to take at least a year to increase our savings, before we try to have a baby. I can't thank you enough for helping me see Owen's side

*of everything and for making me stop and decide what I really
wanted.*

    *I'm sorry that we won't be seeing you again. One weekend
was all we could afford.*

    Thanks again and love to Kim and her babies,

Tish (and Owen, too)

"Wow," Tracy said. "That feels really good. I wasn't sure
that I had told her the right thing."

"You obviously did," Kim said, shifting Boyce to a more
comfortable position on her arm, "but you won't always be
right. I've had a few sad letters from people who weren't satisfied with the way things worked out, but on the whole they've
been very positive. Will you help me with the book?"

"Sis, right now I'd say no, but knowing how you convinced
me to do the weekend, I have no doubt that you'll talk me
into it."

The doorbell sounded, and with Matt comfortably tucked
in her arm, Tracy let Dave in. As Kim rose, he embraced her
and stared at Boyce. "Kim, they're wonderful. Congratulations
for the dozenth time. How are you holding up?"

"I'm totally exhausted," she grinned softly, "but I'm bliss-
ful, or at least I will be when I'm conscious."

As Kim settled back on the sofa, Dave wrapped one arm
around Tracy's shoulders, staring at the baby resting in the
crook of her arm. "That's quite a sight, you and that baby."

Choked by the naked emotion in Dave's eyes, Tracy lightened the atmosphere. "He's such a love. This is Matt and
Kim's got Boyce."

Dave reached out and let Matt grab his finger. "Hi, guy. I'm
your Uncle Dave."

Dear Readers,

I hope you've enjoyed Tracy, Dave, and Kim's story. My book *Velvet Whispers* revolved around a phone sex business, and after it came out, I got lots of letters from women who wanted to know how to break into the business. After the publication of *The Price of Pleasure*, I got dozens of letters about becoming a high-priced call girl.

As with those others, the basis for Kim and Tracy's workshop in *Never Enough* came from my imagination. I'm sorry to say that I know of no weekends like the ones depicted here. However, maybe I'll arrange one myself. It sounds like such fun.

I'd love to hear from you either by snail mail at Joan Lloyd, P.O. Box 221, Yorktown Heights, New York 10598, or by e-mail at Joan@Joanelloyd.com. I know you'll also enjoy visiting my website at www.JoanELLloyd.com. There's information about all my other books, advice, questions, letters from visitors on a myriad of topics, and a new short story of mine every month.

I look forward to hearing from you,

Joan